"BUBBLES WILL POP starts as a Euro thriller that drops you right in the middle of some intrigue and goes like a train. This is part of the Security Through Absurdity series, so it helps if you have read the book that comes before it, "Little Yellow Stickies"—even so, questions are set up in your mind from the start, so it's all good. I got the feeling that book two was much darker in tone than the first, and that's also good— we are embarking into the valley of the shadows here, and things are looking very dark for our now-pregnant, main protagonist Jocelyn McLaren. May I also point out that this novel, and this series, is the REAL DEAL, the consummate insider's view of the US defence industrial complex. The author has lived this from the inside, and you are going to see things from an angle you have never seen before. BUBBLES WILL POP is an ace, well-written read, and I loved the European slant!"

Charlie Flowers. Author of the Riz Sabir Crime Series

"As this is a work of fiction, nothing in this book is true, but it's exactly how things are. Were."

Michael Nystrom, creator of DailyPaul.com and BullNotBull.com

Security Through Absurdity

BOOK TWO
BUBBLES WILL POP

Rachael L. McIntosh

EntropyPress

EntropyPress books may be ordered through booksellers or by contacting:

ƎP

EntropyPress

www.entropypress.com
EntropyPress
PO Box 2254
East Greenwich, RI 02818
USA

ISBN - 13 : 978-1506105956
ISBN - 10 : 1506105955

"FOR A SEED TO ACHIEVE its greatest expression, it must come completely undone. The shell cracks, its insides come out and everything changes. To someone who doesn't understand growth, it would look like complete destruction."

Cynthia Occelli

CHAPTER ONE

October 2005, Switzerland

ETHAN LOWE BLINKED WHILE STARING at his reflection in the bus window. His image merged with the drizzly weather outside, and it kind of fit his mood—if *moods* were what you could call them these days. Everything had sort of mushed into one long-standing malaise. It was only recently that he had started to recognize that maybe this might be a problem. His gray state of mind had originally been an asset for his line of work. But since finding out that he was going to be a father ... a father to twins ...

He shook his head, broke off another chunk of chocolate, and popped it into his mouth. As he sat munching, the bus stopped, and two winter camouflage-outfitted military men boarded the bus, SG-550s slung over their shoulders. He imagined how people would react to the automatic rifles back in the States. *They'd probably grab the kids and push their way off the bus, totally freaked out.* He smirked and watched as the army guys settled down in the seats between an unfazed teenager and an elderly woman.

He liked it here. He had gotten to admire the mountains while on the train ride to the bus and was now sitting comfortably by the window, watching the watery smear of a farm-speckled landscape roll by.

The doors of the bus slid open at exactly 2:15. Like everything in Switzerland, his arrival was a testament to the predictable order of things, as was just about everything having to do with the care and maintenance of the Swiss citizenry. The place was organized and worked like a fine timepiece.

As soon as Ethan's feet hit the ground, the doors closed and the bus hissed away. A herd of sheep stared right at him from behind an antique but well-maintained fence. He looked around and noticed a couple happily holding hands as they walked up the cobblestone path to his left. The drizzle was in full effect, and the leafless trees made it seem much colder than it really was. He pulled up his hood, zipped his black Arc'teryx jacket all the way up, and jammed his hands into his pockets.

Ethan discovered that the cobblestones led directly up a hill to a castle, and he figured that was where he was supposed to go. The message he had received about this meeting had been very vague. Cheese shops, restaurants, bakeries, and cafés lined both sides of the street on his ascent. When he was almost at the top, he noticed it: the polished stainless-steel statue. It was just like the one in Jonas Ledergerber's office (if that was his real name). No, not the castle—this old stone building was definitely where he was supposed to go.

> *Château St. Germain*
> *1663 Gruyères*
> *Museum HR Giger*

He paid his entry at the front desk and headed inside. The place, unlike most museums he had been in, was dimly lit, with pin lights illuminating the artwork. Wandering somewhat aimlessly and uneasily around the building, he was surprised to encounter an enormous cast-bronze statue depicting the creature from the movie *Alien*. It wasn't until he was upstairs and through some arched stone passageways that he took the time to really look at the artwork—large-scale, five-by-five-foot, black-and-white, surreal-meets-technical drawings of pentagrams impaling and/or otherwise violating drawn-and-quartered naked women. There were goat heads and mysterious symbols and lots of mechanical stuff married with the feminine form. The drawings were clearly expertly done.

As Ethan studied one of the more titillating pieces, a tall salt-and-pepper-haired man in a perfectly fitted dark charcoal overcoat and a scented cloud of Clive Christian "V" for Men silently slipped up next to him. "Good day, Mr. Lowe," Ethan heard in a Swiss-German accent. "Thank you for agreeing to meet."

Startled, Ethan turned to the man and replied, "As if I had a choice." And he quickly took the wad of a handkerchief out of his pocket and attempted to pass it over, because after all, that was why he was here—to deliver roughly a million dirty dollars, all of which had been cleverly transferred and fashioned into a very flashy jewel-encrusted butterfly brooch.

Arms folded across his chest and not looking at Ethan, eyes still fixed on the woman being defiled by the top corner of the pentagram, Mr. Jonas Ledergerber answered, "Now, now, it was you who needed me. The neema incident with the colonel," he said, shaking his head, "I regret to say was ridiculous, but you were intelligent enough to accept my help."

Ethan looked at him with restrained disdain as he absently fiddled with the clump he was still left holding. He knew that Jonas Ledergerber was exerting his dominance by making him stand there like a confused child cradling a small fortune, but he also knew he had no right to say anything. He had, in fact, gotten out of hand while working at the "no blood, no foul" operation beneath the Baghdad International Airport, otherwise called NAMA. He thought back on his role as a "translator," the currently accepted euphemism for *torturer*. The Huachuca-trained CIA and Fort Bragg Special Forces had all been professional enough. It had been during a relatively mild session when the guy everyone called "Colonel," with whom he had been partnered for the case, started describing how he had slowly mangled and killed a young Serbian prostitute back in the day.

At first Ethan had figured this was for the benefit of the terrified SOB strapped in the chair, but when the story started to sound a bit too familiar, Ethan lost it. He just lost it and killed, not the guy in the chair, but the "colonel" from Fort Bragg.

Mr. Ledergerber turned to face Ethan. "Now that the regrettable incident is behind us," he made a gesture as if brushing flour off his hands, "it is time that you help me." Without a smile, he patted Ethan's shoulder and said, "Come. Let us enjoy the local fondue before I send you on your way home." Ethan thrust the bundle he was holding into Mr. Ledergerber's hands. Ledergerber took it and, without even looking at it, put it in his pocket. "You will take some time off now, yes? I will call upon you when necessary."

Ethan's head was now officially in the dark-gray zone as he made his way downhill to the anything-but-delightful fondue Jonas Ledergerber had promised. He had no clear idea how he was going to manage any of this. Especially now with Jocelyn expecting.

CHAPTER TWO

The same day, Norwich, Connecticut, USA—6 hour time difference

JOCELYN MCLAREN WAS NERVOUS, EXCITED, and optimistic all at the same time as she locked up her silver C280 Sport Mercedes and headed through the sun-streaked reds and yellows of the tree-lined parking lot to the hospital. She was simply radiant in the new maternity clothes, and she felt surprisingly healthy. Really healthy. More healthy than she had ever remembered being in her adult life. Somehow the hormones of pregnancy had kicked in and countered all the weird physical problems of the relapsing-remitting multiple sclerosis that she had come to know as her normal state of being for the past ten years.

Apparently, these same hormones had also changed her perspective about shopping for clothes. Normally, she didn't like shopping and fussing about her appearance, but now, surprising even to herself, she had a closet full of the lightest pink, very feminine and flattering, not to mention very expensive, mommy-to-be fashions. Her new wardrobe was a huge departure from the black and gray or, if it had been a good day, navy, office attire that she had donned on a daily basis to shuffle into the fluorescent flicker hell otherwise known as the Conglomerate, one of America's "big six" defense contractors. But thankfully, she had peacefully extracted herself from that mess last week, and she was still thoroughly enjoying the buzz of being free. The colors of the autumn morning and the fresh, crispy air were accentuating this feeling of freedom.

She pushed a lock of her strawberry blonde hair behind her ear and unfolded the note Mimi had given her during the going-away party. Walking toward the hospital, she surveyed the layout. Mimi, the receptionist at the Conglomerate, had scribbled it all out for her. According to Mimi, this was the best OB-GYN in the area, and his office was supposed to be in the "new building." Considering that one part of the hospital looked like the mental institution they had shut down back in her hometown—a big, scary, Victorian brick behemoth dating back to the nineteenth century—she instantly concluded that she was supposed to move toward the typically 1980s oversized arches and somehow fake-looking bricks.

Having reached her destination, she smiled at herself in the glass doors as they silently slid open. The unexpected but totally predictable smell of hospital disinfectant wafted past her along with the non-hurried rush of weary hospital foot traffic. When Jocelyn finally found her way through the linoleum and plastic signage scavenger hunt otherwise known as Backus Memorial Hospital, she happily rolled up to the doctor's check-in area and grinned. The dark-haired and very suntanned receptionist sitting behind the beige office cube-like desk reminded her of someone she used to work with—a woman named Nancy.

It was funny seeing a character like Nancy outfitted in colorful nursing scrubs featuring Winnie the Pooh. And she couldn't help but notice that the polka dot-clad clerk, rummaging around in the bank of filing cabinets at the far end of the room, bore an uncanny resemblance to one of the many temps who had buzzed into and out of her division after Nancy died. Jocelyn eyed the bespectacled woman with the pixie haircut, hoping that Ms. Polka Dot would look her way so that she could confirm her hunch, but no such luck. *Maybe those are new glasses or something.* Smiling, she called out over the dim waiting room Muzak, "Hey! Shelly! Shelly Johnson, right?" But the clerk didn't even look up.

Disappointed because she had actually appreciated that temp and wondered if she was just imagining things because of seeing someone who reminded her of Nancy, Jocelyn's attention was soon diverted back to the receptionist.

"You're at ten o'clock?" the tanned Nancy look-a-like asked as she rooted around with her mouse and stared at the computer screen. "Jocelyn McLaren?"

"Yup. That's me," Jocelyn happily answered. However, the receptionist did not possess the same *joie de vivre,* and a silence settled in, forcing Jocelyn to notice the framed, large-format color photographs of mountains scattered around the waiting room. "Nice pictures."

"The doctor took 'em," the Nancy clone replied flatly. "He goes all over the place. Just came back from the Alps." Jocelyn detected a bit of an unspoken "I-hate-my-boss-so-much" attitude before the woman asked her for her insurance card.

"Oh, I don't have one."

The receptionist tilted her head to look directly at Jocelyn and asked, "You mean you lost it?" And that's when the dark, tired bags under the woman's eyes became quite obvious. Given how exhausted this lady looked, Jocelyn wasn't surprised that she could discern the familiar acrid, tangy odor of coffee breath. She was surprised that she could smell it from where she was standing. She could smell everything these days. It was some sort of new pregnancy superpower. This whole being-able-to-smell thing had appeared about the same time as her newfound preference for light pink, and she marveled at what all these new hormones she had coursing through her were doing.

"Well, I had hoped that I was going to be able to get COBRA health insurance after I left my job," Jocelyn said as she placed her color coordinated purse carefully on the counter. "I haven't gotten my card yet, and I don't know what is going on with the paperwork. I had heard that everyone was offered COBRA, so I just figured I'd apply ..."

"Oh, so you got laid off?" The woman seemed to reposition her gaze to a different part of the computer screen she was looking at as she reached over to grab a clipboard to hand to Jocelyn.

Accepting the clipboard and pen, Jocelyn said, "No. I just quit. I couldn't take it anymore. I know stuff takes a long time to get approved, but I—"

Miss Nancy let out a loud sigh, rolled her eyes, and crossed her arms across her chest. "But that's not how it works. You can't apply for COBRA if you just quit."

Jocelyn had figured as much, but she'd also figured she'd give it a try to see what might happen. "Well, I know I'm not getting unemployment, but there's got to be a way to get health insurance. I mean, look at me." Jocelyn positioned herself to showcase her five-month baby bump as the office Muzak softly played a very uninspiring version of *Tiny Bubbles* by Don Ho. The two other women in the waiting area, who both looked as if they were about to drop their precious cargoes at any moment, glanced up but then quickly returned to their outdated *People* magazines.

The receptionist sort of snickered and said, "Yeah, well, I wanna walk outta here too, like every day, but no one's gonna just give me health insurance for being alive. You sorta have to be in on the game, ya know?"

Jocelyn sighed. She hadn't worried about health insurance except for when she had been living in her non-live-in painting studio back in Boston seven years ago, before she landed the job at the Conglomerate. That's when she had just paid money directly to the doctor if she needed to see someone. Sure, it was sort of expensive, but almost everywhere she went had sliding-scale pricing based on income, and needless to say, as an artist she qualified for decent prices. That's just how it was back then. Now the new governor in Massachusetts was doing something different with the state's health care system. She'd heard a little about that from her artist friends back in Boston—some of whom were moving out of the state to New Hampshire because of this new law. And others were frantically trying to figure out whether there was some sort of legal way to become a tax evader. She didn't really know the particulars of it; she just knew it was a new thing back in Massachusetts.

Jocelyn pursed her lips. The woman was clearly correct, but needing to be "in the game" wasn't exactly what she wanted to hear—especially since she had just removed herself from it last week. "What if I made some sort of a payment plan... directly to this office?" she offered hopefully.

"Umm, right. A payment plan. You are getting ready to have twins. You have MS. You are going to be thirty-five when these kids are born. You don't have a job. And you are technically a high-risk pregnancy. Do you know how much a neonatal stay for a preemie costs? Let alone for two? Twins usually come early, you know."

Put off by this woman's confrontational attitude, Jocelyn countered with, "I'm not worried. I have a savings account, and I guess I could sell my house to pay for whatever comes up." She took out her credit card and handed it over in lieu of an insurance card.

"I hope you have a really nice house to put up for sale," the woman said, taking the card. "A neonatal stay could easily run up to a million dollars for twins"—she looked up, held Jocelyn's gaze, and narrowed her eyes, almost smirking—"a million dollars a day."

"Seriously?" Jocelyn asked in disbelief.

"Seriously." An extended and awkward period of silence ensued as the woman wrestled with the clunky credit card imprint machine, swore under her breath when she hurt her knuckles swiping the card, and then asked Jocelyn to sign on the line. As she tore apart the carbon copy of the transaction and handed it to Jocelyn, she said, "I really think you need to start looking for insurance," and handed the credit card back.

Jocelyn primly put the card back into her wallet and said, "Well, I'm having problems locating an insurance company that will take me with the MS and being pregnant. What do you suggest I do?"

"Move."

"What do you mean, move? Like exercise?" Jocelyn asked, somewhat perplexed by the woman's answer.

"No. I mean, like, pack up your stuff and move to another state that has really easy qualifications for state aid," the woman explained while affixing a red dot sticker to her file. "That's what I'd do."

"I never thought of that. People really do that?"

The receptionist looked at Jocelyn as if she had two heads and replied simply, "All the time."

Just then, Jocelyn's cell phone rang, and it gave her the excuse to end the conversation with the sour receptionist. "Oh, I have to take this." Miss Nancy rolled her eyes again, and the other women in the waiting room lazily watched as Jocelyn excitedly answered the phone and made her way to a chair under an impressive photo of the Matterhorn. "Hey! Are you home yet?" she asked as quietly as she could, but still everyone could hear her just fine.

"Umm, no. I'll be home tomorrow morning," Ethan answered and quickly asked, "How's everything going? Is everything okay?"

"Of course. I'm at the new doctor's right now, waiting for my appointment—"

"You have a new doctor? Why?" Ethan asked with audible concern in his voice.

"Oh, Mimi gave me this guy's name, and he's supposed to be really good. I had to use the baby credit card." She giggled. "And—"

"Okay. Listen, I want you to get out of that office, Jocelyn."

"Huh? My appointment is in a few minutes."

"Please."

"But this guy's supposed to be really good, and I guess he's not taking new patients so I'm pretty lucky—"

"I'll find you a better doctor."

"Ethan, what has gotten into you?" Jocelyn asked as a nurse came out to the waiting area and ushered in one of the really pregnant ladies.

"Listen, I already paid for this visit on the card—"

"Don't worry about that."

"Well, that's easy for you to say. The receptionist just told me how much having these kids might cost and—"

"Jocelyn." She could hear him gulp and take a deep breath. "Look, I'm these kids' dad, and I want to be involved. Let's you and I go to a different doctor when I get home. We'll go together. How's that sound?"

"Jocelyn?" a new nurse called while entering the waiting area.

"Oh! I'm up. Let's talk when you get home. I'll make us a nice brunch." Jocelyn stood up and smiled at the nurse.

"Please," Ethan begged.

"Look, I've gotta go. We'll talk when you get home. I can't wait to see you tomorrow!" And she closed the phone.

Jocelyn gathered up her stuff, and just as she was walking toward the nurse, ready to start with the "nice to meet yous," the only other pregnant woman, sitting under an equally impressive photograph of the Eiger, burped and clutched her chest. Jocelyn smiled at the woman, raised her eyebrows, and was ready to make a good-humored joke—if it hadn't been for the fact that the woman appeared to be gasping for breath. Before Jocelyn could ask if the woman was all right, the woman vomited all over herself, slumped, and fell out of her chair, her eyes staring blankly up at the ceiling.

The nurse rushed past Jocelyn and called out to the rest of the staff for help. Not knowing what to do, Jocelyn just gripped her purse and watched as emergency triage kicked into high gear. A stretcher burst through the office door, and more white uniforms came pouring in. The man who looked like he was probably the doctor who Jocelyn had been waiting to see started barking letters and medical terms. AMI, fetal distress, and stat were the only things she picked up on, but it was obvious that things weren't looking good. The woman and three trimesters' worth of extra poundage were hoisted up onto the stretcher, and everyone, the doctor included, filed out of the room, leaving Jocelyn and the receptionist to stare and blink at each other.

"So, umm, do ya wanna reschedule?" the receptionist asked.

"Not really," Jocelyn said. "Do you think we can just forget about that credit card charge?"

The next day over some smoked salmon, bagels, and cream cheese, Jocelyn told Ethan all about the doctor's visit, the woman puking all over herself and having a heart attack, the estimated million-dollar-a-day cost if neonatal care might be needed for the kids, and how the receptionist had told her to move to another state.

Gulping down his coffee, Ethan said, "That's probably a good idea." He didn't seem very interested in eating any of Jocelyn's brunch for some reason.

"What is?" she asked, offering him a little jar of capers. When he declined, she scooped some out for herself and added them to her bagel creation.

"Moving."

"Really? You think so?" Jocelyn was surprised. Ethan seemed very enthused with the idea of her moving away. "Are you trying to get rid of me or something?" she asked, only half-joking.

But the more they talked about it, the more it made sense. She didn't have a job, and this old Victorian house she had was huge. It didn't have a kid-friendly yard, and the way it was decorated and laid out, with twisty, tall stairways, certainly didn't shout "baby safe."

"We can get a little house somewhere together, you and me."

Jocelyn stopped chewing. *He wants to move in with me? Wow.* She was flattered and impressed that he was stepping up to the plate like that.

"But where?" she asked. The plan that she had hatched when she'd first decided to leave her job, when she'd ordered those cassette tapes that taught her how to invest in real estate and be a landlord, well, she could do that anywhere.

So, after some long discussions with Ethan concerning logistics and creative money management, Jocelyn did what any sentient human being would logically do in her situation. She put her house on the market and crossed the border.

CHAPTER THREE

Three months later, Providence, Rhode Island, USA

"I DON'T GIVE A FUCK about Jesus, and I don't want this kid!" Jocelyn heard the only other Caucasian pregnant woman in the busy waiting area whisper ferociously to her mother.

"Sweetheart. It's going to be okay. God has a plan. We just have to let go and leave it up to Him and—"

"I hate you."

Of course, Jocelyn couldn't help but eavesdrop as she feigned interest in the brochures advising pregnant women to get their flu shot. The brochure was somewhat interesting because it was in Spanish, and on the back, almost as an afterthought, the English text appeared.

Looking around the high-risk pregnancy clinic waiting area, Jocelyn observed that she was by far the oldest patient. It also didn't escape her that she was in the minority. Most of these people were Hispanic, so it wasn't surprising that everyone was, on both sides of the counter, speaking Spanish. Moving just sixty-five miles over the state line seemed to have hurled her into another country—at least as far as health care was concerned. A small, brown, and very pregnant girl, who looked no more that twelve years old, waddled by as Jocelyn's phone rang. It was an unfamiliar number.

"Hello?" she answered.

"Hey, Joss! It's me!"

"Me who?" Jocelyn asked, not recognizing the voice.

"Jerry Apario! I'm glad I found you. How are you doing? Did you have your kids yet?"

"Oh. Hi, Jerry," Jocelyn said, not really excited to hear this blast from the not-so-distant past. "I can't really talk; I'm waiting to see the doctor right now. But I'm fine. Thank you for thinking of me." She hoped that this would end the call quickly, but apparently Jerry had other ideas.

"Oh. Okay. But, hey, where are you? I swung by your house the other day, but you had moved, and I couldn't find you on the Internet."

What the heck? Jocelyn thought. He'd never been over before, and she'd never invited him. She quickly responded, "Really? Why, Jerry? What's up?"

"Well, I think I just ran across some weird shit that you might want to know about." Jerry had always been regarded as the in-house conspiracy theorist, and Jocelyn would typically just let him ramble on by the coffee machine for the entertainment value, but seriously, she just wasn't into it. Not today.

"Ahhh, Jerry, look, why don't you just send me what you've got, and I'll look at it. I really can't talk right now." So Jocelyn gave Jerry her new address and happily hung up the phone. She was looking forward to seeing her babies and whether her little boy would be sucking his thumb again during the ultrasound this week.

Jerry, convinced that Jocelyn was onto what he was onto, thought it was pretty smart of her to get off the phone. "They probably have at least one of our lines tapped," he mumbled to himself as he hung up.

Later that afternoon, before he left work, he quickly wrote a note to Jocelyn asking her to contact him as soon as she got the chance. He attached the photos that he had taken and personally developed himself. Not wanting to fold the eight-and-a-half-by-eleven-inch photos, he grabbed a UPS letter package from the shipping department.

Jerry filled out the shipping slip and gave it to Gary, the shipping guy who had helped Jocelyn with the AUSA exhibit. Gary, seeing that the letter was addressed to Jocelyn, smiled and asked, "Hey, did she have the kids yet? I'm still in the running for the big money with the winning birthday date! Tell her to hold those bambinos in for another month."

They shared a laugh as Jerry left the office. And Gary charged the shipping of Jocelyn's letter off to the Indonesia contract, despite (or perhaps because of) the litany of paperwork regarding the tsunami that had blown away millions of dollars' and years' worth of the division's time and effort—thus landing Jerry's shipping expenditure into the hard-to-define state of being otherwise known as "insurance claim purgatory."

Later that evening, Jocelyn, now the size of a Volkswagen Beetle, reclined on Ethan's couch in the little vinyl-sided house he'd found for them in the neighboring state of Rhode Island. The house was small, tucked into an old navy housing development that had been booming with life and barbecues back in the 1950s and '60s. Now, since the base had closed, the neighborhood was filled with old people, and the houses, with their barely maintained lawns, reflected as much. Although Jocelyn owned some beautiful furniture, most of it simply didn't fit into this new house. Her house that she had just left back in Connecticut had been a huge Victorian that she and her ex-husband had rehabbed.

This tiny house that Ethan had recently purchased was a mess—a real handyman special. The roof leaked, which meant the ceilings and walls needed fixing and painting. The bathroom was a certifiable disaster; the vanity and door were all chewed and scratched. Apparently, the former owner would lock the dog in there while she was working as a home health aide, so it had stunk pretty badly the day they'd moved in. The kitchen was several decades outdated. And you could hear squirrels running around in the attic. But it had a really nice, big backyard, and Ethan knew he could fix the house up.

Jocelyn knew that, if she could live through the two-year renovation project at her last house, she could deal with this.

Even though this new Rhode Island house was pretty beat up, at least it was currently sanitary. Jocelyn's mother had come the day they'd moved in and worked her fingers to the bone scrubbing. Ammonia and bleach still hung in the air. It was going to be cute, and more importantly, it was going to be a real home for the kids—a home with a mom *and* a dad. Neither Jocelyn nor Ethan had had a dad around when they were kids, and both felt that this dad thing was important. They also both didn't want to get married, seeing as they both equated marriage with divorce. And divorce was expensive and basically sucked. Learning that Jocelyn would receive better health benefits from the state for the kids by *not* being married basically ended talk of marriage for them.

With her swollen ankles up on a stack of pillows, she (yet again) lovingly flipped through the grainy black-and-white printouts from the day's ultrasound. There they were! Her babies (or at least some reasonable two-dimensional facsimile that she could hold onto). She couldn't wait to meet them.

She glanced at Ethan's digital clock on the floor next to the stack of cardboard moving boxes and the overly ornate, Victorian fern stand. Ethan would be home soon with the Chinese food. She was starving. They were going to have a picnic on the rug and watch her favorite show, *24*, that night. She would show him the ultrasound pictures then.

Having exhausted, at least for the time being, her interest in looking at the black-and-white abstractions, which she adoringly called her kids, she flipped on the evening news. "Blah, blah, blah, and blah. Same old stuff," Jocelyn said as she switched the channel. "Oh, look! There's Veronica's piece!" She sat in rapt attention, critiquing how the reporter handled the two minutes, which just so happened to feature some of the B-roll that she had helped her replacement, Veronica, compile for what she had heard people calling "the liberally-slanted" CNN.

Truth be told, they were all the same. All the major news outlets pushed basically the same products and agendas and, more importantly, *avoided* all the same stories. This would seem unlikely at first blush, but the channels made their money not so much by reporting but by playing off of the psychology of different audiences.

Even NPR. Which was very disheartening to Jocelyn when she finally figured this out. She had always enjoyed her *Morning Edition* as she drove into work. And by the time she left her job at the Conglomerate—now knowing that PBS/NPR and FOX watchers were the most (almost pathologically) loyal to their brands of news because of the way the script and announcers manipulated a very base desire to be perceived as "intelligent and well educated" or "no-nonsense and common-sense minded" (as if the two descriptions were mutually exclusive concepts)—Jocelyn would have to smirk, knowing she was willingly falling into the trap of demographically designed news.

A monotone, detached delivery provided a logical, scientific car ride with the news of the day. Clearly *you*, intelligent person, knew what was going on was the final takeaway. And when smattered with some jazz, bluegrass, or classical music, a perfect nesting place was created for extremely powerful biomed and education interests.

Of course, if your need to self-actualize was not sufficiently fulfilled via the mainline, government-sponsored fix of PBS/NPR, perhaps you enjoyed the more emotionally charged, urgent delivery style of colorful graphics being digitally flung at you as you were talked to (okay, sometimes shouted at) as if you and the announcer were the only intelligent people on the planet and everyone else was a complete moron. Clearly, *you* knew what was going on. It was only common sense. The Pentagon lived here. The liberal media versus fair and balanced. If you bought that, then—bingo—you were hooked!

Jocelyn was pretty impressed with her replacement's spot on CNN, except that the piece talked too much about the Taliban when she knew that they were supposed to be focusing on Al-Qaeda, but that was okay. No one really knew what the heck the difference was anyway.

Just then, Ethan came in carrying two bags of takeout.

"Yum! Thanks, Ethan," Jocelyn said as she eagerly hoisted herself up off the couch to meet him over by the picnic blanket she had set up with plates and cups for their Chinese food picnic dinner. "Here. We'll eat over here," she directed him.

He came over, clearly entertained by the prospect of a picnic, and placed the bags down on the blanket. He kissed her cheek and hugged her as best he could manage around her considerable girth. "How are you feeling?" he asked as he placed one hand on her belly.

"I feel like a beached whale."

"Well, you look beautiful to me," Ethan said. "Are you hungry?" Jocelyn nodded emphatically.

"Good," he said. "Let's eat. I'm famished."

So the two of them settled down on the blanket and started in on the moo goo gai pan. Jocelyn showed him the ultrasound pictures, and they discussed his day at work. He was going to have to head off to Egypt with General Walton soon, and Jocelyn was anxious that he wouldn't be with her when she went into labor.

Before the conversation could get too emotional on Jocelyn's part, the show that she had been waiting for started up. Ethan was not a big TV guy, which was refreshing because her ex would have the television on constantly, like it was some sort of background music or soundtrack to their lives. She had found it really annoying. This, however, was different. This wasn't just any old crappy TV show. This was *24*! And Jocelyn took the opportunity to fill Ethan in on how great the storyline was because it happened in real time. It was like the audience was living through it. And she had placed some of the Conglomerate's products on the show. And, and, and ...

"What's this? A parental advisory at the beginning of the show?" Jocelyn said in surprise.

"Does it always have that?" Ethan asked.

"Not that I remember. This is the first time I've seen it," she said while putting her chicken wing back down on the paper plate.

"Well then, you know all the twelve-year-olds will be discussing this episode tomorrow at school," Ethan said, half-laughing as he snarfed down the rest of his egg roll.

The two of them watched as the main character, Jack Bauer, got graphically tortured for almost a half-hour until Jocelyn couldn't take it anymore and shut the show off. "What was that?!" Jocelyn asked of no one in particular.

"I don't know. It's your show. You mean it's not always like that?" Ethan said as he grabbed for some more spare ribs.

"No. No, it's not. I know that show is pretty good about product placement. I can't imagine which sponsors would be into associating with full-on abuse scenes like that. That just blew my mind."

"Oh, Joss. It's just TV. That was *sooo* not real; it was close, but ..." he said as he rooted around inside the takeout container for more lo mein. "Maybe people want to see that sort of stuff these days. The writers of the show must know what people are looking for. Just relax. It's not real."

"Well, it was real enough," she huffed.

Seeing that she was still visibly upset, he put the fork down and put his hand on her shoulder. Somehow, Ethan's nonchalance wasn't sitting right with Jocelyn. Of course the torture scene wasn't real. But it was the first time she had ever seen anything like that on TV.

That night as she tried to somehow position herself comfortably around oversized pillows, she thought through the situation with TV. There she was congratulating Veronica on a news piece that didn't even get the terms *Al-Qaeda* and *Taliban* right. And just as long as everyone watching at home was convinced that the world's greatest military superpower was vulnerable, Veronica had effectively enhanced shareholder value. Jocelyn was starting to deconstruct what she had been up to for the past seven years, and she suddenly became very, very angry.

I've been deceiving people. She started slowly at first. *Heck, I've been deceived. But by whom?* She paused to think about that and finally concluded, *No. I was kidding myself thinking that I had some sort of important job so that I could live with the fact that I'd been collecting a paycheck for manipulating tons of people like it was cool.* She tried to force herself to stop talking to herself but couldn't. *How the heck are folks supposed to make good decisions about anything— much less things like going to war—if they only have corporate information to base their judgments on? I mean, look at the news and how the Conglomerate does its magic.* Then it dawned on her, and she didn't know why she hadn't really thought about it before. *All the big companies listed on the New York Stock Exchange ... they all do it like that. It's just the normal course of business ... that's just how it's done.* She smirked thinking about that. *It's all marketing make-believe. The money* was *nice though.* She stared at the wall because she wasn't supposed to lie on her back. *It's like they're messing with everyone—preparing everyone for the enemy or something—like TV drama is the new reality. And shows like* 24 *are up to ... up to what? Getting people to accept torture and abuse as something mainstream ... or amusing or ... This is sick!* She really did not like what she was just beginning to touch the surface of. She finally fell asleep when Ethan rolled over and nestled in close.

The next day, perhaps due to an overabundance of pregnancy hormones, or possibly it was a bizarre side effect related to obsessing about her most recent job description, the beached whale, Volkswagen Beetle avatar of Jocelyn McLaren summoned all of its strength and carried the television out to the garbage.

Well, not all the way to the garbage. Jocelyn couldn't complete her trek while hauling the small appliance to the curb as she had envisioned. She was just too fat, and she was just too exhausted. So she settled on leaving the TV in the front yard. With her primary directive of purging the house of the television accomplished, she headed back in to take a well-deserved nap.

Later that day when Ethan came home and found the television positioned curiously in the yard and then discovered Jocelyn unconscious on the couch, his response was beyond his control.

For the average guy, this whole scene might have been a humorous speed bump while on the way to the fridge to claim a beer. But for someone with experiences closer to life and death in an extended, unpredictable situation like a war, Ethan's response was, unfortunately, more typical than most people might realize. He spoke loudly and clearly while checking Jocelyn's pulse. "Jocelyn. Jocelyn?! Are you okay? I'm here. I'm right here."

Jocelyn opened her eyes, confused. The man in front of her seemed to bear little resemblance to the man she had enjoyed Chinese food with the night before. This guy with his hand on her throat, barking at her, was super intense. To the point of being scary. Because of that, Jocelyn slipped into her version of life-saving mode. "Hi, sexy," she provocatively uttered, while producing the most angelic smile she could muster.

"What's wrong with you?" Ethan demanded while removing his fingers from her carotid artery.

Jocelyn quickly sat up (as quickly as she could) and inched away from him. "I'm fine. Just taking a nap. Are you okay? You look different."

"Yeah. I'm fine. What happened here? Why are you taking a nap?"

"I'm pregnant. Remember?"

"Of course I remember," he responded tersely. "Why is the TV in the front yard? Did someone break in?"

"Oh! That!" She started laughing. "No. No. I just didn't want it in the house with our babies—our family. I think it's poison. I don't think our kids, or us for that matter, need to be exposed to that nonsense all the time." Noticing that he wasn't laughing with her, she added, "It's my TV. You don't even watch it. I think I can get rid of it if I want to." When Ethan still did not respond in a way that Jocelyn was accustomed to, she reverted again to her life-saving mode persona. "Look at those muscles!" she said, touching his arm. "You're so strong."

Late that night, Jocelyn went into labor. Ethan was with her and held her hand the whole time. He even sang to her in the delivery room to keep her calm and let her know that he was there. The little boy (five pounds, twelve ounces) came out first that morning. And Jocelyn watched a tear roll down Ethan's face as the new little person, whom they had decided to call William, heartily cried his first breaths. Next came the little girl (five pounds, three ounces). Lillian emerged and cried so quietly that Jocelyn was panicked. She didn't even hear the baby, but the doctor assured her that the little girl was just fine, though born three weeks early. And despite both being tiny, they were healthy and beautiful. They had the same color hair as Jocelyn!

As the nurse rolled her to her hospital room, Jocelyn contentedly held one baby in each arm with Ethan walking proudly beside the stretcher. No special treatment was needed, and they all got to go home together after Jocelyn had had the chance to recuperate.

They might as well have installed a conveyer belt. The house, once the kids came home, became one big production facility of feeding, burping, and changing. Jocelyn, although she had read and heard from more than one concerned, newfound environmentalist the statistics about how many disposable diapers stacked up would reach the moon, didn't much care. It seemed like those giant boxes of Huggies couldn't get through her door fast enough.

It was about two sleepless weeks after the birth of her children. Ethan was in Egypt, and Jocelyn was managing the baby machine solo when she finally took note of the mess of mail stacked up on the kitchen counter. She gathered it all up and took it over to her desk to sort. Mostly junk mail mixed in with some bills. She was surprised to find a UPS letter tucked in with all of the other mail. She recognized the sender's address immediately and tore it open, only to be completely baffled by what it contained.

Hi Jocelyn,

I hope this letter finds you doing well. Smart thinking getting off the phone. NSA would be all over it. Check this shit out. I found it on our server last week. That's not supposed to be there! I don't think Dr. Lambert is behind this. We all know she doesn't have the skills. Ha!

Please let me know when you get this letter.

Very sincerely,

Jerry Apario

"What the heck is Jerry talking about?" She shook her head as she rifled through the large black-and-white photos of a computer screen—some of which were not much more descriptive than the ultrasound printouts she had gotten at the hospital of the kids in utero. Jocelyn started to seriously question her former coworker's mental health. "I don't understand why Jerry is concerned about NASA," she muttered. "Like the space agency would give a hoot about the division's server." She read through his letter again and snorted. "Jerry is so weird. He even spelled it wrong." One of the babies started crying, distracting her from her thoughts. "Oh, someone wants a new diaper," Jocelyn announced. And as soon as she said it, the other baby started to cry. "Yup, right on cue. These two are like clockwork." She stuffed Jerry's photos and letter back into its UPS packaging and tossed it into her bottom desk drawer. Though the bags under her eyes had bags under them, she smiled as she trotted off to comfort her babies.

Jocelyn never got back to Jerry, although he would leave her messages on her cell phone. Eventually, he stopped calling.

CHAPTER FOUR

Two weeks later

SPLASH! AS MUCH AS HE tried, Ethan could not wash the stain away, and it bothered him. The water was still streaming relentlessly into the pedestal sink in their newly tiled, all-white bathroom. His black mock turtleneck was rumpled up in the corner, but he still had his jeans and Doc Martens on. It was nearing 3:00 a.m., 9:00 a.m. Ledergerber's time. *Fuckin' cocksucker. Fuckin' figures. Shithead had to set me up with that motherfuckin' douchebag.* He squeezed his left hand hard into a fist and inspected his knuckles. There were no cuts.

It had been about a year since he had had any interaction with Ledergerber. So much time had passed that he'd even entertained the thought that he might have somehow eluded the man. No such luck. Ledergerber was now making good on his repayment of debt thing. The part that made Ethan uncomfortable was that he really didn't know when the repayment period was going to be officially over.

The water was still running, and Jocelyn knocked on the door again to see if he was all right. "Can I get you something?" she called past the bathroom door.

"No. Please, just go to bed, Joss. I'll be in in a minute." He was getting sick of hearing her voice, and he grabbed for the Clorox as he stared at the stain. It had originally been red and had spilled like an egg being cracked over his head. Then it had turned black as ink and filled his entire field of view. As he stared at himself, a little pinhole in the black opened and grew, allowing him to at least look at himself. It had all made sense when he was a "good guy." Navy SEALs were good. Right? It had even made sense as a

28

contractor working for the good guys. Sure, he hadn't gotten to wear the uniform, but he'd gotten paid a hell of a lot better. Now he was dealing with Ledergerber and vast amounts of wealth. When, exactly, did the same exact stuff become not good? It used to all make sense, compartmentalized and tucked away where it was supposed to be. He splashed the Clorox into his hands and scrubbed his face again.

The creeping black stain would not go away and insidiously burrowed deeper into the cavities of his mind.

CHAPTER FIVE

About a year later

JOCELYN HAD STUCK TO HER plan and was now the proud owner of four income properties. She had bought them all with thirty-year, fixed-rate mortgages. Nothing exotic. She didn't quite understand why people would want to mess with those adjustable rate things. Her credit score was surprisingly great. Like perfect. Better than it had been even when working at the Conglomerate and paying her bills religiously with automatic bill pay. Right now, stores were falling over themselves to offer her even more credit.

She was surprised because it wasn't like she was rich; in fact, she was technically pretty poor, even though, on the books, she was a multimillionaire. The income from the properties and the due dates on her bills had to be timed just right. But she was swinging it month after month. No one had said it would be easy money. Well, maybe Carlton Sheets had said that somewhere on one of those "Investing in Real Estate" cassette tapes she had purchased. But the job of buying, fixing up, and renting property seemed like a decent way to earn a living compared to the BS at her previous job.

She had gotten rid of her silver C280 sport Mercedes as soon as the kids arrived. She and Ethan had had one particularly tedious evening trying to install the baby car seats in the tiny back seat. And both of them had concluded that this was no way to live—collecting state aid while driving around in a Mercedes that they couldn't even install a baby seat in, let alone two baby seats. "This is just ridiculous!" Ethan had huffed while wedged in the backseat and motioning for Jocelyn to hand him a screwdriver.

So she'd researched the car situation and decided to replace the car with a new silver Hyundai Santa Fe. It seemed like an affordable and super-safe baby carriage. She was pleasantly surprised that the Hyundai had all the same features as the Mercedes that she had just given up. And it was silver, so she still felt fancy driving it around—which helped when she would go to the gas station and pay with rolls of quarters that she had collected from the coin-operated laundry machines she had installed at her rental properties.

One particularly tight month, Jocelyn even entertained the idea of cashing in one of those gold coins that she had discovered in her desk at work. They were still a mystery. She had no idea who had left them. Just holding the coins had made her relive a lot of the bad feelings associated with the Conglomerate. *Damn, that place was creepy*, Jocelyn thought as she flipped the coins over with her fingers. She didn't know why, but she had never even mentioned the discovery of the coins to Ethan. She had just buried that episode along with all sorts of stuff she would rather not think about. Of course, she would have happily sold the coins, but having no idea how exactly to do that, although she had looked online, she didn't have anyone to ask for advice; and she felt funny even talking about it. Plus, she feared that she would get ripped off. So she just kept them in her jewelry box—the box where she kept, rather than expensive jewelry, keepsakes like seashells and love notes that Ethan had given her back when, you know, when he was still around, before that night when the babies woke everyone up.

The kids had, thankfully, been sleeping through the night pretty regularly. No problem. But late that particular night, one of the kids had decided to just belt it out and started crying uncontrollably. Naturally, the other twin immediately joined in, and the screaming and crying jolted both Jocelyn and Ethan from a deep sleep. Surprised and blinking herself back to life, Jocelyn did what she had been doing for many nights, months before, and automatically scuttled to the kids' room to pat some backs, check diapers, and hold them. They were both fine, and almost as suddenly as they had awoken, they fell back to sleep.

"One of them must have had a bad dream or something," Jocelyn said as she pulled back the covers and climbed into bed.

Ethan didn't respond. He was just lying there like a hollow log staring at the ceiling. Jocelyn noticed he was breathing in short, shallow breaths, and she reached out to touch his shoulder. She was about to ask if he was okay when he spun over and smacked her hand away.

This took Jocelyn completely off guard. "Hey! I'm just trying to help. What's your problem?"

He just sort of snarled and snapped his eyes shut.

"Oh, like I get up and take care of the kids and you're the one all bent out of shape. Nice, Ethan. Real nice." Jocelyn sat watching him, waiting for a response.

But none ever came. And Jocelyn could swear she saw Ethan sailing away that night—as if he had jumped some sort of metaphysical ship and skated off.

Sure, Ethan was still physically around, but he was not *with* her. Jocelyn would cry to her counselor on a weekly basis about this and try to describe in detail the particulars of Ethan's mental absence. It was often, but not always, triggered by a cell phone ringing and would always end up with a boozy bedtime smell. The thing that mystified her was that she never really saw him drinking—not like her ex-husband, who handled a beer bottle as if it were an extension of his left arm. No. It wasn't like that. "Self-medicating" is what the counselor called it. Jocelyn called it "jackassery," which she attempted to peacefully avoid as much as possible.

Regardless of this intermittent here/not-here thing, Ethan had done some serious work to the little house, and for that, Jocelyn was immensely grateful. The bathroom was completely remodeled in all white. To spiff it up and make it a little more interesting, he had laid the special-order, subway floor tiles in a herringbone pattern. It really was an incredible transformation. And Jocelyn was very proud to relate the gory details of the previous owner's dog's confinement and Ethan braving and conquering the seeped-in dog urine whenever a guest had occasion to visit the room.

The kitchen had new, wide-plank wood floors that Ethan had laid and stained himself. And some decent Home Depot cabinetry had been installed. The whole house had new windows, the leaks were fixed, and the interior painted in Jocelyn's choice of colors. Not as heavy and dramatic as the Victorian she had left in Connecticut but unusual and classy combinations nonetheless. Ethan had even ripped off the vinyl siding and re-sided the house with clapboard. He'd painted the new wood siding "cottage yellow" because Jocelyn had learned that yellow houses statistically had the best curb appeal value. They were both surprised that the color really did make the little house look adorable. In all outward appearances, this was the house that both she and Ethan had envisioned. This was where a real family was supposed to live—a real family that they had both been dreaming about.

Jocelyn's proudest achievement was her kids. They were so happy and bright as they crawled around learning to walk. Sure, it was tedious putting away the pots and pans that they had pillaged from the cabinets for the third, fourth, or millionth time. Or cleaning pureed spinach off the ceiling fan and their faces. But they were so cute when she got a chance to just observe them hanging out in their bouncy chairs babbling with each other. Despite the fact that Jocelyn was sometimes overwhelmed, she came to appreciate the phrase, "God gives you only that which you can handle."

And Jocelyn was stronger than she had ever felt in her life—even better than she had been when she was pregnant and wearing pink all the time. After delivering the babies, she'd started immediately back on her MS medication. And after shedding over forty pounds of baby weight, she felt like Wonder Woman. She could do anything. Even her arms were in shape from picking up the growing kids over and over again.

With no TV in the house and Ethan intermittently floating around somewhere else, Jocelyn started to seek out entertainment in the form of books and on the Internet while the kids slept. There was this new thing called YouTube, and it was really cool! She could watch a music video or a five-minute clip on how to make rice pudding, people bungee jumping in Australia, or a short performance of musicians playing ukuleles at the MET in New York City. And it was free! Who could ask for anything more? Seriously.

One day as her children napped, Jocelyn wanted to revisit her formerly ultracool self and searched to see if any of her old friends back in Boston had produced YouTube videos. Sure enough—*Oh, look at Corey and his band, The Pills!* Making an effort to fight back pangs of regret for abandoning her natural artistic inclinations to take a job at a defense contractor, she mentally congratulated her old buddies for sticking with it. Then she looked for some of the music she used to listen to while she painted in her non-live-in artist's studio, which, naturally, she had lived in.

Oh, Metallica! That's a good one! She clicked on what appeared to be a video for a song by a related band, Pantera. The title, "Don't Tread on Me," was familiar.

Curiously, the video had absolutely nothing do with the band Metallica or Pantera. It started silently with a quote from Thomas Jefferson on a black background and flowed right into a clip from Comedy Central's Jon Stewart interviewing a congressman whom Jocelyn had never heard of. The music kicked in. It was a well-known bass line of an Aerosmith song she hadn't heard in years, and it was enough to grab her and hold her attention for the next eight minutes. She sat and watched with growing interest as snips of nationally televised presidential debates and simply presented text became the backdrop as the congressman spoke about Iraq and the national debt and—

"What the heck?!" Jocelyn would have shouted if it hadn't been for the babies sleeping in the next room. *Who is this guy? And he's running for president?* Jocelyn was very near insulted that she did not know who this congressman was. *Dr. Ray Pierce? I was a paid lobbyist for cripes sake, and I've never even stumbled upon this person?*

She was also intrigued because this man was from Texas of all places. Texas, a Conglomerate stronghold. She had never even seen his name mentioned in any of the memos that came over or down to her. Never. She wondered why.

She was beginning to feel out of the loop not having a television and not having a jobby-job, which of course she had hated. But it had given her some semblance of being among the living. She did a search for the congressman's name and found out he had been in Congress for about as long as her former CEO's best drinking buddy, Stan the Congressman. *Hum. They must know each other*, Jocelyn thought. And she watched the video again.

And again.

And again.

After working at the Conglomerate, she found that she agreed with this Ray Pierce guy's stance regarding Afghanistan and Iraq—especially because she knew more well-paid contractors were marching around over there than were US troops. Many more. From her perspective, the inclusion of the soldiers in the media's storyline was just a cover for the corporations that were already pillaging the place with the blessing of USAID. She knew about that stuff.

But she was enthralled because she'd had absolutely no idea, like none, that the national debt had reached $9 trillion. Nor had she known anything about the interest on that $9 trillion that the federal government was shouldering. She was literally astounded that the grand total was more like $50 trillion and that repayment of that broke down to over $50,000 per person. And that included her kids, and, and, and ... Jocelyn was bounced from this financial downward spiral by the kids, who were, not surprisingly, doing the I'm-not-sleeping-anymore cry.

"Are you guys waking up?!" Jocelyn called down the hall. She knew that her daughter would probably be precariously hanging halfway out of the crib by the time she reached the kids' room. As she headed to stave off a pediatric head injury, she made a mental note to contact Stan the congressman at his new lobbying firm. Maybe he'd give her the scoop on the guy in the video.

CHAPTER SIX

JOCELYN HAD TRACKED DOWN THE number Stan had given her the last time she had seen him and his obnoxious, yellow, midlife-crisis sports car. She dialed the number, hoping to find out more about that congressman from Texas.

However, during the course of their conversation, she found out much more—specifically, why he had basically kidnapped her and brought her to breakfast in DC years ago.

As it turned out, the number for his "lobbying firm" was actually his cell phone. And when he answered, she could barely hear him. So they hung up, and he called back.

"Ah. Jaaaaaaaaaaahhhhhhcelyn!" he greeted her in his familiar way. "To what do I owe the pleasure of this unexpected call from someone as lovely as yourself?"

"Hi, Stan. Looks like lobbying hasn't changed you a bit," Jocelyn said, half-sighing, half-giggling in her customary dealing-with-Stan way.

"Oh, darling, lobbying has only served to hone my unique abilities. I'm so glad you called. I was just thinking about you."

"Really?" Jocelyn asked, honestly surprised.

"Yes, my mind often wanders to pleasant visions."

"Stan, for goodness' sake, please stop."

"At your command." He laughed. "Anyway, it's funny you should call. I was talking with one of my friends who is looking for some help at his agency, and I thought of you."

This piqued Jocelyn's interest. She had been starting to think that maybe she needed a real job. Although the landlord thing made her officially, on paper anyway, a millionaire, the cash flow wasn't going to cut the mustard. "Oh, thanks for thinking of me, Stan. What's the job? I might be interested," she asked, supposing that it would have something to do with press relations or graphic design. And hoping that it had little or nothing to do with proposals.

"Oh, it would be easy for you. You just go to parties."

Disappointed, she asked, "What's the catch, Stan? Am I going to be promoting a brand of vodka or something?"

"Ha! No. You just go to a function looking like your lovely self, mingle, and then type up a report about it after the party. The pay and benefits are decent."

"Who is going to pay me to be a socialite?" Jocelyn asked skeptically.

"Ultimately, the US government, of course."

"Huh?"

Apparently Stan was enjoying this. He seemed to be laughing a lot. "You've already met the person who I'm talking about. He was the gentleman at the Hay-Adams who took your picture after we had breakfast."

It took Jocelyn a moment to place what Stan was talking about and rejigger her memories. "You mean that couple by the flower arrangement in the lobby?"

Stan chuckled, and Jocelyn was confused. "Sweetheart, you seem so well-suited for this. Your reports that I saw were well written and very useful. You don't have to let that go to waste. People would pay for that. The two reports that I was most impressed with were the one about Project LISA and the other about Drumthwacket. They were so interesting that I had you checked out. You're clean. Or at least, you're very good at your job."

"Drumthwacket? The New Jersey governor's mansion? You mean that report I did up from Princeton?" She sighed and rolled her eyes thinking of it. "Well, I'm glad you enjoyed that, but, Stan, I was at the wrong conference."

"Right. And I'm sure you didn't see it in the papers."

Now Jocelyn, although puzzled, started laughing. "What the heck are you talking about, Stan? Look, I was calling to check out a congressman that I have never heard of. Maybe you've met him? Congressman Pierce? From Texas?"

Suddenly, Stan seemed eager to end the call. He quickly explained the reason why Jocelyn had never heard of the congressman in question. It was because Dr. Raymond Pierce did not, like ever, deal with lobbyists, and everyone knew that. "They call him Dr. No," Stan said. "He seems to enjoy just sitting there voting nay on everything." Stan gave a forced laugh. "So that's probably why he's not on your radar. He's kind of an unusual bird. I haven't really dealt with him one-on-one. Listen, I have to go. As per usual, it has been wonderful to hear your voice, Jocelyn. Please feel free to call me anytime."

"Thanks, Stan. Hey, I'll send you a picture of my twins," Jocelyn said with matronly pride.

"I'd actually rather see a picture of you, my dear—perhaps something showcasing your lovely legs and a pair of heels—"

"Stan! What the heck? Stop! Okay?"

Stan laughed unrepentantly as he bid her one of his patented, over-the-top farewells and suggested that she refresh her memory about Drumthwacket.

Jocelyn hung up the phone, exasperated. "What a lecherous ass." She couldn't believe that he had actually said that, but then again, she could.

Still smoldering, she hopped out of the car and headed into her house. The car was the only place she could make a phone call without being interrupted by her kids. Previously, the bathroom had been her call center refuge, but as soon as the kids discovered that it was just good, clean fun to start banging on the bathroom door and shouting at the top of their lungs while she was in there trying to talk to the likes of a bank or a building contractor, she had to relocate. As Jocelyn mentally reviewed the phone conversation, she realized that the whole experience had not only served to confirm that Stan the former congressman was certifiably a grade-A asshole, it had encouraged her to look further into this presidential candidate from Texas, Dr. Raymond Pierce.

Later that night, Jocelyn sat at her computer. It was the computer that she had bought while pregnant and still working for the Conglomerate. She had made sure to buy the latest and greatest with her money because she knew she probably wouldn't be buying anything for a while once the babies arrived.

Recalling her conversation with Stan, she started searching for Drumthwacket. Up came some websites with pictures and a list of the former governors who had lived there and, "Ohhhh ..." Jocelyn furrowed her brow as she read the archived news story.

With his wife and parents standing beside him, Governor Jim McGreevey announced on August 12, 2004, that he was gay, that he had a consensual homosexual adulterous affair, and was resigning effective November 15, 2004.

... It has to do with his affair with Israeli citizen Golan Cipel. Cipel, a former soldier in the IDF, was appointed by McGreevey to head New Jersey's Homeland Security apparatus. In short, the married governor and he had a tryst, and the unqualified Cipel got one of the most important jobs in New Jersey— a state that was identified as one of the targets in the recent terror alert.

Critics claim that McGreevey endangered state and national security by appointing a man who was unqualified for the post and possibly a spy for the Mossad. Cipel also formerly worked in the Israeli consulate in New York.

Golan   Cipel   threatened   McGreevey with a sexual harassment lawsuit.

"No way. He and his wife were married at the Hay-Adams? Wow." She recalled the breakfast and the guy taking her picture. Jocelyn read the story with interest. The former New Jersey governor was now living in a mansion that had eight bedrooms and five fireplaces with his new partner, an Australian investment banker.

"Well, that guy's political career is done," Jocelyn mumbled as she shook her head. She would always remember his speech about the 9/11 first responders. He was really good. She thought for sure that he was on the fast track for national politics. *I mean, I would have voted for the guy. I wonder why Stan thinks I need to know this.* Jocelyn pressed print and reminisced as a copy of the article began chugging out of the printer.

Robert had called her into his office, handed her a stack of business cards, and told her to go to Princeton University the very next morning and come back with as much information as she could.

Jocelyn had gotten there bright and early, and when she'd seen a cluster of business attire moving in one general direction, she'd jumped in.

"You going to the conference?"

"Yup."

"Me, too! Where are you coming from?" Jocelyn had asked.

"RBS."

She gained entry to the auditorium with the RBS gentleman and, not knowing where to sit figured, *Why not right up front?* She noticed a harried woman on the stage attempting to collate a gargantuan stack of papers.

"Hey, you look you might need another set of hands. Want some help?"

"Oh, thank you. Please. Yes. Here, take this stack and start handing them out."

So it was in this way that Jocelyn had met every single member of the audience at the Assessing and Analyzing CyberCrimes at the New York Stock Exchange conference. She had traded business cards with people as she distributed the technical paper, making sure to keep one for herself to include in her summary report for Robert.

She took notes when the guy from the FBI spoke about Internet pedophilia and the online sex statistics happening right on Wall Street and took copious notes about the speed of the latest processors and hardware the NYSE servers were using and made sure to get the correct spelling of the various NYSE board members and Dow Jones dignitaries who spoke. When it appeared that the auditorium session was over, she fell into a breakout working group, where she discussed her perspective of the IBM ThinkPad with its creator. Of course, she didn't have a ThinkPad, but she knew someone who did.

At almost five o'clock, she had plopped herself atop a low stone wall next to the street and started writing her notes about the people she had met while organizing the business cards she had acquired. It was then that a bunch of men with mustaches walked up and asked if this was where the bus was going to pick everyone up from the conference for dinner.

"I don't know, but I sure hope it is—I'm starving!" was Jocelyn's response.

The guys thought that was funny.

"Okay, you come with us. We'll all find out how to get to that dinner. You know it should be good food at the governor's mansion." Jocelyn took time to meet everyone on the bus going to the governor's mansion. Some of the women were very expertly outfitted in designer cocktail dresses. Jocelyn complimented the women, who were not impolite but who did let her know that the men with the mustaches were a bit underdressed for the occasion. "Oh, I'm not with them. I just met them at the bus stop," she'd said. "Am I okay with what I have on? I'm coming from the conference." The ladies assured her that her outfit, although obviously business attire, was probably fine. Jocelyn joked, "Well, at the very least, people might just think I'm part of the waitstaff." They all chuckled politely. The bus soon slowed down to a stop.

The contents of the bus were capably ushered up the front steps past the tall, white columns and into the graciously appointed foyer and sitting room at Drumthwacket, the official residence of the governor of New Jersey, where it appeared that IDs were being checked and invitations collected.

Jocelyn noticed that the well-dressed women had quickly distanced themselves from her and commented, rather disparagingly, about having to show ID. "Is this a new thing?" She also noticed that the men with mustaches did not have invitations and were being questioned but were eventually allowed entry. Not quite sure what to do, she slipped into the sitting room and looked at the portraits of the past governors.

"Might I offer you a drink?"

Jocelyn turned around. "Oh, why, thank you. But no. I am really looking for the ladies' room." She had just realized that she hadn't made time to find a restroom all day, and it suddenly became urgent at the mention of a drink.

The young man taking drink orders must have sensed the import of the situation and quickly led her to the foot of the master stairway. "Here. Go up there." He pointed. "It will be the second door on your left."

After freshening herself up, she headed back downstairs and thanked the waiter, who was loading up his serving platter. "Would you like a drink now?" he said while handing her a glass of Chardonnay.

She smiled, accepted the glass, and followed him out onto the patio, where it was apparent that the real movers and shakers were taking care of the important business.

She set to work, working the crowd. She introduced herself to the mayor and to the governor after they issued their welcoming addresses, which paid tribute to the "true heroes." The governor was a fantastic speaker. *This guy should run for president someday*, thought Jocelyn. She wasn't particularly into politics, hadn't even recognized the guy's name, but Jocelyn was impressed because he was such an eloquent and moving speaker, and she respected that. Being that she was in the proximity of the governor, other men approached her for her business card, and she exchanged cards with them as well. She was racking up a big stack of cards to bring back to the office.

Eventually she headed to the buffet, which had magically appeared in the center of the patio. And magically appearing at the same time from the direction of the porta-potties were the mustached men from the bus stop. "Hey! Strawberry Shortcake! We found you! Great party, huh?" She smiled, happy to have someone at least appear to know her and give her a reason for being there.

All that was the good part of the memory. The bad part had been her boss Robert's reaction to the report she had done up.

"What the fuck is this?! I send you to a NYC First Responders conference—one that the whole goddamn fucking world is going to be paying attention to—and you come home with this *tome* about child molesters, IBM ThinkPads, the stock market and, and, what's this? A full write-up about the history of Drumthwacket? What the hell is Drumthwacket, Jocelyn!? *You* needed to be at that First Responders conference passing out *our* division's business card and getting *your* face in front of cameras talking about *our* proprietary software!"

Jocelyn smirked. *Thank God I'm not working there anymore*, she thought as she looked over the inkjet copy of the news story about Governor McGreevey and Golan Cipel.

Then she stashed it in her bottom desk drawer—the drawer where she put all the stuff she knew was somehow important enough to keep but not important enough to do anything with.

Still not quite sure what to make of the Drumthwacket thing, she turned her online search attention to Congressman Dr. Raymond Pierce. Her searches brought her to more— make that many more—YouTube videos. They all seemed to be thoroughly homemade creations. Jocelyn was pretty impressed with the effort that regular folks were willing to put into making the videos. She had never imagined people getting that creative while thinking about a politician. Some of the videos mentioned a thing called www.meetup.com. Having never heard of it, she checked it out.

Oh, this seems pretty cool, Jocelyn thought as she scanned the website. It was basically an events page. A person could search for interesting things to do in his or her local area. Anyone could create a Meetup group around any topic of interest—hiking, weight loss, gardening, anything. If you saw something you liked, you joined the online group and then RSVP'd for the next in-person group get-together.

It appeared that Congressman Pierce had a vast army of Meetup groups, not only in the United States but in other countries as well. Jocelyn wasn't sure what to make of this, because the other candidates that she had heard of had very little presence on Meetup, if at all. Impressed with what she was learning about the candidate via these online, homemade videos and the support this guy seemed to have on YouTube and on Meetup, added to the fact that Stan, her former senior congressman, had told her point-blank that the man never bargained with lobbyists, she found a local Raymond Pierce Meetup group and pressed RSVP.

CHAPTER SEVEN

JOCELYN WAS PRETTY PSYCHED BECAUSE she finally got to wear those cool boots she had bought on a whim at Discount Shoe Warehouse over a year ago. This was her first time going out of the house solo on a certifiably "grown-up" mission. She brushed her long hair and put on some lipstick.

"Wow," Ethan said as he eyed her through the bedroom door. "You look nice. I haven't seen you get dressed up like this in a long time."

"That's not true," she said, glancing up at him in the mirror. She gave a smile and noticed that he wasn't returning it. "I have to deal with the banks and Home Depot all the time."

"Yeah, well, I've never seen you take as much effort as you are right now."

"Oh, it's just jeans." She poked him in the belly on the way out of their room. "Just you never mind. I'll be home right after the meeting." She grabbed her purse. "I'm really curious about this Ray Pierce guy." She kissed him on the cheek and put on her coat. "I'll give you a full report when I get back." Then both the kids got some mommy love.

As she stepped out of the house, instantly the kids began crying. Walking toward her car, she could hear them wailing, and fiddling with her keys, she felt compelled to go back inside and kiss them again. Ethan finally had to tell her, "Just go, Joss. You're making it worse," as he held both the weepy children on his lap.

In a weird way, she felt guilty as she left Ethan with the crying kids, but she snapped on her radio and sped to the library. She was already late and, while on final approach, had to keep checking the directions she had written down, but she found it. As she drove around the parking lot, she took note of the building. It was new and had obviously been built when she was living in Connecticut. It had that '90s-style architecture, which was basically the same as '80s architecture but with not as much emphasis on arches and columns. That effort seemed to have been redirected into floor-to-ceiling windows in this two-story building. It had the same fake-looking bricks, though.

She hopped out of the car, trotted through the main entrance, and spotted the bulletin board by the closed double doors on her right.

```
6:00 p.m.
Raymond Pierce for President Group
```

She slowly opened one of the doors and walked into the beige-carpeted public conference room. The meeting had already started. "Okay, we're still waiting to hear what the schedule is going to be on signature sheets," said the man standing in front of the forty people assembled. The chairs were arranged in rows, and everyone was seated facing the speaker.

"What's a signature sheet, Kris?" someone in the audience asked with hand raised.

"Oh, in order to get on the ballot, a candidate has to receive a certain number of handwritten signatures. The state wants to know if enough voters are willing to put this person on the ballot," Kris Jung, the man who had organized the meeting, answered as he watched Jocelyn slip into a seat.

"But the election isn't until November. That's almost a year away," a guy about Jocelyn's age interjected.

"Right. But in order to be considered for the presidential election in November of next year, a candidate has to get through the primary. We are a primary state, but most other states have caucuses. We, thank God, don't have to worry about that. That's a different ball of wax. We just have to get Dr. Pierce on our state's primary ballot right now."

"So Dr. Pierce has to win the primary before anyone can vote for him as president?" another woman about thirty-five years old asked.

"Yes."

"And who can vote in the primary? I've never voted in a primary," a young man wanted to know.

Jocelyn noticed that the heavyset organizer of this Meetup was starting to perspire. His formerly controlled tone of voice was starting to exhibit a hint of staccato, which would reach a near crescendo in about ten minutes. Jocelyn was curious about that last question because she had never voted in a primary, either. Sure, she prided herself on having voted in every election since she was old enough to vote, but somehow this primary aspect had eluded her.

The now sweating organizer took a deep breath and continued with a little more intensity. "Any registered voter can vote in our primary. But it's different in every state."

Someone else chimed in. "Can I vote in both the Democratic and Republican Primaries? I'm a registered Democrat."

"No! For goodness' sake! If you want to vote for Dr. Pierce in the primary, you are going to have to disaffiliate." The registered Democrat looked disappointed, and the organizer continued. "What we need now is people. We just need people—people to march around and collect signatures to get the doctor on the ballot." He paused and took a breath. "But we don't have the official signature sheets yet. The secretary of state's office said they would have gotten this information to me by now, but they haven't. I can only imagine why they do this to us."

"Figures. This state can't get anything right," contributed a guy who looked as if he were lounging in his chair.

"Oh, that's just part of its charm," someone added from the back of the room.

It was at this point that a diminutive woman with short, well-styled hair, who looked like she was maybe in her fifties, decided to pipe up. "I think that we should be working on getting people aware of Dr. Pierce and what he stands for. No one knows who he is outside of this little group. I write letters to the editor and try to mention Dr. Pierce, but we need to really let people know who Dr. Raymond Pierce is."

The organizer grabbed a bunch of brochures off the front table and started to pass them out as he glared at the woman. "Look, Samantha, this is what we have! People should be passing these Slim Jims out to everyone they see."

"No!" Samantha said so forcefully that it surprised Jocelyn. "These are horrible! I don't know why the campaign, or *you*, thinks these are helpful. These can only hurt us here. Kris, I know that there are different versions of these available from the campaign. Why do you keep bringing us this version about abortion? The economy and foreign policy is where Dr. Pierce stands apart from the other candidates." She waved her Slim Jim around as she spoke and tossed it on the table where Kris had just picked his stack up. "It has nothing to do with what's going on here in our state. Our state is more independently minded, and there's a huge opportunity to swing this vote. We need to design something that speaks to the people here. Can't someone just take the logo off one of those?" She pointed to her discarded brochure. "I can put together a bunch of bullet points—"

Jocelyn saw this as her chance to say something that might add value. Accepting the passed Slim Jim, Jocelyn responded to Samantha, "I can do some graphic design and deal with the press. Heck, I can put together a whole marketing plan for our state if you want."

All heads turned to look at her. "That's what I did for work, and now I'm out of work. I can do something. Does the campaign have a budget for our state?"

The that's-part-of-the-state's-charm guy was the first to respond. "No. Everyone here is doing this out of their own pocket. We are making our own material because the official campaign's stuff pretty much sucks." He produced some folded papers from inside his jacket pocket and proudly handed them to Jocelyn. "I made these last night. I brought them to share with the group."

Jocelyn looked at the paper. It looked as if it had been produced on a mimeograph (if those were still around), and then she looked at the official Slim Jim. "This is what we are working with?" she asked incredulously.

"I've made a bunch of CDs that I like to hand out to people," a man in a fedora hat added, holding up a homemade CD.

"Oh, those are great!" Samantha said enthusiastically. "Can I get a few more of those?"

Jocelyn's inner brand manager was having a serious conniption.

Who lets a presidential candidate walk out the door with such a mishmash of collateral material floating around? No wonder people don't know who this guy is!

Another person, a graying man wearing a blue down jacket and jeans, held up a hardcover book. "I've bought about twenty copies of this book. It contains all of Pierce's floor speeches. And I give them away."

"Nice."

"Oh, that's a great book."

"I give away Alex Jones movies. I find that really shakes people up."

What the hell is going on?! Jocelyn thought as she watched the Meetup group congratulate each other on what was the equivalent of corporate branding chaos. No, make that a branding disaster. Nope, still not right. This was branding death. Thinking that she had to somehow manage this, Jocelyn said, "How about I check out some demographics and put together a simple marketing plan for us? Just so that we can see how much it might cost. Then we can try and hit up the campaign to see if they can give us some money to pay for it."

People nodded and mumbled in general consent. Someone in the back of the room said, "Knock yourself out."

Jocelyn took that as her green light to fix this car crash of a campaign, and she felt thrilled to have made a little project for herself—one that she might be able to use as a portfolio piece when she finally did start applying for jobs again.

As the meeting format seemed to haphazardly disintegrate and people began fluttering out the door, Kris shouted out the date for the next meeting. "Oh, and don't forget! We need people to step up as delegates!"

"What's a delegate?" Jocelyn heard someone ask the person next to her as people collected their things and headed toward the exit.

Good question, thought Jocelyn as she picked up her purse and the informational material people had graciously given her and started to head out the door.

Kris, the organizer of the political powwow, came up from behind, touched her arm and startled her. "I'm sorry. I didn't catch your name," Kris probed.

"Oh, I'm Jocelyn McLaren," she said as she held out her hand to shake his.

Kris shook her hand and said, "Kristopher Jung. Wow, that's really nice of you to do up a marketing plan. But I don't think we'll need it. The campaign won't fund it."

"We'll see," Jocelyn said optimistically.

"Hey, Clara, can you get a picture of me and Jocelyn? She's doing up a marketing plan for the campaign."

Kris's skinny girlfriend came over and directed them to both stand with their backs almost touching the wall and snapped two pictures.

"Gee, that was almost like a mug shot," Jocelyn attempted to joke, but Kris and his girlfriend weren't smiling.

"Thank you," Clara said as she fidgeted with the camera, not making eye contact with Jocelyn as she spoke. "We'll see you at the next meeting?"

"Yup," Jocelyn replied. "See you in a couple weeks.

CHAPTER EIGHT

Basel, Switzerland

ETHAN BLINKED. IT HAD GOTTEN to the point where he was no longer surprised by the random numbers he would find in his wallet. He had given up trying to remember, but occasionally it did bother him. He stared at the scribble, not sure if it was even his handwriting, and fought the urge to wad it up and toss it away. Then he figured he might as well save it, especially since it wasn't a phone number. *It might be important.* He had gotten himself a couple of safe deposit boxes and stashed the loot that Ledergerber had been giving him in those. *But what would a number, on a pink, lined scrap of paper have to do with the safe deposit boxes?* He couldn't remember, and he couldn't be sure. Anyhow, he didn't need to know right now. He closed up his wallet and directed his attention to the matter at hand.

"Cash. I want US dollars, Ledergerber, or I'm done. I've repaid my debt several times over now, and you know it." He pushed the two kilos of gold that Ledergerber had offered back over the enormous modern art–inspired desk.

"That is your prerogative, Mr. Lowe. However, I would recommend that someone such as yourself, someone as skilled as yourself, be more willing to deal with metals."

"The only metal worth hoarding is lead." Ethan rubbed his shoulder and continued, "No, thank you. You've tried offloading these on me before." He pointed to the two shiny rectangles. "It's nice and all, but I can't buy groceries with that. Cash only."

Mr. Ledergerber did not take his eyes off Ethan and sighed. "As you wish." He stubbed out his cigarette, reached down into his expansive desk, and produced a canvas bank deposit bag. Ethan watched him intensely as he did this and was so focused on Ledergerber that he literally did not blink. The hazy daylight permeating through the full-length wall of a window to his right started doing a crazy thing. It appeared as if Ledergerber was emitting an aura, a white halo, as he placed the bag of money on the desk and pushed it over to Ethan. Because of this, Ethan was not quick to move. Instead, he just blinked. A picture of the entire room in reverse negative was now emblazoned in his mind, and for whatever reason, his brain, within that millisecond of a blink, calculated the angles of the entire space from the perspective of his chair.

"Perhaps you will use this paper to buy some metal, Ethan."

Ethan smirked and glanced out the window at the Art Basel building located down the snow-covered street. *Jocelyn. Art. She'd like that.* He started imagining that maybe he'd bring Jocelyn to the famous art exhibition sometime when things calmed down.

"I am only telling you this because I like you and appreciate your work, Mr. Lowe." Ledergerber sat back in his exquisitely designed executive chair and folded his hands as if in gentle prayer. An original four-by-eight-foot Jackson Pollock behind his desk and the shiny, stainless H. R. Giger sculpture of a baby suited up in welding gear framed him as he spoke. "How is your family?"

That comment snapped Ethan to attention. "Fine. Thanks for asking." He reached over and casually grabbed the money sack. "Look, next time, do me a favor. Don't put me in with that medical school dropout freak again. Okay? I prefer to work alone. If I have to work with someone, I want it to be clean."

"As you wish. But I must commend you on the placement of the jewels. That was superb." He kissed his fingers like someone complimenting a delicious dish of shrimp scampi. "Pure artistry."

CHAPTER NINE

TWO WEEKS LATER, JOCELYN ARRIVED at the library for the second meeting.

```
5:30 p.m.
Welcome Raymond Pierce for President
Group
```

"You! You're an infiltrator!" Kris Jung was screaming. Jocelyn hadn't yet made her way to the conference table that had been set up in the middle of the room. She still had on her coat and executive style courier bag. She was also balancing an oversized Dunkin' Donuts Box O' Joe and a veritable wheelbarrow full of Munchkins, which she had strategically brought with her to ply the group into what she hoped would be submission.

She knew from experience that all serious meetings needed coffee and a yellow legal pad. So that is what she'd brought, seeing as she intended to present her Raymond Pierce for President statewide marketing plan. Jocelyn felt confident that she had, within a week, produced something vastly superior to whatever the heck was currently going on. Plus, she liked Munchkins, so she was pretty sure none of her effort would go to waste.

It took a moment for the smiling Jocelyn to recognize that the shouts of "Infiltrator!" were directed at her. Puzzled, she looked at the others sitting around the table as she put down the coffee and doughnuts.

Standing at the end of the table in a full underarm-sweating frenzy with his skinny girlfriend positioned next to him, Kris had hit what everyone else in attendance was unfortunately already familiar with.

"What's going on?" Jocelyn asked a woman she recognized from the last meeting.

"Oh! Don't pretend like you don't know!" Kris bellowed. "You come sauntering in here from a *defense contractor*, all helpful and offering to take over the marketing effort. Uh-huh. Like you're gonna help us?! Right! Well, Clara checked you out. We know who you are! Do us all a favor and just get out of here!"

For some reason, Jocelyn remembered a lonely piece of forgotten information about body language that she had learned, most likely at one of the Executive Training for Women seminars that she had been forced to endure at the Conglomerate. While Kris was still going off on her and everyone else sat in silence, Jocelyn slowly took off her coat and placed it on the chair in front of her. She turned to Kris and gestured with a palm-down hand for him to take his seat.

"Oh!! Don't you point at me!! Don't point!"

"I'm not pointing," Jocelyn said, looking at her hand and back at Kris. "I'm asking you to calm down." It was at this moment that Jocelyn realized that perhaps this technique only worked on people who were not technically insane.

"God damn it, Kris! Just shut up! What the hell is wrong with you?" a guy about Jocelyn's age started yelling back at Kris.

"What's wrong with me?! What's wrong with all of you! You don't see what's going on here?"

"I see a guy who is losing his shit for the umpteenth time! You're an asshole!"

"Yeah. You're giving us all a bad name, Kris," said a man wearing well-worn Carhartt overalls, who looked as if he had just gotten off work, while indicating that he wanted the Box O' Joe.

Using the pass-me-the-coffee signal to take her gaze away from Kris's tantrum and regroup her thoughts, Jocelyn pushed the coffee and a bag of cups, cream, and sugar down the table.

"I'm giving you all a bad name?! Really?! Like I'm not the one who put this whole Meetup together? And I'm not the one who the campaign vetted and made spokesperson for our state. I'm here to save the republic! Are you people that oblivious to the tyranny around you?!" Kris took a breath and belted out, "Eugenics! Abortion! *They are trying to kill us all!*"

"That's it! Kris, get the hell out!" Samantha said as she stood up and deliberately pointed at Kris and then the door.

Nice, thought Jocelyn, who naturally picked up on the tactical use of the index finger. "You are no longer representing this group! Someone get Jeff on the phone. Let's make this official," Samantha commanded.

As the two guys at the end of the table, who had been busying themselves consuming coffee while all this was going on, searched their pockets for their phones, Kris gathered up his Raymond Pierce for President lawn signs. "Come on, Clara! Let's get out of here! We're obviously not appreciated anymore!"

Clara, looking as if she might cry, glared at Jocelyn as the couple hastily made their way out of the library's conference room.

Jocelyn, still not yet seated, grabbed for a Munchkin in an attempt to appear as nonchalant as possible about the whole Jerry Springer episode she had unknowingly just walked into.

"I'm sorry, Jocelyn," Samantha said. "Kris gets wound up, and he's become a real liability."

"Well, looking at the bright side of my research," Jocelyn said as she patted her courier bag, "no one in this state knows who Ray Pierce is anyway. I guess that technically makes the liability minimal."

"I've got Jeff on the phone," one of the coffee-drinking guys announced.

Samantha looked over at the man holding the phone. "Thanks, Forrest. Can we get him on a speaker phone?"

After some decidedly masculine, overly-technical discussion about how to procure and interface a speaker phone, Forrest and the other coffee-drinking men at the end of the table agreed that they should all just pass the cell phone around as needed. Jocelyn listened with interest as the group took turns describing how Kris had, in a rage, flipped over a table at a recent meeting and scared some "R.P. curious" elderly women out of the room. "They were so sweet," the young woman reported to Jeff. "I think they were Constitution Party members. Uh-huh. Yeah. They were totally on board until Kris just lost it. Yeah. No. We never saw them again."

After about fifteen minutes of Jocelyn listening in on similar stories of Kris's bizarre behavior, she felt compelled to quietly ask the person next to her, "Why, for heaven's sake, was Kris ever made spokesperson in the first place?"

"I heard that he offered to be the Meetup Organizer free of charge in exchange for help with his next campaign," the middle-aged man sitting next to her whispered as he leaned in close. "The campaign probably took him up on it because he's run for office so many times, and he knows all about the technicalities of campaigning."

"He has? Does he hold an office?" Jocelyn asked in disbelief.

"I said he's *run* for office. He's never won."

Jocelyn couldn't help but stifle a laugh and shake her head. "Well, yeah. I guess so," Forrest said as he waved his non-cell-phone-holding hand to get everyone's attention. "Jeff says in order to make this official, we have to document that we are voting in a new spokesperson. What? Okay. Yeah. And he says that someone should take notes and do up some minutes."

"I'll do it," said Samantha as she took a pen out of her purse. Jocelyn passed the yellow legal pad over to her.

Forrest continued to relay what Jeff was saying to him. "Does anyone want to make a motion that Kris be removed?"

The entirety of the group wholeheartedly agreed. "You could hear that from South Carolina, eh?" Forrest laughed and continued, "Okay. Yeah. All right. I understand. I'll talk to you later tonight. Thanks."

Everyone looked at Forrest as he hung up his phone.

"Well?" Samantha asked.

"Well, I guess we have to choose a leader," Forrest said.

Oddly, at least to Jocelyn, no one seemed like they wanted to do that.

The guy sitting next to Forrest in his coveralls spoke up. "This isn't about leaders, this is about ideals. And I think that each person, each individual here has a unique—"

"Oh, for goodness' sake, Palmeri, stop with the Libertarian spiel for a minute," Forrest said, shaking his head. "Ray Pierce is a Republican now, and he's got a chance here. So just deal with it. Okay?"

"I'll never understand how someone could go from Libertarian to Republican." Palmeri shuddered.

"It's just so he can get in on the televised debates," one of the coffee drinkers added. "No one would be allowed to hear any of these concepts here in the United States if he didn't."

Jocelyn was intrigued by this statement and found out later that it was actually true. Only Democrats and Republicans were able to debate on national TV, despite the fact that about fifty different political parties were recognized in the United States. And, more surprisingly, that most Americans did not define themselves strictly as Democrat or Republican.

What Jocelyn was witnessing and had not yet fully understood was how this presidential candidate that she had stumbled upon was attracting such diverse demographic groups. Right in front of her were Democrats, Libertarians, Constitution, and Republican Party members. Age didn't seem to matter, either. What seemed to unify this disparate group was bad teeth. Jocelyn didn't notice it at first, probably because Kris had been exhibiting signs of a full-blown mental breakdown, and that had taken precedence over orthodontics. Now that she had time to really sit back and look at these people assembled around the conference table, it became clear that these were not the same type of people who sat around a conference table in corporate America.

The corporate version of a conference table is pretty much what you imagine it to look like. That archetypal table you see on TV. (Yeah, that one.) Lots and lots of straight, really white teeth, and to a lesser extent, the inclusion of narrow noses or plumped-up breasts outfitted in the latest price-point-specific, ready-to-wear fashion. An expensive watch or some nice eyewear thrown in for novelty sake.

The only thing that makes the "made-for-TV" version and the real-life version different is that the folks at the real-life corporate table really want to look like that made-for-TV version. Naturally, most don't live up to such a lofty goal, but it's the effort that counts. The ones who are able to pull off the made-for-TV look seem to get promoted more quickly.

In blinding contrast, the gang assembled at this library conference table didn't seem to possess the same intrinsic need to look the made-for-TV part that Jocelyn had just accepted as standard operating procedure when positioned at a conference table. At least that's the theory Jocelyn was working with. It was either that or most of these people simply didn't have access to dental insurance. She made a mental note to look into this bad-teeth phenomenon when she had the chance.

"Look, can we just get on with it. I have to get back to the grindstone pretty soon. What's the plan?" Palmeri asked.

Seeing the opportunity to present her marketing plan fading fast, Jocelyn spoke up. "Well, I'm not sure about the finding a leader thing, but I do have a marketing plan for us to look at," she said as she distributed the copies she had brought. The plan included everything from printed brochures to the exact position of billboards on the highway to the timing of radio commercials to a press release schedule to—

"Um ... How much is this all going to cost?" Samantha asked.

"Oh, marketing is like remodeling your bathroom. You can spend whatever you want," Jocelyn said.

"Well, let's say I want a bathroom that works, and I don't want to pay a lot of money. What are we talking?"

"For all this? Probably about $250,000," Jocelyn said, thinking that she was lowballing, since she could buy a house for $250,000. That didn't seem like too much to spend on a state (albeit a very small state) campaign for a presidential candidate. Heck, her budget at the Conglomerate for vaporware products alone had been ridiculously bloated compared to this paltry figure.

The place erupted into laughter and cynical guffaws.

Jocelyn looked at Samantha and said, "No. Seriously. That's what it would be."

"I believe you. But it's not worth it for them," she said. "We don't offer enough delegates." *There's that word again—delegates.* Jocelyn thought that she had better get up to speed with whatever the heck delegates actually do. Samantha continued, "I think we should spend our resources educating people about the stuff coming out of RP's mouth during the debates. I mean, the man is already up there on national TV, but people don't know what he's talking about. And it's too easy for the press to spin this ignorance against him."

"Yeah. Like, if I hear one more person call him an isolationist, I'm gonna snap," said a pretty college-age woman with a charmingly crooked front tooth. "Nonintervention and isolationism are, like, almost opposites. He's saying he wants to trade and deal with everyone but not get involved with anyone's conflicts. Kinda like Switzerland. Like, I'm pro that."

Samantha and the rest of the room nodded knowingly.

"Okay, if we are dealing with a no-money situation, then the best thing to pursue is press relations and guerrilla marketing techniques." Which, Jocelyn realized as she was saying it, was exactly what was already spontaneously happening. It was what had brought her and all these people to this meeting.

"We need to get a spokesperson—someone we can get in front of a camera. With the research I've done about our state, we really need a woman—someone at the younger edge of the baby boomer generation. I recommend J. Jill outfits for the interviews and—" Jocelyn was just about to discuss outfit color schemes when she realized that once again the room was looking at her as if she had sprouted feathers and was speaking a foreign language.

"What?" She scanned the room. "Guys. This is what you do. I've helped people pick out ties, for goodness' sake. It comes down to that sort of detail for a corporate brand manager. If something is working for someone else, steal it. Ride *their* marketing budget. Just put your colors on it. Coke and Pepsi. McDonald's and Burger King. Same stuff, different color scheme and logos. Both companies benefit from their competition because *you don't have to explain* what the product is. Really. People will just buy it."

She looked around, hoping that someone might understand her impromptu marketing seminar. "Political marketing, as far as I can tell, is like the corporate template on steroids. Did you know that one of the Democratic presidential candidates has signed on with The Gap for the whole family during the election? Brand managers from both The Gap and this person's campaign must have realized that they could get more bang for their marketing buck by supporting each other's common cause."

This was going nowhere.

"How about this?" Samantha offered. "I nominate you, Jocelyn, to be the spokesperson."

"No, I'm not old enough. It won't work. We need a boomer," Jocelyn said and countered back with, "How about you, Samantha? You'd be perfect."

"No."

The meeting was going to have to end soon. The next group that had reserved the library's meeting room was starting to arrive. As Jocelyn gathered up the discarded debris formerly known as her breakthrough marketing plan and the Statewide Stitchers had started to file in for their monthly stitch-a-thon, Forrest came up to her and said, "Not bad for your first real meeting, huh?"

Not entirely sure if he was being sarcastic or not, Jocelyn responded, "I guess it could have been worse."

Forrest grunted. "Yeah. Like he could have thrown a chair at you or something." Jocelyn smiled, and Forrest continued, "Hey, are you going to be involved with that thing in Boston?"

"I don't know what you're talking about."

"The thing at Faneuil Hall. It's a fundraiser for RP. They could probably use your help getting some publicity for that. You know Bruce Drewer, right? He wants to do a repeat of that online donation project from last month. He's really into it. He even started a political action committee so that he can advertise and collect funds. They're really on the ball up there."

Forrest took out his phone to retrieve Drewer's number. "Here, you should get in touch with him. Palmeri and I plan on going. If you want to carpool with us, you can."

"Thanks. I'll call him," Jocelyn said as she jotted the number down and stuffed it into her pocket.

The thing with that Kris guy had totally freaked her out, and now she was feeling like maybe she shouldn't get involved with all of this. It seemed like such a mess. But the more she was learning about the economy via Ray Pierce YouTubes, and the more she thought about Stan telling her that this candidate didn't deal with lobbyists, the more she liked Ray Pierce. And, well, here she was.

Jocelyn and Forrest said good-bye and headed off to their respective cars as the Statewide Stitchers officially kicked off their monthly stitch-a-thon. She was driving home thinking about how crazy the whole meeting had been and bemoaning the fact that she hadn't even gotten to keep the extra Munchkins, when her cell phone rang. Anticipating that the call had something to do with the kids, she answered.

"Is this Jocelyn?" a man blurted out before she could even say hello.

"Hum. Yeah. Who's this?"

"Bruce Drewer. I just got your number. We need you. This thing is gonna be big, and we need help. I want this all over the news. All over the place. It's gonna be bigger than the last one, and—"

Jocelyn cut him off mid-sentence, "Bruce, I'll have to call you back. I'm driving, and I—"

Now he cut her off. "Do you have any contacts with national media?"

"Well, yeah. But I'm driving. I want to talk to you, but..." Jocelyn said with a hint of growing anxiety in her voice. "Can I call you back? I just realized how icy the roads are becoming."

After promising to call Bruce back, Jocelyn put both hands purposefully on the wheel as she approached what was colloquially referred to as the cursed death trap S-curve.

Everyone was a mess when she got home. The kids were crying, and Ethan seemed totally at a loss as to what to do. "Oh, look who made it home, kids," Ethan said as he got up, not to hug or welcome her, but to get his heavy wool coat.

Jocelyn, still in her coat, ran past him and scooped up both the kids and plopped down on the couch with them. "What's the matter, my babies?" she cooed while rubbing both their backs. She looked over at Ethan and said, "It's really, really icy out there. I'm sorry I'm late, but I had to take a different way home. That S-curve—"

"Well, you could have called. We were worried sick about you."

"I guess you're right. I'm sorry. But I wanted to keep both hands on the wheel ..." She watched him open the front door.

"I'll see you later."

"Huh? Where are you going? I just got home. I want to tell you about the meeting. It was—"

"Gotta go. Sorry." He made a face like he really wasn't sorry and slammed the door behind him. It was dark, and the sleet had picked up.

The light emitting from the lamppost in the front yard completed the chiaroscuro effect as she watched him through the living room windows purposefully hopping into his truck. She felt totally deflated. "Why does Daddy have to be like this?" she asked the kids, who were now calm.

CHAPTER TEN

SEEMINGLY OBLIVIOUS TO THE WEATHER, Ethan whipped out his cell phone and clicked on his lights as he pulled out of the driveway. He glanced down to see if he had any text messages before he put the phone to his ear. "Is he still there?" he shouted into the phone as he rounded the corner and pulled onto the deserted main road to the highway.

"Yeah."

"Hang on. I'll be there in about twenty." He slapped the phone shut and jumped on the pedal as sleet and now hail hammered the hood of his black Dodge truck. The adrenaline pumping through him made sense. He was late. The truck fishtailed around corners. He had to focus, and that felt good—even though his vision had closed in on itself and his field of view was the equivalent of looking though a paper towel roll at a staticky black-and-white television.

Oddly, what he was experiencing felt more normal than anything else these days. Nothing was normal anymore, and what used to be enjoyed as "normal" felt quite uncomfortable.

As Ethan plowed on through the icy weather, songs of the past were sung to him by what he imagined to be white-robed, winged cherubs. Little angels. But then his heart skipped a beat and his stomach dropped when he recognized that the angels were laughing at him and were the same devils in disguise as they always were. The paper towel tube he was looking through collapsed on itself a little more, so that now it was as if he were peeking through a Cheerio as he pulled into the fairly empty parking lot at the Foxy Lady.

He parked next to an ice-encrusted Cadillac, hopped out of the car, and made a beeline for the entrance. His shadow skated silently after him on the black ice. With sleet and hail pelting him, his singular objective took on epic proportions. He was on a mission.

"Oh, look who made it!" a friendly voice called out from the lonely lounge. "Someone give this man a drink!"

Ethan looked at the greasy-looking, twenty-something man sitting at the runway. He did not recognize him, but he sat next to him anyway.

"Only four girls tonight, the weather and all. Guess that means more for us!"

Just then, the music started pumping, and a young brunette pranced out on stage. She was so lovely that Ethan didn't even notice when his favorite drink magically appeared in front of him. He plunked a fifty-dollar bill on the stage and watched as the woman locked in on it. She sauntered over, gyrating to the beat, hit the floor, and crawled over to pick it up with her teeth. The man sitting next to Ethan slapped a one-dollar bill in front of him, but the stripper didn't seem to notice. She was focused on the money man. She rolled around a bit, rubbing and caressing herself, and then hopped up while snatching the one dollar bill and headed over to the pole—all the while her eyes bolted to Ethan.

"She's such a cutie!" the man enthused.

Ethan noticed his drink for the first time and took a gulp. His field of vision was coming back. The Cheerio was expanding, and it had fully evaporated from view when an older, bleached-blonde woman, about Ethan's age approached. She wore a full-length, low-slung, tight, turquoise gown. The woman started rubbing Ethan's shoulders. "You really shouldn't have made the drive. I would have kept it safe for you."

Ethan grinned. "I'm sure you would have." He swiveled around in his chair, grabbed the woman by her waist, and plopped her down in his lap. It wasn't a kilo, but it was more than enough for everyone in that club to have a great time until the ice melted the next day.

CHAPTER ELEVEN

WITH ETHAN INTERMITTENTLY COMING AND going, stopping in to sleep and staying only long enough to kiss the kids and make some coffee, Jocelyn had thrown herself into working with Bruce Drewer for the past three weeks straight to get his RP fundraiser some publicity. She had done up professional press releases, created top-notch press packs, and written radio ad scripts. Other people from all over the country, having caught wind of the excitement of the fundraiser on the Internet, started putting together simultaneous events in their states. YouTube videos from all over the world started to get posted to promote the thing. It was really exciting to watch and be a part of.

The good news: Bruce had collected money to buy radio ad time to promote the fundraiser. The bad news: He had collected money to buy ad time. This wasn't acceptable. The radio station couldn't take money directly from Bruce. That was against campaign finance laws. Apparently, there was going to be some lag time in moving the money from his business account, Bruce's Custom Cabinetry, to the political action committee. Naturally, the radio station wasn't going to do the spot until it had its money in hand on a Political Action Committee check. Of course, the check from the PAC was going to take some ridiculous amount of time to clear, so Bruce was going to drive into Boston and give the station a cash deposit to hold and return to him when the PAC check finally went through.

It was amazing that Jocelyn was even able to swing that sort of deal, but she had hit it off pretty well with the salesperson at the radio station, and she got the drive time slots she wanted. Everything had seemed to be going well, until she started getting calls from the PAC members who were really upset with Bruce for totally ignoring the wishes of the PAC. As much as she tried to understand what these PAC people were saying, she had a hard time understanding what they were upset about. It had something to do with some sort of legal technicalities with the state or with the official campaign or both. It was hard to tell because the whole thing seemed pretty disorganized. Of course, she couldn't do much but listen to them complain, but it added to the drama of the whole scene.

Then she started getting calls from the Raymond Pierce Campaign reminding her that they were in no way involved with Bruce's Faneuil Hall fundraising event. The campaign stressed the importance of making sure that an appropriate statement saying as much was attached to the script of the already-recorded ad. This meant the radio station had to redo, basically for free, the whole ad literally the hour before it was supposed to run.

Jocelyn cringed thinking about what she had put that saleswoman through. But everything got done, and everyone seemed happy with the results. Jocelyn was really excited to learn, only after the fact, that there had been some ardent RP supporters at the station; that was what had helped the whole messed-up process along. Naturally, this was great news! But it did make her realize that just about anyone running for office could easily pull off a number of tricks to bend election finance rules—especially a candidate with real money. Heck, all she had in her pocket was her warm phone demeanor and her "people person" self, and that was more than enough to help along the "I like you" part of the ad buy.

The national news outlets part had been more fun. She got to catch up with all sorts of people she hadn't spoken with in a long time. Jocelyn had gone down to the basement to look for that Conglomerate proprietary media contact list that she had been issued. She'd pulled out the box that she had packed up almost two years ago. Everything was there, just as it had been when she left the Conglomerate for the last time.

Flipping through the contents of the box, Jocelyn had to laugh as she looked at the brochures she had spent countless hours of her life fussing over.

While scanning the contents of the box to find the media list, she noticed her beige "insurance policy" diskette—the one that she had created just in case her old boss, Robert, tried to set her up on that Malaysian proposal thing. She grabbed it, not really knowing why. When she finally laid her hands on the media list, she headed up to her computer.

She spent the better part of two days calling around and rekindling old connections. Most of the contacts on her sheet had changed positions within their network. Some were still hanging onto whatever it was they had going on and seemed more than harried but happy to hear from her.

"You mean this is happening all across the country on the same day?"

"Sounds like a cool story."

"Send us over the pack."

"We'll get someone on it."

These were the responses she had received from pretty much everyone she had called. Jocelyn had just expected that they would do a story. Why wouldn't they? Nearly every time she'd tried to place a story when she'd worked for the Conglomerate, she'd gotten the same sort of positive response with excellent results. Things were looking good, and she was feeling very accomplished.

That night, Ethan came home with a Christmas tree. Of course, she detected a slight boozy odor, but he was into hugging her and decorating the tree with the kids. So Jocelyn joined in the fun and put on some Christmas carols. They hadn't all hung out as family like this in a while, and they all went to bed happy that night. Jocelyn fell asleep contentedly going through her mental checklist. She knew she was doing a decent job, and she knew she could easily use this experience as a résumé enhancer later on. *Just two more days until the event in Boston.*

Jocelyn woke up extra early the day of the fundraiser and packed her desktop computer into her Hyundai Santa Fe mommy mobile. This moving the computer around, with all its various cables and extension cords, was a pain, but it would be worth it. The plan was to bring it to Boston along with a bunch of press packs and set up in Faneuil Hall so that she could act as an on-site media contact during the concurrent rally that Bruce had organized during the online fundraiser.

As soon as the babysitter arrived, Jocelyn headed out. Music blasting—check. Hot coffee in purloined Conglomerate stainless steel travel mug with ill-fitting lid—check.

Bring it on! Whatever was going to happen with this fundraiser, Jocelyn knew she had done all she could to make it a success. She was happy—happy about everything but the weather.

The weather wasn't looking so great. In fact, it was pretty miserable. Icy rain and snow slowed traffic to a near standstill. The intermittent flashing of hazard lights should have alerted Jocelyn to the danger at the cursed death trap S-curve, but she was too lost in thought about how the online donation process was going to work. Would they have to use her computer? Is that why Bruce was so adamant about her bringing it? Not that she minded, but—

Bam!

No lead-up with tires screeching. No frenzied panic of knowing that she might actually die. Just your basic blunt-force trauma with a radio still blaring and coffee flying all over the place.

Once Jocelyn figured out what had happened (namely, that her car had operated under accepted Newtonian laws of physics and slid sideways into some trees that lined the aptly nicknamed icy road as it turned and began its uphill climb) she reached over to shut off the radio and—

"Awww, shit!" Jocelyn braced herself for the impending impact of the clearly out-of-control purple Honda Civic she spotted in her rearview mirror. Again, no high-pitched screeching of brakes accompanied the Civic as, practically in slow motion, it neared its point of collision.

Bam!!!

"Okay. Not cool," grumbled Jocelyn between clenched teeth. Her car was now trapped between some trees and one of the most obnoxiously loud vehicles she had ever had the misfortune to find herself wedged up against.

Like Jocelyn before she'd shut her radio off, the operator of this car had his music cranked up. Unlike Jocelyn's, the windows of this purple car with its complementing blue-neon ground effects were viciously rattling in response to its subwoofer's beat. Jocelyn could clearly make out the digitally altered lyrics—"Feel the bass ... Feel feel feel the bass ... Can you hear me?"—repeating over and over again.

At first, this auditory redundancy irritated her as she watched tiny balls of hail spring off her windshield in what she imagined should have been a solitary, tranquil time to reflect upon how lucky she was to be alive. But no. *Like who doesn't automatically shut off the music at a time like this?!* Jocelyn huffed as she rubbed her elbow.

When the music kept going for what seemed like way too long, it dawned on Jocelyn that maybe something bad had happened to the driver. She clicked off her seat belt and crawled into the backseat. Of course, two matching, ridiculously large, and (Jocelyn thought) tremendously overpriced car seats occupied what would have otherwise been a navigable area. She peered out the window, hoping to catch a glimpse of the driver. This was hard to do because of the Civic's black-tinted windows. So Jocelyn opted to crawl over the backseat and into the rear of her Santa Fe, where she had stowed her computer and a box of her Raymond Pierce fundraiser press packs. She opened the only exit that wasn't pinned between either a tree or another car, the hatchback, and hopped out.

"Feel the bass ... Feel feel feel the bass ... Can you hear me?"

Regaining her footing as she slipped on the wet slope of the hill, Jocelyn made her way over to the passenger side of the quivering purple mass and knocked on its trembling window.

"Feel the bass ... Feel feel feel the bass ... Can you hear me?" Nothing.

Jocelyn opened the car door, only to unleash twenty thousand watts of pure, unadulterated techno whoop ass.

"Feel the bass ... Feel feel feel the bass ... Can you hear me?"

"What the hell!" Jocelyn shouted as she reached in and snapped off the music. Once inside, she was quick to notice that the driver appeared to be unconscious. She slid into the passenger seat to get out of the weather.

"Hey. Hey, are you okay?" she asked as she touched the young man's arm. With no reply, she assumed that he was not. Jocelyn took out her cell phone and dialed 9-1-1 while glancing at the kid's gold chain and crucifix. *This guy looks like an extra from* The Sopranos. Jocelyn gave the particulars of the accident to the 9-1-1 operator and hung up. After what seemed an eternity of silently waiting and watching snow gently cascade onto the hood of the purple Civic, Jocelyn was finally able to enjoy that moment of reflection she had yearned for earlier.

But it got old sooner than she had envisioned. So, she called Bruce Drewer and left a message that she had gotten into a car accident and would not be at Faneuil Hall for the fundraiser. Then she called 9-1-1 again, only to be reassured that an ambulance was on its way.

As she craned around to look down the hill in anticipation of an approaching ambulance, the driver began rousing himself and grunted, "Dude. What happened?"

"Oh. Hi," Jocelyn said, surprised to hear from him. "You hit my car."

"Shit. I'm sorry," he said as he slowly straightened himself out in his seat.

"I called an ambulance for you. You looked like you were in a coma or something."

Jocelyn's statement seemed to inject some sort of vital life force into the guy. "Umm. Are the cops coming? I don't need an ambulance. I'm fine."

"Ahhh, to be young again," said Jocelyn. "They might. We probably just need a tow truck."

"Naw. We can get out of here," the formerly unconscious driver said as he slammed his foot down on the clutch and thrust his stick shift into reverse. "Hold on." In a minimally messy decoupling of their vehicles, the purple Honda Civic reversed its way back onto the road.

"Pretty slick driving there, mister! Can you help me get my car out of there?" she asked, pointing to her unbalanced Santa Fe, which was teetering on the precipice of a formidable ravine. All that saved her car from a full-fledged rollover were the skinny trees that she had slid into.

"Yeah. I think so. Let's do this thing!" the driver said with an admirable amount of enthusiasm as he backed the Civic across the street and parked it.

The two of them jogged over to the Santa Fe. The driver climbed in on the now accessible passenger side and started up the car. Jocelyn stood on the side of the road and attempted to make herself seem somehow useful as she observed the valiant extraction efforts of the young driver. Finally sensing that the Santa Fe was doomed to remain where it was, Jocelyn signaled for the driver to stop.

"Dude! This isn't working! I need to get a tow truck!" she yelled while waving her arms.

It was at this moment Jocelyn noticed a gray, older model pickup truck slowly lurching its way up the hill. Its bed was piled high with what Jocelyn mistook as lobster traps. The defeated driver, shaking his head, got out of the Santa Fe and joined Jocelyn as the gray pickup stopped in the middle of the road.

"You guys need some help?" a bearded man in his late fifties shouted out the window.

Jocelyn waved and smiled as she and the driver walked over to the newcomer. What Jocelyn had mistaken as lobster traps were now discernible as stacked crates full of live chickens, clucking and fussing.

"Looks like you've got a full load there," Jocelyn commented, gesturing to the poultry as the curious driver walked around to inspect the birds. She continued, "Yeah. I could definitely use some help. But I think I'm going to need a tow truck."

"Oh, my brother, Manny, has a towing company. I can call him if you want."

"Sure! Why not?" Jocelyn consented, and the poultry man quickly produced his cell phone and proceeded to call his brother.

"It's days like today that I really wish I had gone into the towing and storage business like Manny," Poultry Guy said as he waited for his call to connect.

Jocelyn, pulling up her collar in a useless attempt to stay warm, smirked, thinking the business generated by the cursed death trap S-curve was probably more than enough to generously feed a family of five. That's when she heard them before she saw them—the familiar wailing and yelping of sirens.

Up rolled not one but two fire engines, a police car, and an ambulance. The emergency vehicles were not expecting a poultry truck to be parked in the middle of the S-curve and swerved to make their way around it. During the course of the swerving, the second fire engine drove with its sirens blaring and lights flashing, quite unceremoniously, directly off the road; and the ambulance, emitting a hyper-pulsed, phaser-type siren blast, fishtailed and skidded sideways into Jocelyn's Santa Fe.

Two and a half hours later

"I just wanna go home," Jocelyn whined.

It had been a long morning. The fire department had sent out four more engines and two more ambulances in response. The police department had sent out six more cruisers to close the road, help direct traffic, and take statements. All the sirens were finally shut off about forty minutes into it, but for some reason, the lights stayed flashing, making the place appear not much more inviting than a drizzly and cold outdoor discotheque. Measurements were taken with long yellow tapes, and a whole slate of questions was repeatedly asked. Jocelyn was just about ready to start crying when the crisis management commissary truck pulled up.

"Look, can we just go home? You've got all of our information," Jocelyn said, glancing toward her new cohort of the driver and the poultry guy. "Wherever my car ends up, just let me know. I'll pick it up."

The officer sighed as he took his coffee from the commissary truck while clicking something on his radio. "Yeah. Okay. You need a ride?"

"No," all of them said in unison.

"I just have to get some stuff out the back of my car," Jocelyn said, speaking more for the benefit of her cohort than the officer. Driver offered to help her take the stuff out of the car and load it into Poultry Guy's truck. The three of them had concluded about an hour ago that Poultry Guy would take Jocelyn home because he was going to be heading back that way when all this was over. His day was effectively shot, and Jocelyn felt bad for him. He had just stopped to lend a helping hand, and the next thing you know, he was getting grilled all over the place. Even the chickens sounded like they were getting weary as she and Driver headed over to unload the Santa Fe.

"Nice monitor," Driver commented as Jocelyn removed her coat to cover her black, wide-aspect flat screen.

"Thanks. Here, try and cover that CPU," Jocelyn said, gesturing toward one of the kids' blankets. "I don't want that computer to get messed up. We'll come back for that other box and the cords."

"Dude, so you're, like, into computers?"

"Not really. I actually don't like them at all. But I had a job where I needed one. I just sat in front of a computer, and they paid me," Jocelyn said, attempting something of a grim joke. She continued, "I figured I'd splurge on this one so I could feel more like I was at work when I was at home."

"Oh," said Driver. "You sound like my sister's old boyfriend. He had a job that sounded just like that. They broke up after he proposed to her. He gave her a nice ring and everything."

"That's nice," said Jocelyn as she carefully positioned her foot on the icy slope leading back up to the road.

"Yeah, it *is* nice! She kept it. You should see it. Some sort of precious gemstone. Really big," he said as he covered the computer with a blue blanket and hoisted it out of the hatchback.

Succumbing to her girly, conversationalist side as she carefully surveyed the position of the crooked ambulance she would have to navigate around, she asked, "Then why'd they break up?"

"Because he found out she really wasn't pregnant. My sister's such an ass. I mean a guy can only go so long before noticing something like that."

"Uh-huh," Jocelyn said, now fully regretting having probed further.

"I kind of felt bad for the dude. He was all about computers. Like, all about them. You know, kind of a geek. He took me to Hooters once. He was trying to stay friends with me after they broke up. Lame. But the wings were okay."

Having successfully circumvented the ambulance and conquered the slick, grassy slope, they both automatically stopped by the side of the road to look both ways. That really wasn't necessary though; the road was closed and disco lights illuminated the icy drizzle. They loaded the stuff into the cab of the chicken truck as Poultry Guy looked on. Then they trotted back to the Santa Fe.

"Dude, I am so glad those cops didn't search my car," Driver said as he snatched up the box of computer cords. Jocelyn took inventory of what was still in the vehicle. "I don't even want to know what's lying around my car after that party last night."

Jocelyn smirked at his youthful boast and grabbed the box of RP fundraiser press packs.

"Yeah. I'm supposed to be at a party right now in Boston." Jocelyn sighed and slammed the hatch. "That's where I was heading. Guess I'll just have to watch it online now."

"What? Like the party is doing a webcast or something? That's cool."

"I'm not sure if we found anyone in Boston to do that. But almost every major city in America is holding a party during this big online fundraiser today. I'm sure if you have access to the Internet, you'll find something about it."

"Jerry could set up a webcast. No problem. He'd be into it."

"Who's Jerry?" Jocelyn asked as she instinctively grabbed for Driver's arm while starting to slip down the hill.

Driver caught her grasp, helped steady her, and continued. "You know, my sister's ex who I was telling you about. Jerry Apario. He's like Mr. WebCam. Seriously."

"No way." Jocelyn took a sharp breath in. "Did you say Apario?"

"Yeah," Driver confirmed.

"I used to work with him," Jocelyn said, a little taken aback by the coincidence. Now she wished even more that she hadn't learned details of the breakup between the sister and her ex. "Small world," she muttered.

After a few rounds of "No shit!" and an exchange of cell phone numbers, Jocelyn parted ways with Driver, but not without giving him his own personal press pack as a farewell thank-you gift.

CHAPTER TWELVE

NOW TUCKED INTO THE PICKUP with her feet on the boxes stacked in front of her, and the monitor sitting on her lap, Jocelyn took in a sigh of relief as the policeman moved the orange cone, allowing the poultry truck to exit from the crash site. She and Poultry Guy sat in silence for a while until Jocelyn said, "Hey, thanks for offering to help. I'm sorry it turned into a giant nightmare for you."

"Ah, it's definitely not *your* fault. Guess God wants me to do this whole delivery tomorrow. Gotta believe he has a plan here."

"Guess so." Jocelyn nodded. "I'm just glad that no one was seriously hurt. That S-curve really is dangerous."

Poultry Guy sort of grunted in agreement as the windshield wipers squeaked in time like a metronome. Jocelyn looked out the window, grateful she wasn't driving. After an extended preview of the minimalist symphony that Jocelyn had entitled "Wiper 82," Poultry Guy cleared his throat. "Mind if I smoke?" he asked, while reaching into his chest pocket for a tiny cigar.

"Oh, no. By all means. It's your truck," Jocelyn said. "But thanks for asking."

The two sat in silence while Poultry Guy deftly sparked up his Zippo and sufficiently puffed up his Romeo y Julieta mini. The smell, which she had initially perceived upon entering the vehicle, was soon taking the form of whimsical swirly Qs, which ultimately blossomed into a full, thick fog. The headache she now began to appreciate started to officially knock as Poultry Guy began speaking.

"Raymond Pierce? He's still goin', huh?"

"Yup," Jocelyn said.

"I used to get his newsletters back in the day. I would imagine those might be collectors' items now. Should have saved 'em."

"Oh, they probably are. I didn't realize that he sent out newsletters."

"Yeah. I enjoyed getting those in my mailbox. The man called it like he saw it. I appreciated that. I loved it when he told off Reagan and quit the Republicans."

This was new news for Jocelyn, and she wasn't quite sure what to make of it or Poultry Guy.

"Well, he's running for president as a Republican. There's this huge online fundraiser for him today. Here," Jocelyn said as she awkwardly reached over the widescreen monitor and down between her legs to dig into the box of press packs. She put one on the seat between them. "Here. Look this over later. If you liked him then, you'll like him even more now."

Poultry Guy smiled a wry smile. "I'm not so sure about that." And after a long pause he said, "Thank you, though. I'll be sure to look it over."

Finally, they pulled up to her house. The precipitation had slowed down, and the sky was an unfortunate shade of gray. Jocelyn could see the kids' heads peeking out from behind the curtain, clearly enchanted with the arrival of a truck full of chickens.

After the long unload and thanking Poultry Guy profusely for the ride, Jocelyn ultimately entered her house holding his generous gift of two Rhode Island Reds.

"Chickens! The gift that keeps on giving!" Poultry Guy had exclaimed, smiling as he thrust the crate containing the live hens toward her. She had awkwardly accepted them. He wouldn't let her say no. "Your kids are gonna love 'em. You'll see. They make great pets. Just don't name them if you intend to eat them."

The sitter looked confused as Jocelyn instructed her to get some newspaper to spread under the crate. They all joined in the process of feeding the chickens Italian flavored bread crumbs and an apple. Jocelyn's daughter had the bright idea that the chickens might enjoy a ramekin of fresh water. Seeing as all they were doing was staring at birds eating, Jocelyn told the sitter that she might as well go home. The kids watched the Reds picking at the apple seeds for a while. Eventually, the kids left the kitchen, where the birds' crate was stationed, and started orbiting around Jocelyn as she reassembled the computer on her desk.

Once the Internet was back up and running, Jocelyn checked her e-mail. CNN had sent her four e-mails already. *Sweet.* She quickly got their reporter in Boston on the line. It was clear that this woman had not received her press pack, so Jocelyn spent some time clueing her in on the pertinent talking points: Bring the troops home immediately. Eliminate the federal income tax. Return to sound constitutional money. Implement a noninterventionist foreign policy. Secure our borders.

"Uh-huh. So where does he stand on abortion?" the reporter asked as if that was the most important issue of the day.

"He is personally against abortion but feels that the only legitimate, constitutional way to handle the issue is to leave it up to each state, and let the people decide how they want to deal with it."

"Umm ..." Jocelyn imagined the woman writing it all down during the pause. "Okay. So you're with the campaign. What's your title?"

"No. I don't have a title. The campaign has made it very clear that they are in no way involved with what is happening today."

This seemed to short some sort of crucial circuit for the reporter. "Then who is doing this? Who are you?"

"I'm Jocelyn McLaren, and this fundraiser was planned online by people I've never met."

"Uh-huh. Okay, so how'd you get—"

"Oh, I used to work at the Conglomerate, and I offered to help with the public relations for this event today."

Still seemingly confused, the reporter asked, "So where did all these online people hear about this?"

"Beats me. I'm guessing at websites like The DailyPierce or the forums. Or maybe at their Meetup groups. I don't know. MySpace? Word just spread. People have made some really nice YouTube videos that have been passed around."

Jocelyn could hear the reporter putting her hand over the receiver, and then when she returned, she asked, "What's a Meetup group?" Jocelyn tried to bridge the digital divide for the cable news reporter and was attempting to direct the reporter to a graphic showing all of the RP Meetups compared to the other candidates when she realized that she hadn't heard the kids in a while. She took the cordless phone so that she could continue her conversation and started heading, with a modicum of concern, to the kids' room. She knew full well that too much quiet, typically, was not a good sign. She walked past the seemingly content chickens and curiously eyed how much of the apple had been eaten. "No, see, the other candidates, they don't have *any* Meetups. No. It's not just because they are Republicans. Look. Look at the Democratic front-runners. They have almost none as well. This is a new thing and—oh, my God!"

Bubbly water was steadily cascading out of the bathroom into the hallway. "Look, I have to go! It's my kids." Jocelyn ran to the bathroom.

When she rounded the corner and entered the room, she saw her two little ones engaged in some serious experiential learning. Her son had inventively used several rolls of toilet paper to dam up the sink in order to create a wondrous waterfall, which he made only more captivating with the inclusion of all the shampoo available within his tiny arm's reach. The hair care empties were strewn around the room, one of which was floating into the hallway.

Meanwhile, her daughter had miraculously procured a Sharpie marker, previously stashed away from little fingers on top of the refrigerator (or at least that's where Jocelyn thought she had last seen it) and was efficiently producing a full portfolio of abstract gesture drawings, in mural form, all over the white, tiled walls.

"No! No! No! No! Nooooooo!" Jocelyn wailed, running in to shut off the waterfall. The kids looked at her, crestfallen, as she shuffled them out of the bathroom while berating them and then, finally, herself for letting it happen.

Once all the available bath and paper towels had been used up and nothing more could be done to prevent further flood damage, Jocelyn called her mother and, holding back tears of frustration, requested that she come and take the kids.

"Mom, look, I'm trying to do some PR work. It's the first time I've had the opportunity to do something like this since ..."

Mom did not need any more of an excuse to hop into her car and immediately buzz over to pick up her grandchildren. Jocelyn told her mother that she didn't really want to talk about it when the latter looked up inquisitively as she stuck her finger into the chicken crate in the kitchen. So Mom just said, "Well, the Christmas tree looks nice."

"Please. Just get the kids out of here for the next few hours. I just have to make some phone calls."

As soon as the kids had been packaged up and were out the door, Jocelyn hit the phone. Hard. She got CNN back. She wanted an AP reporter. If she could just get AP to pick the story up—anywhere. She had lost a ton of time. She was frantically e-mailing and answering calls from California at this point—a bad thing. She had lost the East Coast news cycle. Lots of little local papers had questions. That was okay but wasn't going to help. Jocelyn opened a second web browser window to monitor the outlets.

It was starting to crack. They were running with it. She would have to wait to see what was going to appear on the news, but typically, when she'd worked for the Conglomerate, they'd just cut and pasted directly from her press release. Nice! Boston.com was interested, and *The Boston Globe* was only moments behind. The *Globe* was AP, and it was at that moment the RP fundraiser was officially official all over the world.

By the time Jocelyn's mom finally brought the kids back home, Jocelyn was mystified. Why hadn't the media cut and pasted like they always did? Sure, Raymond Pierce had collected $6.1 million dollars with the average donation being $20. And sure, he'd broken the record for one-day donations to a political campaign. Astonishingly, this all happened on the heels of a similar one-day fundraising event that had yielded him over $4 million only a month before. Clearly, people were interested in this guy. Every nook and cranny of this campaign offered a story opportunity, but no one was biting. The press didn't seem to want to actually discuss any of RP's talking points. What was that all about?

CHAPTER THIRTEEN

"SOMETHING'S STRANGE HERE," JOCELYN muttered the next morning as she scanned the news outlets for mentions. When she saw the CNN piece, she burst out, "A friggin' pet monkey in an RV?! That's all I got?! That was pretty damn near close to a hit piece!"

CNN had aired a feature-length interview of a woman who had driven up to Boston through the snowstorm with her diaper-wearing pet monkey for the fundraiser. And the other outlets? Where were they? *This doesn't even make sense*, she lamented.

Jocelyn sat blinking in absolute disbelief. She couldn't help but blame her dismal performance on the death trap S-curve. "It really is cursed. It's got to be. This is crazy. The whole freakin' day was a complete and utter nightmare." She shut off the computer in disgust. Yeah, the bathroom was still a certified disaster, but whatever. It was the car she was more worried about. How much was that going to cost?

Sure, stories about the breaking of fundraising records had appeared, but they weren't really about Raymond Pierce. Many of the stories led off with the Ray Pierce event of the day before but closed with fun facts, conveniently highlighted in the sidebar, about Republican and Democratic campaigns collecting ludicrous amounts of money in a single day, only briefly mentioning the source of those funds. These articles seemed to downplay the difference between cold, hard cash-in-hand emanating from an average person's credit card or PayPal account and "pledged donations" from PACs and corporations, and they certainly did nothing to elaborate on the significance of that difference. It was apples to oranges.

Press relations crisis management at its best. She recognized it, but still, it irked her.

Trying to brush off nagging feelings that "something isn't normal here," she decided she had to deal with the Sharpie marker situation and the flooded bathroom scene. Ethan had pretty much snapped his mental carrot, right next to the chicken crate, the night before. She promised him that he wouldn't have to deal with any of it. Of course the chickens wouldn't be living and shitting on the kitchen floor.

She'd take care of it. She'd take care of everything. Not to worry. She also noticed they were running low on just about everything in the house. Food was her primary concern. She hadn't been grocery shopping in the past few weeks since having been involved with the fundraiser. It was time for her to "snap back to reality," as Ethan was eager to point out after seeing the bathroom and listening, with mouth agape, to the story of her car.

She had to admit that she probably wasn't really good at the whole "work-life balance" thing. But Ethan took it upon himself to explicitly spell it out for her that it wasn't really "work" that was distracting her from the kids, and him, and the house.

"They aren't paying you, Jocelyn! That technically means *it's not a job!*"

True.

So that day, she tucked the kids into the Toyota that she'd borrowed from her mother. She was borrowing her mom's car because the Santa Fe was impounded somewhere, not so conveniently, really far away. Mom had outfitted the Toyota with her own car seats after the first time Jocelyn had asked her to take the kids. Trying to get Jocelyn's car seats stuck properly into place was just a frustrating, giant pain, and Mom refused to keep dealing with it. So she bought her own and drove around with them all hooked up and ready for grandkid action. Just in case.

Once everyone was securely latched into position, Jocelyn and the kids headed to the grocery store to gather supplies for "Operation Restore Domestic Tranquility," as she had dubbed her mission for the day. When they pulled up to the house with the car full of food, household items, lumber, some window screens for the coop she was going to craft, and chicken food, Jocelyn was surprised to see the front door wide open.

"That's weird," Jocelyn said to the kids as she parked the car in the driveway. "Why would Daddy leave the door wide open?" His car wasn't around. "Maybe he came back for something and forgot to shut the door." This seemed unlikely. "You guys stay here. I'll check and see what's going on in the house. Stay here. Okay?" As if the kids could actually extract themselves from the restraints of the car seats.

"Hello!" she called out before entering the house. Nothing except random clucks from the chickens. She hesitantly entered her own house. "Hello?" she said again.

Cluck, cluck, cluck, cluck.

"Oh, shit. Christmas!" she said as she hastily approached the Christmas tree they'd set up a few nights before. The presents they'd put under the tree were still there, seemingly untouched. But what was that smell? Just a whiff. It seemed familiar.

Bauch, bauch, bauch, bauch, baaaawck!

"Hello?" she said again as she wandered down the hallway checking the bedrooms. Nothing. Everything seemed just as she had left it. She turned around and headed through chicken territory, the kitchen, toward the basement door. She knew what was down there. It was like honey to a bear. She bit her lip as the obvious began to roll over her. Ethan had his gun stuff stored away in a sizable safe down those stairs, along with his reloading equipment and ammunition.

Cluck. Cluck. Cluck.

She headed down cautiously and slowly circled the reloading table that Ethan had set up. It reminded her of some sort of a chemistry lab with its little electronic scale, plastic jars full of different powders, and everything meticulously organized by weight and caliber. Nothing seemed disturbed. Feeling distantly disappointed after her mental lead-up to the Hollywood-style horror scene she had imagined, she redirected her thoughts to her kids strapped into the car outside. She jogged up the stairs only to be welcomed by the now all-too-familiar smell of burning plastic. Why was it always so hard for her to detect that?

"For goodness sake! It's burning plastic." For whatever reason, her brain hadn't been able to register the scent until it was quite obvious—just like back at the Conglomerate in the new marketing area when the duct work had been all messed up and they hadn't had heat.

She grabbed the little kitchen fire extinguisher kept by the stove as she hurriedly made her way back to the Christmas tree. She figured that's where it was coming from. On her way, she passed the entrance to what had become her improvised office. Black smoke was slowly curling its way up from the back of her desktop CPU, which was sitting on the floor next to the desk.

"Oh, my gosh!" Jocelyn said as she ran over to it. She was more than relieved that she didn't have to deal with a homicidal, gun-toting maniac. At the same time, she was grateful she didn't have to break the news of a criminal Grinch stealing Christmas. And best yet, she wouldn't have to tell Ethan that the Christmas tree had burst into flames due to some Chinese-made, piece-of-crap lights she'd gotten at Walmart.

Nah ... it was just some sort of weird fire in her computer. She quickly unplugged the computer and yanked the case off the thing. Tiny sparks were still visible, but they were dying out. Convinced and happy that everything was okay, she headed out to unload the kids and the groceries.

"These Mr. Clean Eraser things are amazing!" said Jocelyn as she scrubbed the tiles in the bathroom. That and, curiously, baby wipes were doing most of the work getting the bathroom shipshape again. Her computer and her car, well, there was nothing Mr. Clean could help her with there.

The phone rang. It was Bruce Drewer, who was ecstatic, just ecstatic about the news coverage the fundraiser had gotten. While Jocelyn appreciated Bruce's call and his gratitude, it bothered her that the media had not responded to her as it usually did.

It also bothered her that she had just come home to a house with the front door splayed wide open. *Maybe I got so distracted by the kids that I didn't lock the door on the way out ...* But try as she might to recall whether that was true or not, she couldn't be sure. *But why would the door just fling open like that? It isn't even windy.* This is what occupied her thoughts as she and the kids finished scrubbing the bathroom walls.

That night she made the best dinner ever and got the kids to bed precisely on time. Operation Restore Domestic Tranquility was seemingly a success—except that Ethan wasn't really as excited about it as Jocelyn. They went to bed without saying anything to each other.

The next morning at approximately zero five hundred, the entire household was awakened by the signature sound of a helicopter batting air against their roof. The kids were screaming.

Wawp Wawp Wawp Wawp Wawp Wawp Wawp Wawp Wawp Wawp.

Jocelyn jumped out of bed and headed to her kids' room to comfort them. "Oh, it's just a helicopter—a whirly bird," she said in that cutesy voice only used for children. "Don't worry," she said soothingly over the ruckus. "Don't cry. It will go away."

But the helicopter wouldn't stop. It just hung there in the air, right above their house. Jocelyn went up to the window and peered out, trying to see it. It sounded like it was literally on their roof. Holding her wailing son, she walked to another window and looked out with the same result. She couldn't see it.

"Assholes!" she heard Ethan shout out from their bed. She took their crying daughter out of her crib and gave her a squeeze, hoping to calm her down. The helicopter was not going away.

"Ethan, what is going on?" she asked as she marched back into their room with crying children hanging onto her pajamas. She headed directly to the window to see if anything of the craft was visible from that vantage point. Still nothing. Getting really disgusted that she couldn't see who or what exactly was messing with her family, she quickly unlocked the window and lifted it open. She was just about to stick her head out in an attempt to get a good look at whatever it was that had awoken them, when Ethan unexpectedly grabbed her, hard, and pulled her back in.

"What the hell do you think you're doing?! They'll pop your goddamn head off!"

Jocelyn looked at him in stunned silence. The helicopter continued beating, and the kids kept screaming. He stared back. They stayed locked in each other's gaze until the helicopter decided it had had enough and departed. They never got to see what type it was.

Of course, Jocelyn could not stop talking about the incident, and Ethan didn't say a word. He made his coffee and eventually headed out. As she watched him leave, it dawned on her that she had not told him about the open door scene of the day before. During the Operation Restore Domestic Tranquility dinner the night before, she had wanted only to focus on how fantastic the bathroom looked. Which led her to expound upon how weird it was that baby wipes could not only gently clean a baby's tender bottom but also remove

Sharpie marker from ceramic tiles. "What type of chemical does that?" she had asked a clearly unenthused Ethan while passing him a bowl of sweet and savory Moroccan couscous.

Now she wondered if the open door had any relationship to their new friend, the Early Bird Whirlybird.

CHAPTER FOURTEEN

"YOU RANG?"

"Mr. Lowe, you are disappointing me."

"Well, I'm disappointed that you sent a helicopter to my fucking house. What the hell was that all about?"

"If I am unable to reach you by traditional means, I will revert to more direct measures. Stay away from your local mafia. I am referring, of course, to a private party you recently attended. You are one of us, and we will not associate with that element. We do not need muddy water. This is God's work."

"Oh, okay, Dad. Whatever you say. What the ...? God's work?! Give me a break."

"You are smarter than this, Mr. Lowe. You are free to socialize with whomever you wish. However, mentions of your association with me or the company are very ill-considered and may result in termination. Of course, that would be unfortunate for all parties involved. You are very lucky that those in attendance at your party the other night were such small-time players and have been easily silenced.

"Ledergerber, I need you to leave my fucking family out of this. My kids, not to mention their mother, were out of their minds. But then again, I'm pretty sure that was your point. Fuck with me all you want. Whatever, I don't care. It's kind of fun actually. Just leave them out of your grandiose plans. Seriously. Fuck with them again, and I'll kill you. It's as simple as that. You have been warned, Ledergerber."

"As have you, Mr. Lowe. Have a pleasant day."

CHAPTER FIFTEEN

WHEN SAMANTHA BALLENTINE CALLED THAT morning, happily letting Jocelyn know that she had seen a lot of the coverage of the RP fundraiser, Jocelyn mentioned that her computer had blown up. Samantha gave a weird sort of snort. "Figures," she said.

Somewhat confused by the response, Jocelyn assured her that she planned on taking the computer over to Staples to see if it could be fixed up. "That was an expensive machine. I want to try and make it last if I can." After Jocelyn had disclosed the circumstances of the open door and, most recently, the helicopter, Samantha became quite serious and strongly recommended that Jocelyn not take the computer to a place like Staples for repair. In fact, Samantha insisted that she use her computer guy. "He's one of us. He knows what time it is. He's safe," she said.

"He's safe?" Jocelyn asked.

"Well, he's been locked up. He's out now, and he doesn't want to screw up again. He knows a lot about a lot of stuff. He just happened to be an easy fall guy. Here. I'll call him right now and send him over to your place. I insist."

"Uh-huh, well okay, thanks. That would be great," Jocelyn said, not fully following what Samantha was getting at, but she was happy to have someone come to the house because she still didn't have the Santa Fe. It was undergoing some "minor" body work, which Jocelyn anticipated being not so minor when she saw the final bill.

"I use him at home and at our office. I trust him implicitly," Samantha said.

Four hours later

"You think it could have been the National Guard?"

"At 5:00 a.m.?" Jocelyn said doubtfully to the computer tech Samantha Ballentine had sent over.

"Well, Camp Fogarty is just over there," the pale, wiry, and incredibly fast-talking tech said as he quickly thumbed over his shoulder. If Jocelyn didn't know better, she would have put money on this guy being a crack addict. But maybe he was just janked out on tons of coffee. She trusted him enough to stand or sit near him the entire time he was in her house. He seemed to know his way around a computer, and Samantha had recommend him, but she wasn't into allowing this guy out of her sight—not after the door thing and the helicopter experience.

"Well, it looks like your hard drive is fried. It's not letting me do anything."

"Great. Just great," Jocelyn sighed as she plopped herself down on her desk chair.

"Mind if I take the case off and look inside?"

"Please, go right ahead. I took it off when I discovered the fire." The wiry guy slipped the case off the computer with lighting speed.

"Hummm." The guy squirreled up his brows. "When did you last take this thing in for repairs?"

"I never have."

"Are you sure?" he asked while rubbing his nose.

"Of course I'm sure. I bought it straight from HP. It came out of the box, and the rest is history."

"Hummm." He sniffed and rubbed his nose again. "Well, I hate to break this to you, but it looks like someone has been doing some soldering in here."

"What?! Soldering?" Jocelyn jumped up, only to crouch down next to him to look at the mysterious inner workings of her computer. "Where? How can you tell?"

"Here and here," the tech said as he pointed his shaky finger at some silvery, blobby lines on the green motherboard.

"This wouldn't have left assembly looking like this. I can assure you."

"You have to be kidding me." She hadn't taken that computer anywhere. "Maybe it's just bad quality control at the factory or something?"

They both sat in silence for a moment as the tech continued his hardware forensics. "I'm actually surprised that you had been able to use this thing. Were you having memory problems with it lately?"

"No."

"How many memory cards did you have?"

"What do you mean?"

"Right here." Out came the shaky finger again. "It looks like you have enough space for four memory cards. There's only one in here. You said you paid a lot for this computer. Usually, it's the processor or the memory that bumps up the price.

"I got the best that money could buy at the time. I don't know how many memory cards it's supposed to have."

"You said you got it from HP. You don't still have any of the paperwork that came with it, do you? It would list everything you bought."

"As a matter of fact, I do! Hold on." Jocelyn went over to her filing cabinet and deftly flipped through her manila file folders. She triumphantly whipped out her order with the receipt stapled to it and handed it to him.

"Hummm," he mumbled as he perused the papers. "Yeah. Okay. You are supposed to have three memory cards. You only have one now."

"So what are you saying? Someone broke into my house right before Christmas." She pointed to the Christmas tree. "Didn't take any of the presents or typical stuff that crooks would want and went straight to my computer and started soldering? Then took two-thirds of my memory? Not all of it? That makes no sense."

"Maybe they just left enough to kill your hard drive. Or start a fire. I don't know."

The way the situation was unfolding was blowing Jocelyn's mind. It made absolutely no sense to her. "Why would anyone bother? Just take the whole freakin' machine. Steal it. Why leave it here?"

"Maybe they wanted to watch where you were going—you know, online. See who you were talking to."

Jocelyn was having a hard time getting her head around all of this. So she asked the only question she could think of that was somewhat grounded in normalcy. "Can this computer be fixed? Or do I need a new one?"

"Sure. Your monitor and sound system are pro. You are going to need a new hard drive. Obviously, you can add as much memory as you want. It's up to you."

After they discussed the particulars of fixing the computer and the importance of backing up the hard drive (which had just as much impact as the dentist telling her to floss), Jocelyn agreed that he might as well take the damaged machine back to his place and start rebuilding it.

"If you want, while I'm at it, I can try and recover anything that might be still on that frazzled hard drive. If I'm able to extract anything, I'll put it on a disc for you and bring it back when I deliver your computer."

"Sure. That would be great. There's a lot of stuff on there from the Raymond Pierce fundraiser and the Meetup group that I'd like to save if I can," Jocelyn said as she looked around for her checkbook. "How much do I owe you for coming out here today?"

"Oh, don't worry about it now——"

"No. Really. I want to give you some money," she said as she riffled through her pocketbook. And the tech, for reasons unknown, started speed rambling about his pet iguana.

Not finding the checkbook and wanting to just shut this guy up, she patted around on her desk as if she might actually feel it before she saw it. She opened the top desk drawer and, while continuing with the patting around approach, noticed the two-year-old UPS letter from Jerry Apario stashed under a notebook. "Oh! I forgot about this thing!" she said as she excitedly extracted it. "Hey. While I have you here, do you mind looking at this? This guy I used to work with sent me these photos, and I don't know what they mean." She slid the black-and-white photos of the computer screen and the accompanying letter out of the envelope and handed them to the tech, who apprehensively took them. "Here, read his letter first; that might help you. I had no idea what he was talking about. I guess he had been trying to hunt me down to tell me about this. But I had just had the babies, and I guess I really didn't—"

"Oh. It looks like the root directory," the tech said as he flipped through the pictures. He stopped to read Jerry's brief letter. "The NSA?" He looked up quizzically at her.

Jocelyn, thinking he thought this was just weird too, replied, "I know. Like, why would the space agency be interested?"

"No." He laughed. "Not NASA, the NSA—the National Security Administration. It's creepier than the CIA. They collect all sorts of information. They like to monitor communications and ... wait, where did you say you worked?"

"At a defense contractor."

The tech raised his eyebrows and looked at the photo. "Oh, I get it. He took pictures and sent them UPS so that no one would see that he was communicating this to you."

Silence as he looked at the root directory.

"Well, what does it mean?" she asked.

"Do you know what the name of your e-mail server was? Or its IP address?"

"No."

"Hummm ..."

"Why?" she said, positioning herself so that she could see the photos too.

"I'm just guessing here, but if I didn't know better, I'd think that maybe this is telling one computer to copy and forward all the e-mails coming to it over to this other computer." The shaky finger pointed to Computer A and Computer B as they appeared in the lines of code.

"He said in his letter that it wasn't supposed to be there," Jocelyn offered with brow furrowed.

"Why don't you just ask him what it means?" the tech said.

"I guess I will," replied Jocelyn.

After they had figured out when and how to get the repaired machine back to her and Jocelyn had decided to take him up on his offer of not worrying about paying him anything now, the tech left, cradling her crippled computer.

Jocelyn knew Jerry's e-mail address at work. All the employee e-mails had the same format. But of course, Jocelyn couldn't e-mail Jerry; she had no computer. And naturally, she had not saved his phone number. Then it dawned on her. "The kid in the purple Civic! I'll call him. His sister might still have Jerry's number."

She picked up the phone and realized that she didn't even know this guy's real name. That didn't stop her from making the call, which was answered on the first ring.

"Yo."

"Umm. Hi. Are you the guy with the purple car?"

"Depends who's asking."

"It's the chick with the Santa Fe you crashed into."

"*Oh*! Hi! How's it going?!" he greeted her warmly. "I saw that fundraiser you were talking about. I gave twenty bucks. You were involved with that? Cool."

"Yeah, I was. And you did? That's great," Jocelyn said encouragingly.

"Yup. I heard about it later that day on one of the car forums that I go to, and I realized that it was the same thing you were talking about."

"A car forum? Who woulda thunk it?" Jocelyn smiled as she said it.

"So I figured that it must be cool, and I gave some money. It was pretty serious watching the donations roll in. I saw my name on the website. That was cool how they did that."

"That's awesome," said Jocelyn. "Yeah. I liked how they did that too. Hey, listen. You know how you were telling me about Jerry Apario? You, or your sister, don't happen to still have his phone number do you? I need to call him." Jocelyn was ready with the pen and paper, eager to get the number.

"Oh, jeez. I haven't talked to him in like two years."

"This is kind of important. Would your sister know how to get in touch with him?"

"Maybe. Do you want to hold on? Or do you want me to call you back?"

"I'll hold."

Jocelyn heard the phone drop on the table and then waited as Driver and his sister verbally assaulted each other. There was lots of high-pitched complaining interspersed with well-placed profanity, and then a lower, louder voice came through shouting at both of them. Something about trying to get some sleep, which Jocelyn heard very clearly. After things had quieted down, Driver came back on the line and gave her Jerry's number. Jocelyn thanked him and proceeded to call Jerry.

She felt a little awkward because he had tried to call her so many times, even sent a package, and she'd never returned his call. But she sucked it up and dialed. She sat waiting for him to pick up. No such luck. Not even an answering machine.

"Hmmm ... maybe that's not his number anymore," she said as she placed the phone back on its cradle.

As soon as she had done that, the phone rang. Half-laughing, Jocelyn picked up the phone.

"Jerry?"

"Uh ... no. I'm looking for Jocelyn McLaren. I'm Joel Belanger, legal counsel to the Raymond Pierce campaign."

Jocelyn instantly got that old, all-too-familiar pit in her stomach that she would get when Mimi would patch through one of the Conglomerate's lawyers.

"Oh, hello. Hi. This is Jocelyn. I'm sorry. I was expecting a call from someone else."

"Well then, I'm glad I got you on the line. I understand that you have done up a marketing plan for the campaign."

"Well, I did do something up for my state. But—"

"Would you be able to send a complete copy of it to me?"

"Sure. No problem. What's your e-mail address?" she said, automatically grabbing a yellow legal pad. The fact that her marketing plan and her computer would not be making contact with this lawyer had been temporarily forgotten.

After she had quickly written down the address she read it back to him.

"Camp@mandolinalaska?"

"Yes. I run a music retreat up in Alaska."

"Seriously?"

"Oh, it's quite a wonderful experience for musicians in the summertime. We have very accomplished mandolin players come in from Belgrade to give workshops."

"Belgrade? As in Serbia?" Jocelyn was completely confused. "You are the lawyer for the Ray Pierce campaign, and you run a music retreat? Shouldn't this summer be the busy season for the campaign? I mean, the election is in November." She could just about hear him smiling on the phone. "Wait. Where did you get my number? And how did you hear about the marketing plan?"

"I'm *one* of the lawyers. I'm not the *sole* lawyer for the campaign. Lawyers need a life too, you know," he paused as if anticipating laughter. "Jeff Truellson in South Carolina has you listed as the RP Meetup organizer for your state. And apparently you passed out a marketing plan to the group when Kris Jung was voted out."

"Jeff in South Carolina?" Jocelyn squinted as she attempted to look into the recent past. "Oh. Okay, yeah. Forrest was talking with him on the phone. Yeah. That was some meeting."

After they discussed the situation with Kris and the Meetup, the lawyer went on to ask Jocelyn about herself.

Of course, she filled him in on all of her qualifications and her involvement with the online fundraiser.

"Oh, wasn't that fantastic?" he said. "Just outstanding. It surprised everyone."

But it got weird when he started to ask her if she liked music. And if she played any instruments. And if she would like to come to Alaska to learn to play the mandolin that summer. So she decided to end the call by letting him know that she would send the marketing plan in the regular mail, as her computer was undergoing some maintenance. After he gave her the mailing address, he promised to forward her document over to two other people who handled the campaign's advertising.

She hung up, not really sure how to feel about the conversation. She was pretty convinced that he was who he said he was, but why didn't he give her a campaign e-mail address? And why would the campaign's lawyer be planning a summer retreat? Weren't these people in it to win it? She was thinking that she should maybe call Samantha to confirm that this guy was who he'd said he was. But she really didn't want to bother her. Samantha had already sent the tech over, and Jocelyn didn't want to appear completely helpless.

Plus, the happiness she was feeling that her plan was going to go to someone who made decisions about advertising was winning out. Maybe someone from the campaign would offer her a "real job." That would be great! She could use all the stuff she had learned at the Conglomerate and help the country get back on track, instead of peddling implements of doom and vaporware. She figured Ethan would prefer her getting paid for her time as well. Maybe then they'd have something to talk about at dinner.

Jocelyn rooted around for the paper copy of the marketing plan when her body started to experience a sensation that was not unlike that which she had endured on a daily basis when she was back at the Conglomerate. She couldn't pinpoint it, but she recognized it. It started in her gut and almost imperceptibly radiated out to the rest of her body. Maybe she needed some coffee.

The phone rang.

"This is Jocelyn," she said in her corporate voice.

"Joss! You finally got back to me! It's me, Jerry Apario. Man, I can't believe it. It's been so long. I don't want to talk on the phone. When and where can we meet?"

CHAPTER SIXTEEN

"YES. I'LL HAVE THE ROOTY Tooty Fresh N Fruity, and she'll have ..." Jerry paused and looked up at Jocelyn, his breakfast companion.

"An English muffin," Jocelyn said, finishing the order.

When the waitress finished scribbling their selections and walked away, Jerry, still wearing his Wayfarer sunglasses, leaned in close. "Look. I'm not supposed to be here. I'm a ghost."

"What?" Jocelyn said with amusement. Then, perceiving that he was serious, she became concerned not only for him but, more importantly, for herself. Maybe it was good that she and Jerry had lost contact a couple of years ago. He had already exhibited some strange behavior earlier in the parking lot. After they had welcomed each other with a hug, he had skittishly glanced around, pulled up his jacket collar, and pulled down the hat to nearly cover his sunglasses.

"Being a ghost is the safest place to be. Everyone thinks you're dead."

"Do people think you're dead, Jerry?" Jocelyn asked, impersonating her own counselor's voice.

"I hope so. I torched my car just before they shut down the division."

"You started your own car on fire!?" she said in a whisper/yell, which instantly snapped her out of the counselor impersonation. "Why? For the insurance money?"

"No. I wanted people to think I had gone missing. You know. Without a trace."

Jocelyn looked at him hard, trying to figure him out. "Dude, you're like the worst ghost in the world. I just called your ex-fiancée and got your number."

"Well. I didn't answer. Did I? And I called you from a pay phone."

"Yeah, well, someone's paying that cell phone bill."

"It's a disposable phone."

What Jocelyn imagined being an enlightening meeting about the meaning of the mysterious photos had quickly devolved into the equivalent of a verbal slap fight. The two continued to one-up each other about whether or not Jerry was a convincing ghost until the Rooty Tooty Fresh N Fruity arrived.

"Okay, fine. You're a ghost," Jocelyn conceded as her English muffin was placed in front of her. "What were the photos about? I didn't know what you were trying to tell me with those. That's why I had to hold a séance to summon you."

"Very funny," said Wayfarer-sporting Jerry as he dug into the Rooty Tooty part of his breakfast.

"No, seriously. Did you send me the pictures because you didn't want to communicate with me via e-mail?" Jocelyn watched him chew. He was clearly a bit miffed that she wasn't buying into his ghost thing.

"Look, Joss, if they were trying to kill you too, you'd think twice about what I'm doing. And you might even think twice about why I'm here to see you today."

This caught Jocelyn's attention, and she stopped messing with him. It was only a little while ago that Ethan had cautioned her about a guy in a helicopter possibly having the intention of popping her head off.

"Okay. You're right. I'm sorry." She leaned in close to him and, in a hushed voice, asked, "Why do you think someone is trying to kill you?"

"Because I was a mule, and then I saw the code."

"I thought you were a ghost."

"No. No, Joss. I'm a ghost *now*. I was a mule *then*. But I didn't know I was a mule until later. And then I found the code and told someone about it."

Jocelyn thought he was going to cry. And right now she was pretty convinced that she was sitting with a crazy person. Jocelyn figured she'd just calmly finish her English muffin, politely say good-bye, and hopefully never have to deal with Jerry Apario again.

Jerry looked around the International House of Pancakes and took off his sunglasses. He rubbed his eyes with one hand and then leaned in very close to her. He was looking at her with such intensity that it caused the hairs on the back of her neck to bristle. Finally, he spoke. "Joss, I didn't know what I was doing. I swear. But at the time, I was happy to do it. I got a Post-it note right before I left. It told me to go to an address in Algiers and pick up a package; I guessed it was for one of Adam's businesses. The Post-it said to claim the package for some sort of wine company. I was confused, but sure, why not? Right?

"When I got to the address, it was a shop that sold all sorts of random stuff—everything from magazines and hookahs to computers and cameras and gold necklaces. You name it. I told the guy behind the counter that I was there to pick something up. Of course, my French isn't that great, and I didn't know what he was saying. I just asked for the package again, and luckily, I had the original yellow sticky note in my wallet. I showed it to him. Dude nods, reaches under the counter, and brings out this little box."

Jerry formed a little rectangle with his hands. "He just gave it to me. Nothing exchanged. And I just walked out like it was cool. So I figured everything was already taken care of. That night, I go to my hotel and end up getting sprayed with all sorts of shit."

"Oh, I remember this," Jocelyn said. "This was a long time ago. I was still there. Wasn't it the hotel's exterminators or something?" Jocelyn asked, but she was starting to get aggravated because she wanted to know about the photos, and Jerry was relaying ancient history at this point.

"Exterminators, my ass. They were trying to exterminate me!"

"Yes. Yes. I remember. Obviously, this event affected you." Jocelyn was back to believing that she was dealing with mental health issues. "But, Jerry, what does this have to do with the photos you sent me?" she asked before taking a bite of her now cold English muffin.

"I'm getting to that. Anyhow. As you know, I came back and complained. I gave the little box to Adam's assistant, Sharon. Next thing you know, I'm getting sent all over the world to install bullshit demos that people didn't even want. Oh, and while I'm at it, I might as well pick up, or drop off, a little box for that wine company." He looked at Jocelyn to see if she was still following him.

"Go on," she said as she applied grape jelly to the other half of the cold, crunchy, and decidedly not delicious English muffin.

"Yeah. So that's when my girlfriend gets pregnant."

Jocelyn raised her eyebrows and pursed her lips.

"I tell Adam that I'm not going to be able to go all over the place anymore because my girlfriend is going to have my kid. That I want to marry her. And that I might have to quit my job for something more stationary. You know, in the middle of the layoffs and all and people getting sent to other divisions in Colorado and Utah, I figured I was doing him a favor. And you know what he does?"

"No."

"He gives me a raise! And sends me back to Algeria to that weird shop. Tells me that Akbar, or whatever the hell his name is, will hook me up."

This story now had Jocelyn's full attention.

"So I go trotting back to Algeria purportedly to install the same damn demo that no one even wanted the first time I installed it. I head to that same crazy little shop, and the guy seems to know I'm coming. He takes out a bunch of gorgeous rings. I mean over-the-top stuff—diamonds literally fit for a queen—and basically tells me, in so many words, to pick one. I'm not really going for it because I know that I can't afford any of the ones he's showing me. So, and I'm not sure why he does this, he takes out all these loose gems and invites me to look at them—you know with the special tweezers and the jeweler's loupe. Like I know what I'm doing. So I play along, because why not? Right? I look at the gems. He sees that I am tending to purple and pink stones. He whips out this amazing ring—a twelve-carat oval purple amethyst surrounded by another carat and a half of little pink sapphires with another carat of tiny diamonds thrown in for sparkle's sake. I know my girlfriend is going to freak. Totally her scene."

If she's anything like her brother, Jocelyn thought. But she remained silently engrossed as Jerry continued.

"Anyhow, long story short. He gives it to me! Like, just gives it to me! Then he swoops up all the gems that I just looked at, adds a bunch of diamonds, packages them all up in a little box, and hands it to me. I leave like I usually do with the box and with a ring for my girl in my pocket. No payment, nothing."

Not really sure what to say as she imagined Driver's never-pregnant sister proudly featuring such a ring, Jocelyn said, "Wow. Did anyone try to poison you that night?"

"No. I left going to that shop until the very end of my trip. I went directly to the airport and slept on a bench until I got on my flight home."

Jerry picked up his fork and took some hungry bites of his breakfast as Jocelyn silently processed what he had just told her.

"So anyhow, when I get back, I decide to tell Robert about the whole scene and—"

"What?! Why would you tell Robert?" Jocelyn almost yelled.

"Well, who was I gonna tell? It's not like the HR director was going to do anything. And I was starting to feel, you know, kind of weird about it. I know it really wasn't my business to know what was inside those boxes. But goddamn it, when I ended up knowing, it freaked me out. I wanted to tell everyone, but then I didn't, and then I wasn't sure what to do."

Jocelyn believed him now. "What did you want Robert to do? What did he say?"

"Oh, Robert mostly focused on how great it was that I had gotten that ring for my girl. And how I should propose to her. Which restaurant I should bring her to. That sort of stuff. He kind of blew off the diamonds and gems thing. He just said, 'You know how Adam is.'"

"Uh-huh. I can totally picture him saying that. He would never rock the boat. That's for sure," Jocelyn commiserated.

"So that's when I called the FBI."

"Seriously?!"

"Yeah. Why not? Like when you and I called them the day after 9-11. I called them."

"Okay. So did they respond to you?"

"Not really. Well, I take that back. They might have gotten involved. But I didn't talk with an agent if that's what you mean. This was about the time you were leaving. After you left, so many temps were coming and going that no one really got any work done. I had to constantly train the new temps, and then they would end up not coming back. I eventually got stuck just dealing with the servers. That's when I saw that code. I didn't know who else to tell. So I took the pictures and developed them myself. You know, you never know who's gonna be looking at your stuff at those photo lab places," Jerry said before he took another giant bite of his breakfast.

"Right," said Jocelyn. "So what does the code mean, Jerry? You're killing me here."

"Someone was copying all the e-mail communications and sending them somewhere else." Jocelyn nodded. "I checked it out. And I'm not a programmer, but I think they were also making copies of the proposal files stored on Nancy's computer and sending everything to the same place."

"Wow. Okay, now I see why you wanted to find me. Proposals. You think it's corporate espionage? I know that Adam was totally paranoid about that."

"Maybe. But I think all this stuff might have been sent to an FBI server."

"Oh, so they did respond to you. That's a good thing, right?"

"Umm. Not really. If it was the FBI, then they didn't do it the right way. They can't just show up and install something on someone's server in the middle of the night. They can't just look at private communications like that. That's totally illegal. Even if it is a corporation. Corporations have the same rights as walking, talking, real people in this country. However messed up that is."

"Well, maybe they had a warrant."

"No, they didn't. I checked."

"Well, you did call them. Maybe they had probable cause or something, and it prompted some sort of secret sting operation."

"*Well*," he said, imitating Jocelyn, "maybe they might have wanted to talk with me, you know, the guy sitting right there, right next to the server—the guy who actually called them to report diamonds and gems being smuggled into the country, the guy that *actually did the smuggling*. No one personally contacted me for follow-up, Joss. I called them three times and gave my story to the person who answered the phone. I know they have a file on me because the person I'd speak with always knew what I was talking about." Jocelyn just looked at him, not knowing what to say.

"I've come to the conclusion they don't want to hear about it. And that's what is freaking me out. It's so cheesy, this code. Like, if it was the NSA, I probably wouldn't have seen anything. With the NSA, whatever they wanted to see would have just been scooped up somewhere along its journey through the Internet, you know, like when it traveled through Southern Bell or something. Hell, the NSA is probably already doing it anyway. This was a hack. If the FBI got busted for violating the Fourth Amendment, I'd make a perfect fall guy. If it was someone else, I'd still make the perfect fall guy."

"Maybe it's not the FBI. Maybe someone was trying to trick you into thinking it was the FBI so you wouldn't touch it. Did you remove it?"

"Yes, I did. And guess what?"

"What?"

"A new, enhanced version showed up again the next day! That's when I noticed that Nancy's computer was specifically involved. That was new in the code. And that's when I decided that I had to get lost. I mean we all know what happened to Nancy. The woman just dropped dead, for Christ's sake. It's pretty obvious that she was murdered." He searched Jocelyn's face for some sort of confirmation. "Look," he continued, "me and my girlfriend had broken up. She told me she'd had a miscarriage and didn't really want to marry me. So fine. What did I have to lose? That's when I decided to become a ghost."

CHAPTER SEVENTEEN

"NOPE. NOTHING. I COULDN'T GET anything off that," the tech said as he handed her the remnants of her hard drive.

Jocelyn took the useless piece of machinery and looked at it. "Seriously?" she whined. "But all the Raymond Pierce stuff—"

"You could try to bring that hard drive to someone else—someone with better equipment who does recovery for a living. They might be able to find something. But I'm sorry; I didn't have any luck."

"Well, at least you tried. Thanks."

The two of them set up her new computer on her desk. It was blazingly fast. "Sweet," Jocelyn said, smiling. "How much do I owe you?" she asked as she looked around for her checkbook.

"Nothing, Samantha already gave me some money," the tech said as he stuck his hands in his jean pockets and shuffled his feather weight uncomfortably.

"Oh, *I* want to give you something. Like a tip. I'm really glad you were able to do this for me. Hold on. My purse is out in the car. I'll be right back."

She left the tech tidying the wires as she ran out in search of her checkbook. At this point, Jocelyn felt okay leaving the tech in the house. He seemed sincere enough and obviously knew what he was doing. She was contemplating that until she got about five feet from her mother's car, the one she was still putt-putting around in, and she stopped.

The sun visors were down. She hadn't used the visors. She couldn't even remember the last time she had entertained the idea of using a sun visor. She slowly approached the car and opened the previously locked door. Yup. It had been broken into—right there in her own driveway. There were no broken windows. Nothing like that. It was almost worse. Everything inside of the car had been ransacked—the glove compartment was open, and its contents haphazardly strewn around. The little center console armrest had been busted open, and a fine collection of both her mother's and her own CDs had obviously been perused and scattered about the car. Even the floor mats and the kids' car seats looked as if someone had been curious about them and had made no attempt to hide it.

Oddly, her purse was still sitting on the passenger seat. She reached into it, expecting to find her wallet missing. Nope. *The cash and the credit cards must have gotten snatched*, she thought as she tore open the wallet. Negative. Her purchasing power was still intact. Admittedly confused, she started slipping the CDs back into their little slots in the arm rest compartment and discovered that they were all still there too. *Is this some sort of weird prank?* Jocelyn wondered as she put a map, random receipts, and the car registration back into the glove box. Nothing appeared to be missing. Nothing. Not wanting to leave the tech alone for too long, she grabbed her purse and headed back into the house, shaking her head.

"Hey, you didn't happen to see anyone over by my car, did you?" she asked the tech when she rejoined him over by the computer.

"No. Why?"

"Someone broke into it and messed everything up. How weird is that?"

"They probably wanted your CDs. That happens. The losers think they can sell them or trade them for a fix."

"No. I don't think so," Jocelyn said as she took out her checkbook and started writing the check. "Nothing was stolen. I mean, I'd call the police, but they didn't steal anything, and they didn't damage the car. I can see why they didn't want my mom's audio books or her *Aretha Franklin's*

Greatest Hits CD. But come on, what kind of modern-day crook doesn't take *Rage Against the Machine*? They didn't even go for that. In fact, they didn't take any CDs. The strangest part is that they didn't even touch any cash or credit cards."

"Honey, you've got some weird luck," the tech said as he accepted her payment.

Jocelyn had to agree and thanked him.

Once he left, she jumped right into her e-mails.

There were lots of e-mails thanking her and letting her know that the RP supporters on her growing contact list had seen the fundraiser coverage. There were a ton of e-mails asking her, now the de facto Ray Pierce Meetup organizer, when the next Meetup was. And there was an e-mail from camp@mandolinalaska. The Ray Pierce lawyer had received her marketing plan and wanted to speak with her.

Fretting that she hadn't responded to his e-mail within what would be a reasonable, accepted corporate time frame, she replied back, apologizing. She would call him, at his convenience, of course, any time that day. Camp@mandolinalaska replied back within fifteen minutes letting her know he would appreciate a call at three-thirty.

Bingo! This was exciting! Jocelyn had about two hours to get ready for the call. She made sure that she knew the particulars of her plan and had a copy of it on hand. She knew that she would have to communicate with him from her child-free call center, aka the car. She looked around for her cell phone, wanting to check the battery. She had time to charge it before the call if need be.

"Where could I have put that thing?" she wondered aloud as she began to search her purse.

"Shit," Jocelyn said as it finally dawned on her what the whole car thing had been about. *My phone. They took my phone. Great.* Jocelyn sighed. Okay fine, now she was going to have to call the cell phone company and report it stolen. She tried to think back to when she had last seen the phone. *I haven't even gone out since I saw Jerry at IHOP.* "Pathetic," grumbled Jocelyn. *How messed up is this? I'm so housebound with these kids I didn't even think of missing my purse. Someone could have called the whole world by now on my phone, and the bill—*

The deductible on the Santa Fe still hadn't hit home. Oh man, she did not need this. She called the cell phone company and went through the typical question/answer thing with customer service. The woman Jocelyn dealt with was amazingly accommodating. The phone company changed her phone number for her and put some credit on her account.

Not expecting such a generous response from the cell phone company, Jocelyn said, "Oh, thanks for the credit. I hate to ask this, but out of curiosity, how much did they actually rack up?"

"What do you mean?" the customer service woman asked.

"The credit. I'm assuming you're giving it to me because I didn't make the calls. I was wondering how many calls the thief actually made. What's my bill going to look like?"

"Oh, no. We just gave you the credit for having to go through the inconvenience of not having a phone. It has nothing to do with your bill. If you hold on, I'll check for you."

Jocelyn braced herself for the worst.

"When was the last time you made a call on that phone?" the customer service woman asked.

"Three days ago."

"It looks like no calls have been made since then."

"Really?" Jocelyn said in surprise. "Why would someone take my phone and not call anyone?"

"I don't know," said the kindly customer service woman. "Maybe they just wanted to see who you were talking to."

CHAPTER EIGHTEEN

"HERE. THIS IS WHAT YOU wanted." Ethan tossed the file onto Ledergerber's desk. Man, he hated that little baby-wearing-welding-goggles statue. It was creepy, and he wanted to punch it in the face every time he saw it. The Picasso made sense. It was just a friggin' dude whippin' paint around in some sort of drippy, drizzly, cigarette-smoking frenzy like it was cool. And it was cool. The colors made sense too. Just gray and black and tan with a random blob of red like it was a mistake.

Like it was a mistake.

Ethan knew better. It wasn't a mistake. It was a career move. And once you've committed yourself to that mistake you can't go back. *Like friggin' "Hotel California."* The famous Eagles song blasted out of Ledergerber's mouth, in stereo no less, when he began speaking. Ethan had to really focus in and concentrate on what the man was saying. Two tracks were playing at the same time, and it was confusing.

"Thank you, Ethan. I know this was difficult for you. Please understand that this is important information, so I called up the captain. Please bring me my wine."

Ethan strained to rip the statements apart from the lyrics. *He wants wine?*

"Your woman is going down an interesting path; wake you up in the middle of the night. Such a lovely face."

He didn't know if he should sit down and wait for a drink or agree that Jocelyn was lovely or just leave now that he had delivered the file containing a full report regarding Jocelyn's digital footprint. He had been genuinely impressed that it was she who had reported the curious spam emails to the Generals back at the Conglomerate. He felt heavy—as if his limbs were made of lead, the lead that knew he should be making into more bullets.

"Bring your alibis. The diamond exchange was a disaster waiting to happen. You should be very proud of your service to humanity. We are all just prisoners here of our own device doing God's work."

He began to perspire. Heavily. This was just too messed up, and what made it more messed up was that he knew he was slipping. He was losing it, and that was the scary part. He knew that he had been having problems, but fuck the VA or any of that shit. Hearing the music coming out of Ledergerber's mouth was entertaining, like tripping on acid when he was twelve, but knowing that he was going full-on bat shit was not. He had to get out of there.

"Mr. Lowe, you do not look well. Would you care to sit down? You can check out any time you like, but you can never leave."

Ethan blinked and without making eye contact with Ledergerber, he snatched the money sitting on the desk. With almost military correctness he turned on his heel and promptly left the office.

CHAPTER NINETEEN

"ALASKA IS SO BEAUTIFUL AT that time of year. You'll really love it. I can make arrangements for you—"

"No. No, thank you. Look, did you read the marketing plan?" Jocelyn asked, much more than a bit miffed. "Are we able to access any campaign funds to execute even a part of the state plan?"

"Oh, I did. It looked wonderful. But I don't make decisions about advertising, nor do I have anything to do with the checkbook."

"Did you give it to the two people you had mentioned the last time we spoke?"

"I did."

"And?"

"They will contact you when and if they need to. But back to Alaska ..."

Jocelyn was sorely disappointed. Her idea that maybe she might prove her worth in some capacity other than feeding and bathing was effectively shot. At least for the time being. *I should probably just call Stan and find out if that job he was talking about is still around.* But she didn't, considering that the band camp/Pierce campaign lawyer was only communicating with her because he was just as lecherous as Stan. Jocelyn just didn't have it in her to deal with her former congressman and his inappropriate innuendoes right now.

She figured she might as well start getting the kids fed and then think about what to make Ethan for dinner. He had said he would be home tonight. She really wanted to tell him about the cell phone. She really wanted to tell him about that jerk of a lawyer over at the Raymond Pierce campaign. She really just wanted to talk. And although she stayed up until

1:00 a.m. waiting for Ethan, she would not be talking to him that night. Her children were effectively her world, and maybe she should just accept it.

She went into their room and watched them as they slept. Jocelyn silently promised that she would do everything in her power to make the world better for them. She was sleepy and not quite sure what she even meant by that, but she kissed their dream-filled heads and then shuffled off to bed herself.

That night, she had her own dream. A very vivid dream. It went like this:

She was dressed in high heels and black thigh-highs; a short, black skirt; and a tight, crisp, white blouse. She was changing her son's diaper. She knew it was a dream while she was in it because her kids had been potty trained for a little while now. In the dream, her son was crying, and Ethan was downstairs in the basement yelling. She couldn't tell what he was yelling about, but she shouted back, "I'll be down in a minute! Don't worry! I'll be right there!" She proceeded to calm the little boy in front of her and change his diaper. Once that was done, she headed to the basement stairs. She opened the door. Ethan was still yelling at the top of his lungs. A boy about nine or ten years old with brownish hair, not anyone she recognized, came running up the stairs toward her holding what looked like a little plastic briefcase. He gave her an impish grin, but there was panic in his eyes as he rushed past her and out the door.

"Ethan," she called out. "Ethan, I'm here."

Ethan rounded the corner. Apparently, he had calmed down. His face was very placid—almost a relaxed smile. She smiled back. Then she saw it. He was holding a black pistol. She cocked her head, not understanding. And then he lifted it.

He pointed it, and—

Bang!

He shot her. All the while, he wore the same placid, I-told-you-so smile. She looked at him in confusion as she slumped against the wall and slowly slid down into a sitting position on the top step.

"You ... you shot me," she said in mild surprise. "I thought you were a better shot than that. You should have killed me. I'm so close." He didn't say anything but maintained that same creepy calm.

Then everything went black, but she was still there in her dream. *Is this what it feels like to be dead?* Then contemplating that in silence, she realized that she was dead. *Oh, I see now,* she heard her voice say. But it wasn't the voice that comes out of your mouth. It was that voice in your head that you just know is your own.

Everything was black. Nothing. It was the strangest sensation for Jocelyn to know that she was in a dream while dreaming, and even freakier to not see anything in the dream but pitch blackness. All this while somehow appreciating, with every fiber of her being, that she was seeing something that she had never seen before.

Jocelyn awoke from this dream thoroughly confounded and more than a bit disturbed. She checked the clock—not quite 4:30 a.m. She lay there for the next few minutes not able to fall back asleep. As she was staring at the ceiling contemplating this dream, her son suddenly burst out, "Wahhahahah! Mommy! Mommy!"

Jocelyn hopped out of bed as she had done countless times before and went to comfort her son. Her daughter, amazingly, slept through all of her brother's fussing.

"Oh, honey," Jocelyn said as she picked him up. "What could be so bad?"

The toddler had tears rolling down his cheeks and said, "Loud bang, Mommy. Bang!"

She looked at her son in amazement. "You heard that?"

He nodded. Jocelyn hugged him, wondering if they had somehow had the same type of dream. As she embraced her child, she saw Ethan stealthily enter their bedroom, and she froze. It would be days before she told him about the cell phone or even felt comfortable enough to speak with him at all.

Monday of the next week, when she finally decided it was time to talk, she cornered him at the kitchen counter as he was making his morning coffee. "Look, Ethan, we've got helicopters, burnt-out hard drives, and stolen cell phones. Add that to what Jerry Apario told me, and I'm getting kind of creeped out."

"Joss, don't let Apario freak you out. That guy is kind of a weirdo. You know that," Ethan said as he put the coffee can back in the fridge and started searching for his Mensa International coffee mug in the dishwasher. "Are these dishes clean?"

"Yeah." She nodded that they were clean and continued. "But, Ethan, what he was saying ... I think he was telling the truth."

"Or at least he *believed* he was telling the truth," Ethan corrected her. "Honestly, Joss, the guy isn't a programmer, and he's a little tapped."

Jocelyn cocked her finger into the universal signal for "wait one moment." She hustled over to her desk drawer, got the UPS letter package, and presented the contents to Ethan.

"What is this?" he asked.

"Jerry sent it to me a long time ago, but I didn't look at it until the computer guy came to fix my computer," she said as she circled around behind him to look over his shoulder while he studied the large black-and-white photos. Ethan sat down at the kitchen table and remained silent as he flipped though the images and then read the brief letter.

"And then you went to breakfast with Apario?"

"Well, yeah."

"And you didn't feel the need to clue me in about your date?"

"Well, it wasn't really a date," she tried to explain.

The whole conversation quickly, and almost inexplicably, turned into Jocelyn defending Jerry Apario while Ethan angrily spiraled into accusing her of everything from having an affair with the guy to spending way too much time focused on Ray Pierce.

"You know, all this shit with the helicopters and your computer and your phone all started when you got involved with that campaign, Joss. You know that, right? Why don't you just let other people deal with politics? You can't handle it with the kids and the MS ..."

Okay, right there: "You can't handle it." Ethan had pushed the button. She'd show him. She didn't know exactly how, but it was officially on. She left him stewing and went straight to her computer and scheduled the next Ray Pierce for President Meetup.

She and Ethan did not speak for the rest of the day.

The next day, Jocelyn came home to find Ethan on the roof. "What are you doing up there?!" she shouted out as she unloaded the kids from the rehabbed Santa Fe.

He smiled, waved, and unsteadily made his way over to the ladder. Jocelyn walked over, concerned about his balance (or lack thereof) and held the ladder as he climbed down. When both feet were on terra firma, he gave her a big, warm hug and pointed up to the tree next to the house.

"I've installed cameras. Look," he slurred.

Not only could she hear it, she could smell it. He had been "self-medicating." *What's up with me and drunk guys?* She'd have to mention this recurring theme to her counselor. He held her hand as they walked around the tree looking at the motion-activated camera that he had installed.

"It's wireless. When someone walks by, the light goes on, and I can watch it on my computer," Ethan said, dizzily leaning back to admire his work. "I put it up for *you*. You said you were getting creeped out. I would give you a gun, but I know you won't carry it. So here. Here you go!" he proclaimed proudly with a grand sweeping motion of his hand.

Jocelyn was getting flashes of Jerry Apario installing webcams on her computer at work. Yet another topic of discussion for the next counselor's appointment—why did cameras make people feel safer? All they had the ability to do was capture images of someone committing a crime. Someone could be possibly stabbing her in the eye or raping her or breaking into the house, and another person far, far away could watch the whole thing from the comfort of his or her own home. Heck, someone could even post the whole sordid scene on YouTube. This did not make Jocelyn feel safer. It actually made her feel more like a piece of meat—a victim before anything nefarious had even occurred. But she appreciated Ethan's attempt and squeezed his hand. He was trying.

That afternoon as she de-cluttered the kitchen counters and Ethan and the kids were napping, she came across one of Ethan's credit card bills. She glanced at it. It included a charge for the Cozy Inn Motel. *Oh, how sweet.* She smiled. *He must be keeping this as a reminder of the time we stayed there. That was such a scene. I'll always remember that.*

Her smile, soon replaced by furrowed brows, was eventually completely deconstructed by tears when she noticed a charge, that same day, for five hundred dollars at the Cadillac Lounge, a local strip club. She and Ethan had been at the Cozy Inn over three years ago. This bill was from last month. She crumpled the bill and threw it at the wall.

"What a freakin' douche! Oh! And he had the audacity to go off on me about Jerry! Nice deflection technique there, Mr. Couple-a-Drinks," she hissed.

If it hadn't been for the kids' nap inducing some sort of motherly don't-wake-the-baby thing, she would have just marched up to the sleeping Ethan and gone off on him in your basic hell-hath-no-fury kind of way. The kids sleeping provided her with a moment to think things through.

As she wiped tears from her cheeks, a country music song started to compose itself in her head. Yup. Her life had somehow devolved into the equivalent of a country music song. Jocelyn initially thought the music she was hearing was more of a blues tune, but she knew that all good songs about a woman getting screwed over, persevering, and overcoming were country.

Yeah, this was a country music smash hit, she decided. She didn't have to put up with this joker. She and the kids could move into one of her houses. Or she could sell one of the houses and get some money. Oh! And she had those gold coins! Yes. She could sell them to fund her escape. She knew this would take some time. But screw it. She did not have to deal with this jackass! *Fuck this shit! Fuck him.* She was better than all of this.

But ... oh yeah, health insurance. Friggin' health insurance. What was she going to do about health insurance? The medicine she took every day for the relapsing-remitting MS she had been afflicted with since she was twenty-five years old cost over $3,000 a month. It seemed to be working, and she wasn't about to go off it. She knew what those relapses were like. Ethan had been providing her with health insurance since the babies were born, so that her copay was about $350 a month. That snappy country song that had been playing in her head on a vinyl record just got really badly scratched up and skipped back to the blues tune.

She honestly didn't know what to do about Ethan. If she confronted him, she would have to leave. She saw no other option. It was *his* house after all. She couldn't kick one of her tenants out and move into one of her income properties because her cash flow was that darn tight. That was even if he was able or wanted to keep her on his insurance plan with her not living in the same house. She simply wouldn't be able to swing it if one of the renters was not paying rent. Maybe if she didn't mention it, maybe if she never brought it up, she could make peace with the new situation—that he was just a roommate—and that would be okay. Maybe. But she decided to talk to a realtor anyway and see about selling one of the properties.

Needless to say, things got colder and colder at the little "cottage yellow" house. After the wireless, motion-activated camera was installed, Jocelyn spent more and more time interacting with people online in the RP Meetup as she fed and dealt with the kids and the never-ending housework and laundry. She spent more and more time reading alone in her bedroom. And she escaped to places like the DailyPierce, an online community of people who supported Ray Pierce and posted news stories and YouTubes, keeping each other informed on things like the election, the economy, and foreign policy. Her log-in name was LadyLiberty70, and she was a regular there. It was nice to know people were concerned about the same things she was concerned about. It gave her hope and the feeling of being proactive as she lounged comfortably in her own home. And almost equally important, it gave her the ability to forget about other things.

CHAPTER TWENTY

"WHY DON'T YOU JUST GO to the VA? You were in the service," the pretty redhead said while massaging his back. "They deal with this stuff all the time now. I'm sure they could get you in with some counseling—"

"The VA is the very last place I would go to get counseling," he mumbled. He was thoroughly enjoying the Swedish massage.

"For goodness' sake, why?"

"They'll take my guns away."

"No, they won't!" She kneaded harder on his shoulders and giggled.

"Oh, yes they will. Folks never thought they'd ever do background checks on people wanting to buy a gun, considering it's a constitutional right to own one. But of course they do background checks now—health records, specifically psych health records ... Well, I don't need that mess, especially not from the VA."

"Well, I think background checks are probably a good idea." She started doing the karate chop thing on his back and continued speaking. "I mean my daddy showed me how to shoot when I was a kid. We've always had guns. But honestly, the way things are today"—she paused as she worked a knot in his neck—"I think background checks are smart."

Suddenly, Ethan's Swedish massage wasn't quite as enjoyable. He had been hoping for a "happy ending" finish, but now he wasn't particularly into this chick. In fact, the urge to debate her and explain how wrong she was seemed to overpower him. He held his tongue and glanced over at the digital alarm clock positioned next to the Macintosh-scented

Yankee Candle. He only had ten minutes left anyway. *If she could just keep her mouth shut ...*

"I mean, look at all the kids who are dying because of guns. It makes me so sad."

He let out an audible sigh. He couldn't let that one slide. "More kids die in swimming pools each year than get killed by guns. And background checks are not going to stop kids from messing with guns that were presumably bought by someone who had a background check."

She had moved down to his glutes and was vigorously rubbing in circles. "Seriously? Is that true?"

"Yes."

"Wow." She picked up his hips and did some sort of mild adjustment thing as she jostled him around then started massaging the backs of his legs. He was surprised by how strong she really was. "Well, those gun-free school zones are good though—especially in the inner cities."

"Okay! That's it! Would you please just be quiet and finish this massage."

The woman was absolutely silent for the next eight minutes. Ethan had to admit it was a very good massage. He was able to think. He was able to see. And he was very relaxed. When she had finally finished by therapeutically caressing his head and temples, she asked, "Would you be wanting any extras today?"

He sighed, shook his head, and begrudgingly replied, "Yeah, sure. Why not."

CHAPTER TWENTY-ONE

JOCELYN SIGNED UP TO BE a delegate for Ray Pierce, although she still wasn't quite sure what being a delegate entailed. She collected signatures in order to get him, and her, on the ballot. Positioning herself in freezing cold rain in front of the local grocery store, she thought that, if people saw her, they might feel bad enough and just sign. Everyone else in her Meetup group was doing the same thing.

It must have worked. Amazingly, when the secretary of state released the final numbers, Raymond Pierce had gotten the most legitimate signatures of any candidate running for president. The signatures didn't mean that people were necessarily going to vote for him. But it showed there was a significant interest in this candidate, and people wanted to see his name on the ballot.

She felt she owed it to herself to learn as much as she could about the US system of government. This naturally, like a domino falling over, led her into wanting to learn about money. Jocelyn figured you can't have a government without money being involved. Of course, as she learned more and more about the US economy and, more importantly, about what money actually was, she began to slowly see that Ray Pierce wasn't even speaking the same language as the other candidates. She became more and more impressed with how he was able to toggle the divide between people who had a clue and people who were just interested in the spectacle of politics.

She read *A History of Money and Banking in the United States of America* by Murray Rothbard. It was a tough, tough book, basically a college textbook, but it challenged her, and she liked learning about such an important subject.

She read another really long book that was easier, *The Creature from Jekyll Island*, and watched an exhaustingly long documentary called *The Money Masters*.

She was so astounded by what she saw in the documentary that she swallowed her pride and invited Ethan to watch it with her. It took two nights to fully watch it with him, but once they finished it, Ethan wanted to watch it again. In a way, they sort of bonded over that film. A bunch of stuff was in the documentary that neither of them had ever learned in school and that corroborated what she'd found in the books she had been reading.

It was right about then that Jocelyn started entertaining the idea of homeschooling the kids. *Why would public school leave this information out?*

Finally, the primary came. Ray Pierce did not win, and he dropped out of the race. Incredibly, that did not stop his supporters, who decided to show their support for Ray Pierce's ideas and go to Washington, DC for a rally! Not surprisingly, the campaign did not have anything to do with it. Jocelyn had attempted to get the press to cover the supporter-sponsored rally, like the one-day bombshell fundraiser. But interestingly enough, when she called the numbers on her list, the same exact list that she had called to push the story of the fundraiser, no one knew who she was.

"No," Jocelyn tried to explain, "I'm the woman you dealt with on that story you did in Boston." Silence. "About the Raymond Pierce online fundraiser? The one where he broke all sorts of fundraising records."

"I'm afraid I don't recognize you," the female reporter said flatly. "You'll have to go through the main number."

"You know," Jocelyn was getting angry but tried to remain professional. "Remember you interviewed a lady with a monkey in an RV. She had driven all the way to Boston? It was snowing. Remember? "

"I'm on a deadline, and I have to get off this phone. Call the main number if you think this thing in DC is important. Good-bye."

Incredible. All of the calls she made went pretty much like that. Jocelyn had become a *persona non grata.* No one in the media wanted to talk with her. What just happened?

"Well, the guy didn't win the primary, Joss," Ethan said coolly. "He's not going to run for president. He's called it quits. Now can you just relax? I, for one, am glad this thing is over."

Jocelyn took Ray Pierce's loss very personally. She shoulda, coulda, woulda done more was all she could think about.

"I'm going to DC," she announced the next morning.

CHAPTER TWENTY-TWO

SUSTAINING HERSELF ONLY ON BEEF jerky and bottled water, Jocelyn carpooled with twelve other people in a rented van. Naturally, the GPS unit that the driver of the van relied upon was not spitting out very good directions, and a trip that should have taken about ten hours ended up taking closer to twenty. But it was fine. She had brought enough beef jerky for everyone who was jammed into the van with her. And they only had to live through one serious round of bickering between a Catholic woman and a born-again Christian as the two heatedly and emotionally debated proper interpretation of Bible scripture.

The atheists in the rear of the van held their own conversation while this was going on, and everyone else just talked about the particularly cool attributes of Jim Morrison and the Doors or the new music of the Flobots. Of course, everyone would chime in about RP when his name came up. The tired and hungry group arrived only a few hours before the rally was to begin.

Suffering somewhat from sleep deprivation, Jocelyn and the van pilgrims walked to the Washington Monument. The crowd was smaller than Jocelyn had hoped, but it was still impressive. The group that had assembled under the trees around the famous obelisk was some sort of hybrid mix of Mardi Gras meets the debate team. Jocelyn noticed that everyone appeared simultaneously extremely happy yet dead serious—a weird dichotomy. But it worked. And they marched.

They spilled onto the well-manicured lawn in front of the Capitol building. At least a few hundred more people were already there mulling around before their parade got there. It was hot. Ridiculously hot. Jocelyn sat under a tree to apply some sunscreen.

It was here, on the Capitol steps, that she heard the former CIA officer in charge of the Bin Laden unit speak. He supported Ray Pierce. She heard a Marine deliver one of the most moving and powerful speeches she had ever heard in real life. Men all around her had tears in their eyes, she noticed as she dabbed her own. She listened to a pretty female author, admittedly a Democrat, but supporting Ray Pierce, who was concerned about warrantless wiretapping and the loss of a whole menu of civil liberties. She heard from a famous economist who talked about why Ray Pierce's proposed financial plan was the only one that didn't completely suck and that, even under the Pierce plan, Americans were going to have to adjust to some changes economically. "America is in serious trouble, and none of the other candidates are even attempting to talk about this!"

More and more people kept arriving. It was hard to judge how many people were there because it was so hot. People were hiding under trees and in all sorts of nooks and crannies to get out of the sun. Jocelyn saw that people had brought their Ray Pierce for President signs, which was kind of heartbreaking, and they were using them as giant sun visors.

She couldn't help but notice the group of people in Ray Pierce for President T-shirts trotting back and forth with a large banner that read, "Read *Atlas Shrugged.*" And the guy standing next to her was toting a sign that said, "Required Reading: *The Road to Serfdom.*" Handheld personal camcorders were all over the place. The mainstream media was nowhere to be found. YouTube videos of the event were posted in close to real time, and black helicopters flew overhead.

You were just as likely to meet a person selling water as you were to bump into someone selling silver coins with Raymond Pierce's image on the front. Jocelyn would have bought one, but she couldn't be sure it was real silver. While she was inspecting the silver coin, Raymond Pierce finally took the stage. He was flanked by his two granddaughters. An eager and enthusiastic crowd rushed out from all over the place and instantly converged on the lawn in front of the stage.

"I bet he thinks he's gonna get hit," a beer-bellied guy on her left commented as he applauded.

"Hit with what?" Jocelyn asked as she clapped in admiration.

"You know. Shot. He's surrounding himself with his grandkids. They are blocking the shot."

"Maybe," she said as she smiled up at the stage, still vigorously clapping. But she started looking around and noticed some guys up on the roof. *Too obvious to be bad guys. They must be keeping an eye on him ... or us.*

"Well, there are a ton of people here who'd be honored to take a bullet for RP," a college student said as he clapped enthusiastically while watching Ray Pierce adjust the microphone on the podium.

"Yeah. You're probably right. You go first though, okay?" the guy who brought up the thing about the granddaughters quipped back while still clapping and cheering.

Then, when the applause of the five thousand or so in attendance died down, Jocelyn listened in rapt attention as Ray Pierce laid into one of the best non-teleprompter speeches she had ever had the pleasure to listen to. He ended it by announcing that his campaign was organizing an even bigger rally the same week as the RNC. His rally would be right across the river, not ten miles away, from the Republican National Convention.

"Dude! That's the balls!" she heard someone exclaim.

Ray Pierce continued and said that he would be holding political training for those interested and that he hoped that everyone in attendance would spread the word.

And spread the word they did.

"Feel better now? Got that all out of your system?" Ethan asked after Jocelyn excitedly relayed her experience in Washington, DC. She had only been gone for three days, but Ethan and the kids and the house all looked like they had lived through some sort of natural disaster.

"Ummmm. Not quite. There's another thing coming up at the end of August—"

"Oh, for cryin' out loud, Joss! Seriously! Give it up already!"

Tired and feeling really beat up by the van excursion, she laid into Ethan without really knowing what she was even saying. The kids were crying, and Ethan was yelling, and the only thing that could have made the whole scene more confusing was a tea kettle whistling or a smoke detector going off.

Her cell phone rang.

Looking to escape the mess in the kitchen, she grabbed the phone and basically ran outside to answer it. The motion-activated light that Ethan had installed flashed on, and Jocelyn grimaced, knowing she was being recorded.

"Hello?" she said as she walked out of what she imagined was camera range.

"Hey, Jocelyn, guess what? We've had three offers on one of your houses." It was Jocelyn's realtor—the one she'd contacted right after she'd discovered Ethan's credit card bill and hatched her plan, which she had dubbed Operation Easy Extraction, or OEE for short. Little did she know at the time that the real code name should have been something closer to E-I-E-I-O. But for now, this was great news considering the shit storm in the kitchen. "Well, all the offers are short sales," the realtor continued.

"That's great!" What's a short sale?" Jocelyn asked.

"They're offering less than what you owe on the house. Short sales are pretty rare in this market. I don't know if Countrywide is going to go for it. We can keep trying for your asking price if you want."

"Yeah. Keep trying. It's great that we've had such a positive response so far though, don't you think?"

"Absolutely. I'll keep on it. And honestly, the highest bidder was only a few thousand off from your asking price. I think we'll be able to sell it."

Totally uplifted by the call from the realtor, as it provided evidence of hope for escape, Jocelyn went back inside and, with a Herculean effort, bit her tongue, letting Ethan just verbally go for it.

She picked up the kids and put them in their high chairs and started putting together food for them. Finally, when she was able to get a word in edgewise, she promised that August would be the last RP event she would be involved with. After that, she would call it quits with the Raymond Pierce campaign. Apparently at a loss for words, Ethan stormed out of the house. A beam of light from the tree-mounted webcam flashed on as he slammed the door behind him.

Jocelyn stared at the door for a moment and then turned around to face her children. The kids seemed to calm down almost instantly. She was very happy to be with them. She had missed them. She was also extremely happy to be snacking on something other than beef jerky.

CHAPTER TWENTY-THREE

ETHAN NOTICED THAT HE WAS trembling. He needed something—something he lost. He looked around the cab of his truck. Was it here? But then he remembered that he couldn't remember what it was that he was looking for in the first place. A Möbius strip of anxiety twisted around the core of his being and was about to consume him entirely when a text message alert slapped him across the face and halted his downward trajectory.

"Where r u? Starbx @airport now."

That's when it all came back to him like a dry heave—that pink, lined scrap of paper that had been sitting in his wallet since forever. A date that had been assigned so far in the distant past that it had lost meaning until this very moment. He threw the Dodge truck into reverse and peeled out of the commuter parking lot where he had taken refuge. Zipping in and out of traffic on Route 95, he was fully focused. It was this very aspect of channeled adrenaline that was missing from everyday life. This felt great! He was in control and knew what he was supposed to be doing, finally.

Ethan knew at that very moment the reason why he had no memory of this. It was because it was her. And it was because when he'd gotten the information, he had blocked it. Just shut it off. His brain had simply compartmentalized it and stored it away out of his mental sight. He was good like that. He could see and experience everything, and simply, *poof!*—just like that, it was gone. Never happened. He could easily pass a lie detector test, no sweat—which was ironic considering the amount of sweating he'd had to endure on a daily basis because of this memory-eraser technique, implemented unconsciously, right after the botched old lady job with that scalpel-wielding freak. The job that had basically sent him over the edge.

"Look, asshole, we're here for an enhanced interrogation job, and you're just cutting her for the fun of it at this point. Let the woman speak!"

"Oh, she's talking," Dr. Freakshow sung as he waved the scalpel around in front of the old lady's face. "Aren't you now, honey?" But then he stopped and considered something. "Maybe she's not afraid." He scratched his pockmarked chin. "She's been under the knife before." He grabbed her by the hair and yanked her head back violently. "Ta-ha! I knew it! Look! Look under her chin. Look at that scar." He moved in very close to study the mark. "She's had a facelift. I'd wager more than one." Pleased with his astute medical observation, he let go of the woman's hair, and her head dropped with full force directly onto the scalpel that Dr. Shitshow was holding. "Oh, dear. I'm sorry about that," he apologized as he twisted and yanked the scalpel out of her eye. The woman shrieked as her eyeball literally flung out of her head and onto the Oriental carpet.

"Oh! Nice, fuckface! Real nice!" Ethan threw his hands up. "You're killing me here. We have real information that we need to extract from this subject, and you're fuckin' around!" He walked over to the woman and sighed. "Are you all right?"

The lady pleaded with him via her one teary, elderly eye and died. Right there. Just up and died without so much as a confirmation of anything.

The doctor started laughing. "Oh, you are a stitch!"

"And you're a fucking moron." Disgusted, he grabbed the damn butterfly pin, scrubbed it of fingerprints, and finished off the job. "There! That should make you happy," he growled at his accomplice as he started to collect his gear.

Within moments, the cleaners came in, and that was when he was handed the note. At the time, he had known it was from her and that it was the date she wanted to be in America. She was saving up for it. It was also the exact same moment that he erased every fucking thing about that job.

Now sitting in the driver's seat, both hands on the wheel as yellow lines blazed by, his head started to throb. His heart ached, and he felt as if he might throw up. He hadn't seen her since she was twelve.

He parked the truck and hastily made his way into the concourse. There were three Starbucks coffee shops on the premises, and luckily, she had decided to plant herself at the one closest to the entrance of the parking garage. He spotted her before she saw him. Ethan almost cried, she was so beautiful. He had not anticipated this. She was a full-grown woman now. Her lithe but muscular, olive-skinned shoulders were supporting the spaghetti straps of her bright floral sundress. A slate of luxurious black hair, in which she had tenderly placed, above her left ear, the most precious specimen of a white flower, fell over her shoulder. He gulped, took a deep breath, and purposefully strode up to her. He hadn't felt this nervous about approaching a woman since he'd been in junior high school. Announcements of gate numbers and instructions not to accept gifts from strangers filled the coffee-perfumed air. He took in one more deep breath and greeted her simply with, "Hello, Stojanka."

She quickly glanced up at him, and Ethan thought he felt the equivalent of thirteen different emotions being broadcast from her before she stood up and, steely-faced, shook his hand. "You take me now to a gun."

CHAPTER TWENTY-FOUR

THINGS WERE NOT GOING ACCORDING to plan. One of Jocelyn's houses, the one by the Ivy League university, had been completely trashed by her renters. You know, the kids who drove the BMWs and had dads who were doctors from Nigeria and famous psychologists? Yeah, that place got disrespected to the tune of nearly ten thousand dollars. Within a week of discovering that, another of her properties literally went up in flames.

The fire was caused by an older gentleman nearing retirement. Nice enough guy and very responsive, but he was what people would call a hoarder. He had so much stuff crammed into the basement of the house, not to mention his living space, that Jocelyn had to write a letter letting him know that he was required to keep a minimum clearance around the furnace and hot water heater. Of course, he dutifully complied and reorganized the antique pillars of what could only be called unnecessary piles of junk. Fortunately, she had that letter when the fire chief and the inspectors came to investigate the source of the fire. The prognosis—some paper had slid under the hot water heater, started on fire, and eventually ended up burning down about a quarter of the house.

"Good God! The guy had fourteen propane tanks down here! You're lucky the fire didn't reach that!" the clipboard-toting inspector exclaimed, while using his foot to shove a large Tupperware container full of salad tongs out of the way as he explored the burned-out labyrinth of curiosities in the basement.

Naturally, the fire had exposed a whole host of problems within the structure of the house, which caused the building inspector to declare the place "officially a teardown."

The insurance she had been paying on the house would only cover $38,000 of the damage, despite the fact that fire had basically rendered the house unfit for human habitation. Soon, she began to wish that the fire had reached the fourteen propane tanks.

She called her realtor and told her to list all of her properties—all of them—and to accept a sale no matter what. Even if it was a short sale, she'd figure out how to pay the difference. Whatever. Just make it so.

This was easier said than done. Remember, they were dealing with Countrywide home loans. Jocelyn had to hire a lawyer to actually get anyone from the mortgage company to talk with her or her realtor on the phone. Eventually Countrywide wouldn't even return her lawyer's calls when he personally attempted to contact them with offers of a sale. It got to the point where her lawyer had to finally break the news to her.

"Look, the only thing I can recommend here is that you declare bankruptcy. We can say that you live in one of the properties—like that one over by the university; it's the most valuable. And that way you'd be able to keep it."

"Yeah, but that one is trashed, and I won't have money to fix it up ..." She trailed off while she attempted and failed to do quick math. Frustrated, she blurted out, "This is bullshit! If Countrywide would just let me sell that first house, even if I have to pay them the extra to cover the short sale, I might be able to make this work." She looked directly at the lawyer. "I want to sue Countrywide. I want you to take them to court. Sue them! They are ruining my life! How can a mortgage company do business like this? I have the offers, and they aren't even answering the phone! This cannot be legal!" Jocelyn noticed that she was shaking, she was so frustrated.

The lawyer sat back in his cranberry leather wingback and said, "Jocelyn, I'd love nothing more than to represent you in court while you sue a huge financial organization. But I'm afraid that, even if you won the case sometime down the road, let's say a decade from now, you'd lose. Countrywide will have no problem dragging this out forever. I would be the only one making money off the case, and I don't think I can do that to you. I say let's just get this over with as quickly and painlessly as possible. So, which house do you want to keep?"

"I don't want any of them."

"But, Jocelyn, when you finally pay off that mortgage, you will be holding a very valuable piece of property. Let's just say that it's your primary residence and—"

"Wait. You're telling me to lie in bankruptcy court?"

Her lawyer continued as if he did not hear her question. "Do your renters pay their own utilities or do you include it in the rent?"

"Huh? I include it in the rent."

"Great," he said as he checked off something on the paperwork in front of him. "Just make sure that you have the bills sent to the property and then have the post office forward them to you. That way, we'll have a record of you living there."

"But I don't live there."

"Jocelyn"—he leaned over the stacks of paperwork on his desk—"this is what bankruptcy is all about. Legally reorganizing and preserving your assets. Heck, I have clients who have done this multiple times. Look at Donald Trump." As if that was supposed to impress. "The couple that was here, right before you, they each bought Range Rovers because they know that they are going to be able to keep their cars and their primary residence, a waterfront home they just built on a cliff overlooking the ocean. It's an incredible house," he absently enthused as he scribbled something on a legal pad. "It has a wall made entirely of bricks from Fenway when they did the renovation at the ballpark recently. The guy is really into the Red Sox. Anyway, once we get rid of their debts with a Chapter 7, well, her debt—they planned that she would do the 7; we had to switch a lot of stuff over to her a few months ago. She's a mortgage broker for Countrywide." His face contoured into a painful-looking half-smile as he let out a decidedly unjovial chuckle, almost as if he had just now realized the irony of it all. "The husband already did a Chapter 11 and ..."

Jocelyn felt like she wanted to punch someone. She had been receiving a lot of e-mails lately about welfare moms and illegal aliens taking advantage of the system. But what about all of this? Weren't those Range Rover people just like the welfare moms, only different?

"No. No, thank you. Screw it. I don't want any of the properties. I can't keep them up and in the black. I mean, it's obvious, isn't it? I was not meant to be a landlord. This is a disaster."

"Right. Now let's get you out of it and make it all go away. You are going to feel so much better when it's all over," he said while giving her the human-services nod.

Before she left his office, he handed her a stack of papers that he wanted her to fill out regarding all of her assets and debts. "Just sleep on that university property. You don't want to do anything rash."

Jocelyn took the quarter ream of paper and told him that she wouldn't be back until early September. She was going to the political training at the big rally that Raymond Pierce was holding across the river from the RNC.

"Oh, Ray Pierce! That guy's great. Do me a favor; take notes at that political training thing. I'm thinking of running for city council. I would love to pick your brain about what you find out."

Jocelyn half-heartedly smiled and agreed.

"Is he going to be speaking at the RNC?" the lawyer asked.

"No. They won't even let him into the RNC. Imagine that," Jocelyn said.

"Seriously?" the lawyer asked incredulously.

"Yeah. I guess so. That's why he's holding his own convention across the river at the Target Center."

"Wow."

Then Jocelyn, almost as a mental breather from all the bankruptcy talk, spouted off in rapid succession all the stats she had accumulated about the economy and the wars. Somehow, turning the conversation away from her own financial disaster and focusing on the impending doom of the country at large was somehow comforting.

"Well," the lawyer said, getting up to walk her to the door, "looks like bankruptcy law will be keeping me busy for a while then if all the stuff you say is true."

Jocelyn nodded.

"When you get back, if you still want to get rid of that house, I know a judge who might be able to help you. He buys up properties like yours."

"Oh, then let's call him now," Jocelyn said, confused as to why he hadn't mentioned it before.

"Well ... see, it's like this." The lawyer stuck his hands in his pockets. "It depends on what type of bankruptcy we decide to do for you. He buys your house from you to get it off your asset/debt list. Then after your bankruptcy, when your credit score is in the gutter, you can buy it back from him. The catch is that he would be your bank. And he charges a significant markup with his interest rate—"

"Is that even legal?" Jocelyn interrupted. "Sounds like a Mafia thing. Is he a loan shark?"

"Of course it's legal. He's a judge." He smiled and said, "Don't hate the player, Jocelyn; hate the game."

CHAPTER TWENTY-FIVE

STOJANKA WAS A GOOD SHOOTER—a very good shooter. He knew that she would be, and he was proud to have recognized that talent in her at such a young age back in '98—back when he was in Serbia spreading the joys of a humanitarian war and she and her older sister were working for a living. She was just little then, and Ethan had told her that she could make real money, US dollars, by learning how to shoot. At first, his suggestion was just for shits and giggles, but soon he found himself committed to her training. It was a good diversion, and it kept him focused on why he was even there in the first place. No one seemed particularly averse to this, especially since the place had been completely bombed to smithereens by unsanctioned NATO airstrikes, and the gray fog of war obscured everyone's vision.

She was a natural—sure-footed and deliberate. Amazingly, she had better eyesight than Ethan's 20/15, and even as a child, she had been intensely methodical as she approached the target. With each bull's-eye struck, Ethan would swell up with pride. But today it wasn't pride Ethan was feeling. It was awe. The woman was a machine.

"All I have to say is that you'd definitely be in the winner's circle at Camp Perry," Ethan remarked as he pushed himself up from the dangerously dry grass, removed his earplugs, and squinted at the target six hundred yards away.

She glanced over at him and nodded as she started packing her gear. "That is what Mister Timothy Brucker says also. That my skill is the best."

"Brucker?" Ethan did not recognize the name, but, then again, maybe he had erased that, too. He quickly broke down his setup and stashed it all expertly in its case.

"He did contract with me in Italy," Stojanka said. Ethan still looked left out, so she added, "You must know this man. He is one of you. He is also a colonel."

Upon entrance of the word *colonel*, Ethan's stomach dropped. She hadn't mentioned *that* yet, and that was more than fine by him. Let bygones be bygones. But now, standing on the sun-splashed hill with the little white moths dancing in and out of the tall, tall grass with this beautiful woman, this beautiful killer of a woman, he was ashamed. Humiliated. If he had been wired to do so, he would have broken down in tears and said, "I'm sorry. I'm so sorry." Instead, "I hope he paid you well," fell out of his mouth.

"Oh, yes. Gold coin. Better than US dollar. Krugerrands." She took a deep breath through her nose and finished her packing.

"Here, want me to carry that for you?" Ethan offered.

"No." She slung the entire kit over her shoulder and followed him down to the dirt parking lot where he had parked his truck. She was about to put her pack in the bed of the truck, but he stopped her. "We have to go over a couple state lines. Let me lock that up inside the cab. I don't think we are even supposed to drive through Massachusetts with these things."

Stojanka shot him a look of concern, and Ethan remarked as he locked up the guns, "You know what we need? A motorcycle."

"Motorcycle?" she asked in her heavy accent.

"Yeah. Nothin' says America the Free like speeding around on a Harley Davidson. I want to take you on a nice ride on a good bike someday—you know, before you leave," he said as he checked the lock to make sure it was secure. "I have some stuff I have to deal with first, so I'll be out of contact for a while. But I really want to do that with you. We'll make a real date."

Stojanka did not smile. Instead she blinked, nodded at him, and jumped in the truck.

CHAPTER TWENTY-SIX

"WHAT?! YOU BROKE HIS NOSE?!" Jocelyn shouted as she lay on the floor in the living room. She hadn't been able to walk right; her balance had been all messed up since she got home from political training and the big rally at the Target Center. It felt like she was on a boat swaying from right to left and back again. Lying down was the only thing she could do, lest she fall over. The kids were playing on the floor next to her as she tried to prop herself up to hear what Ethan was saying.

"I think so," Ethan said as he walked into the living room. "I took the camera out of the tree. The last thing we need is footage of that."

"You got it on camera?" Jocelyn asked.

"Yeah," Ethan said as he rubbed the back of his neck.

"Can I see it?"

"No."

"Why?"

"Because it got written over by me coming and going for the rest of the week. I didn't save it. I mean, why would I? It's me punching Apario in the face. Not a pretty scene. I actually feel kind of bad for the jerk. What kind of asshole shows up at 10:00 p.m. with a bag of loose webcams and a ring?"

"A ring?"

"Yeah. And I'm supposed to believe that you two weren't fooling around? Right."

"Wait. You're talking about me and Jerry? Oh, for the love of God, Ethan! I only saw him that day at the pancake house. I haven't spoken to him since. Why did he come here?"

"I don't know. Why don't you ask him," Ethan said as he causally walked out of the room.

Jocelyn flopped back down. The mental boat she was on was rolling recklessly now. The past year of riding the ups and down of the Raymond Pierce campaign and now this thing with Jerry Apario showing up and getting punched in the nose, not to mention the BS with Countrywide and her impending bankruptcy, all of it had really thrown Jocelyn and the multiple sclerosis into a tailspin. Her mother was starting to look for home health aides for her.

"Oh, they'll just pop in and help you take care of the kids—"

"And what? Change *my* diaper? Seriously, Mom. I'm going to be okay. It will pass."

But the rocking didn't stop.

Jocelyn's mom had driven her, the kids in tow, to her neurologist appointment.

Jocelyn had taken a significant amount of time to research and seek out this specific doctor. Her one requirement—this special doctor had to be ranked as one of the best in the state. Leaving the kids and her mom in the waiting area, Jocelyn hobbled in to meet the doctor for the tenth time since the kids had been born three years ago.

The doctor entered the exam room. A medical student from Kenya, who was just going to observe, followed behind. This observation thing had happened pretty regularly over the past twelve years since she had been diagnosed. Feeling like a lab rat had become part of the whole coming to visit the neurologist experience.

"Ah ..." The doctor flipped through the file he was holding as he sat down next to the computer on the desk. The med student stood in the corner, notebook in hand. The wide aspect monitor on the doctor's desk was positioned so that Jocelyn could see what was on the screen—namely, the MRIs of her brain. "Jocelyn," he said as he located her name on the file, "it appears that you have several new lesions." He pointed with rapid, cursory motions with his pen at the computer screen. "When was the last time I saw you?" He flipped through the file again as Jocelyn stared at the image of a spotted brain. Her eyes began to well up. "Okay. It says here three weeks ago. How have you been feeling since then?" the doctor asked, not looking at her. Jocelyn went to answer, but her voice cracked. The doctor looked up. "Have you been feeling depressed?"

"No. Not really. I mean—"

"But you are crying." The neurologist was starting to remind her of Dr. Spock from *Star Trek*.

"Well, look. Look at that picture on the screen. That can't make anyone feel very good," Jocelyn said.

The doctor quickly wrote something on a small pad of paper. "It looks as if the medicine that you have been on, Capaxone, has stopped working. I am going to move you up to a new drug, Tysabri. It just got approval from the FDA, and it is proven to control MS exacerbations better than anything on the market."

Jocelyn looked around the room in confusion. "Does this mean the disease is progressing?"

"Yes. You've had a pretty good run of it so far—better than most, really. So, it's about time to change your meds."

Images of herself in a wheelchair and not being able to feed herself and all sorts of things started to fly by. She started crying. The doctor took out the little pad and rapidly scribbled something else.

"Tell me about this Tysabri," Jocelyn said, accepting the tissue the doctor offered. She noticed that the tissue box was branded with the Tysabri logo.

"Well, it has been tested extensively and ..."

Then her gaze wandered to the Tysabri calendar hanging on the wall. A nurse came in and offered her a plastic bag with the Tysabri logo printed on it. The bag was filled with a gorgeously designed and finely printed booklet about

Tysabri. The paper itself, a thick cotton stock, Jocelyn noticed, must have priced this booklet out to something far more than her budget at the Conglomerate would have allowed for. It was an impressive piece of marketing collateral material. Along with the printed stuff, a sun visor, sunscreen, and a T-shirt were included, all bearing the Tysabri logo.

"Oh, a marketing fun pack," Jocelyn said, looking through the stuff as the doctor continued his spiel about how great Tysabri was. He concluded by mentioning, almost as an afterthought, the one rare but troubling side effect of the drug.

"It's extremely rare, so I wouldn't worry about it, but I do have to mention it. There have been fatal cases associated with the drug in a very few test subjects. It's a type of brain infection."

Jocelyn did not like the sound of that. She'd rather just deal with the crappy symptoms of MS than deal with a fatal brain infection. *How does someone even get an infection that affects only the brain?* If more than two people got it in the test group for this drug, Jocelyn reasoned, then it was more than mere coincidence. Jocelyn wondered about this. But since she was pretty sure she would not be taking this drug, she didn't even bother to ask about this unfortunate possible outcome.

"What if I just try a different diet? I've read on the Internet that diet has a lot to do with it."

"Why? What are you eating?" the doctor asked, glancing up at her.

Jocelyn gave a brief rundown of her usual meals as the doctor scribbled some more.

"No. Diet has nothing to do with it. Of course, a balanced diet is beneficial, as it is for anyone. But dietary changes are not going to make you feel markedly better."

"Do I have to wean myself off the Capaxone? I mean I've been on it for more than a decade. It doesn't seem like you can just yank yourself off something you've been injecting yourself with every day."

"No. It shouldn't make any difference."

Jocelyn sighed. "I like Capaxone because—"

"Well, it has stopped working for you," he said with a certain type of finality that bothered her.

"Okay, I guess I'm just skeptical of this new drug." Then she hit him with what she had really wanted to ask him for the past five minutes. "Are you getting paid by the drug company to promote Tysabri?" Jocelyn asked as she put the sun visor on and pointed to the calendar. "Looks like the rep has been here."

The doctor looked at his watch. "Do you have any other questions before I go?"

"Yes, actually. Why is this fun pack full of sunscreen and this sun visor? I know I'm a fair-skinned person, but why would a drug company spend this much money on marketing their product by branding sunscreen?"

"Oh. I'm glad you asked. When you are on Tysabri, you are not allowed to be in the sun—at all."

"That's a strange side effect. I'm glad I asked, too. Not that I ever sunbathe, because I only burn, but that seems like a critical piece of information. I thought vitamin D from the sun was one of the best treatments for MS."

"Did you see that on the Internet, too?

"Well, yeah."

"Okay, we've got to get you off the Internet."

Jocelyn couldn't tell if he was attempting a joke or being serious.

"So you are telling me to stay indoors, eat anything I want, and take Tysabri, and I'll feel better?"

He gave a sideways nod.

"But there is a slight chance that I could get an extremely rare brain infection that could instantly kill me?"

He kind of rolled his eyes, did something weird with his eyebrows, and said, "You are more likely to die in a plane crash than to die from this drug, Jocelyn."

"My dad died in a plane crash."

The neurologist looked down as he rolled the pen between his fingers. The pen, which Jocelyn noticed for the first time, also bore the Tysabri logo. "I'm sorry to hear that," the doctor said.

"What else besides this new drug would you recommend?" Jocelyn was convinced that the neurologist was getting a kickback, or at least some Patriots or Red Sox tickets with parking and a dinner thrown in.

"Chemotherapy."

"Chemotherapy?! For MS? You're kidding me!" Jocelyn, for whatever reason, couldn't shake the very real sensation of trying to decide between a root canal and an IRS audit. "Can I think about this?"

"Of course," the doctor said as he closed up his file and tucked it under his arm. "Be sure to make an appointment for next week on your way out."

As Jocelyn watched the neurologist and the med student from Kenya leave, the student turned on his heel and walked over to her. "I think you may be onto something with diet," he said with an accent that Jocelyn would have placed as coming from somewhere in the Caribbean if she hadn't know his actual origin.

Now it was the neurologist's turn to spin around. "Excuse me," he said to the student while ushering the young man out the door. "I'm sorry, Jocelyn. He's just interested in you because they don't have MS where he's from."

The student nodded. "I have never seen this before."

"Oh, you will when McDonalds finally comes to Kenya," the neurologist said as both he and the student left Jocelyn alone in the exam room surrounded on all sides by the Tysabri logo.

"Really? McDonalds? I thought you just said diet had nothing to do with it," Jocelyn grumbled as she gathered up her fun pack and headed out to the front desk to make her appointment for next week.

The appointment clerk happily handed Jocelyn five prescriptions that the doctor had written out for her during their visit. One was for Zoloft. She recognized that, an antidepressant. The other was for Lipitor. Lipitor?! *Wasn't that for high cholesterol or something?* But she didn't recognize the other three. What had they talked about that prompted the others? She could sorta, kinda, see the connection to Lipitor, sort of. They had discussed diet. But seriously? She ate more healthfully than most people she knew. She had told him that. And what the heck? Hadn't she said she didn't want an antidepressant? He clearly wasn't even listening to her. Or maybe these weren't her prescriptions?

"What day would you like next week?" the cheery clerk asked.

"Um ... I'm not sure," Jocelyn said as she looked over the little slips of paper bearing the neurologist's signature. "I don't think these are my prescriptions. What are these medicines for?"

"Oh, I'm not really the person to ask. Would you like me to get the nurse over here for you? If you just wait, I'll—"

"No. No, thanks," Jocelyn interrupted her. "My mom's a nurse, and she can probably tell me."

"Don't worry. I'm sure they are all covered by Medicare."

"But I'm not on Medicare."

"You're not?" The appointment maker looked up in surprise. "How have you been paying for all these MRIs and the drugs that the doctor has been ordering up for you?"

"I have insurance. But yeah, monthly copays and deductibles are taking a real bite," Jocelyn answered honestly.

"Oh, I bet he thought you were on Medicare." She sighed as she flipped through Jocelyn's paper file while trying to find the corresponding information on the computer. "I don't think he would have prescribed all this if he thought you were dealing with copays. I'm sorry, honey."

"Are you kidding me?!" Jocelyn asked in alarm. "You mean I don't need all this stuff he's been prescribing for me?"

"Well, I didn't say that, exactly ..." Appointment Maker Clerk, attempting to change the subject, said. "Okay. So what day would you like to make your appointment for?"

"I'll have to call you and let you know," Jocelyn said with absolutely no intention of calling.

Holding the wall for support, she shakily made her way back out to the reception area, which was jammed with people who looked equally as messed up as she was. Walkers and wheelchairs were parked in front of the TV. Her mother and kids looked up from the *Highlights* magazine they were reading. Their eyes were wide with quiet concern for Jocelyn. Her mom, without saying anything, gently grabbed her by the waist while her son held her hand. Her daughter held the doors and pushed the elevator button for all of them as they slowly and silently made their way back to the parking garage.

"Well, what did the doctor say?" her mom wanted to know before she started the car.

Jocelyn sighed and handed the prescriptions over to her. "He's no good. I'm not doing it."

Jocelyn could tell her mother was blinking back tears. "Look, sweetheart, the man is the best we have here. I know he probably said something that you didn't want to hear, but this is what we have to deal with—what *you* have to deal with. You have children now, and you have to think of them too. You can't just ignore the facts or the science behind—"

"Mom! The guy is ripping the government off! He's getting kickbacks from the drug company, too. I just know it.

He's probably causing a ton of adverse side effects for his patients who think they're suffering from just another weirdo symptom of MS!"

Jocelyn's mother replied, "I have some money. I can fly you out to that doctor in Colorado. We can get a second opinion."

"No, Mom," Jocelyn practically whined. "It's not that. You don't have to fly me anywhere. We all know I have MS. He just wants to put me on some new drug."

"Well, that should be great news! There's something out there that some genius has developed that might cure this thing!"

"I think that's doubtful, Mom. These drug companies make way too much money from this disease. Just like diabetes. Just like ..." Instead of breaking down into tears like she wanted to, unfortunately for all trapped in the car with her, she got angry. "Mom! No one wants to cure any of this! Don't you get it?! They want to *treat* me, not *cure* me! No one would make any money if I was cured! It would be the end of the gravy train if I somehow woke up tomorrow morning and felt just fine. They want to keep throwing me into that MRI machine. Why? So that they can look at some cool pictures on their computer screen? No! It generates jobs and paperwork and the need for more databases, and thousands and thousands of dollars get moved around just because of me. No! Make that millions! I'm a goddamn economic engine for everyone involved in this friggin' scene! Just by virtue that I am certifiably not feeling well, it's in everyone's best financial interest to keep me hooked on whatever treatment they've got going. Hell! The whole country's economy would probably fall apart if everyone was miraculously cured! It's like a bad joke! The stuff he wants to put me on admittedly kills people!"

Her mother looked as if she was about to say something, most likely having to do with probability and statistics, but then apparently thought the better of it.

Jocelyn leaned up against the window and put her hand on her forehead. She just wanted to put the seat back into full recline, but it would squish her kid sitting behind her, so she didn't. Her internal boat was rocking pretty hard. "I'm not doing it, Mom."

"Honey," her mother said, almost pleading, "you have to think about it. How about you call that doctor you like out in Colorado and just get his opinion? Ask him what would happen if you didn't take it. What other treatment would he recommend?"

"Oh, I asked the doctor that today. He said he'd put me on chemotherapy."

"Seriously?" her mother blurted incredulously.

"That's exactly what I said."

"Okay, get that doctor on the phone. Promise me." She grabbed Jocelyn's wrist. "Promise me you will call him before you say no to this new treatment. Please?"

Jocelyn agreed, and this seemed to calm her mother down. Mom turned the key in the ignition, and "Red skies at night! Red skies at night! Woa-ohhh. Woa-ohhh. Oh. Oh. Oh"—a louder-than-expected broadcast of the classic Fixx song from 1982—startled them all. Jocelyn quickly turned down the volume. Mom, or she, must have forgotten to shut off the radio when they parked.

Once on the highway, Jocelyn asked what the prescriptions were supposed to be for.

"Oh, one is basically a sleeping pill, one an antidepressant. I'm not sure, but I'm thinking one might be some sort of laxative based on its name. And another is a type of gentle upper. Lipitor is—"

Jocelyn groaned. "So I take the upper, and then I need a sleeping pill. I told him I wasn't depressed. Yet this is the third time I've left his office with an antidepressant prescription in my hand. And what the heck with the laxative?"

"Maybe one of the other pills has a side effect of constipation. Or maybe people at this stage of the disease need a little help—"

"Mom, do you see how ridiculous this is? I'm like a sitting duck for these drug companies. And if someone is on Medicare ..." Jocelyn didn't even bother to finish her thought.

The sky.

The sun was beginning to set, and it was such a vibrant, dazzling, not to mention unusual sight that most everyone on the highway began slowing down to appreciate it. Some people were even pulling over into the breakdown lane to stare or take pictures of the brilliant red of the sunset. Incredibly, the luminescent vermillion clouds, in varying stages of puffiness, appeared to be intersecting, almost as if making a grid pattern occupying the entirety of everyone's field of view. It would have been downright breathtaking if it hadn't been so freakishly unnatural.

CHAPTER TWENTY-SEVEN

"DUDE! DID YOU SEE IT? I was trying to drop off some webcams for you, you know, to add more live feeds to my ChemTrailTales website when Ethan ... well, I'm sure you heard."

"I did. I'm sorry that happened, Jerry. Are you okay?" Jocelyn said, not entirely excited to hear from him. She had been kind of hoping that the meeting at the International House of Pancakes would be the last of him. She didn't really need to rekindle a hardly-there-in-the-first-place friendship with him—especially now since Ethan was on a jealous tear about the IT guy showing up at their house. Ethan's behavior was confusing at first, but Jocelyn quickly recognized it as some sort of mechanism to create for himself a one-way ticket to the magical destination of Whatever-The-Hell-I-Want-To-Do-And-You-Don't-Have-Anything-To-Say-About-It Land.

"Yeah. I am now. But he did break my nose."

"Oh, for goodness' sake!" Although unhappy to hear it, Jocelyn wasn't really surprised. She shook her head, imagining Jerry touching his bandaged nose as he spoke to her. "I'm so sorry, Jerry." And feeling the need to explain/defend Ethan's actions, she added, "I think that ring and you coming over at ten o'clock kind of irked him. By the way, how did you know where I lived?"

"I just followed your computer's IP address. I probably shouldn't have come over so late."

"Yeah, well, I wasn't home anyway," she said as she clutched the side of the bed. She'd have to remember not to shake her head like that. She stayed absolutely still as Jerry continued.

"I was just really excited about what I had found out! I picked up a ham radio frequency. It sounded like they were discussing a lithium additive test right here in New England! Like, how often does that come around? Usually it's barium. So it sounded like it might be cool; lithium should glow red. Right?"

"I don't know," Jocelyn said, when she was really thinking, *I don't even know what you are talking about, Jerry.*

"Well, I thought, this is gonna be killer! I listened for a long time, and they never actually said when the test was going to be. But they mentioned that they would publicly broadcast a signal, 'fix 82,' at T-minus thirty minutes on the day of the test. I've never heard of 'fix 82,' and I know all sorts of signaling protocols and codes. It's probably some weird ass, dark project language."

"Probably."

"Anyhow, I wanted to make sure someone caught it on camera. I started handing out webcams to anyone who would take them. I drove over to Gino's house, and—"

"Who's Gino?"

"Gina's brother, of course. I thought you knew him," Jerry said.

"No."

"Yes, you do! The guy you got my phone number from—my ex-fiancée's brother."

"Oh! Driver! Yes. Yes, of course." Jocelyn laughed. "I had no idea his name was Gino."

"Yeah, well, I went over there to see Gino and give him some webcams for the ChemTrailTails thing, and—"

"Wait a minute. Are you still a ghost?" Jocelyn interrupted. "How can a guy who's trying to disappear be working on web sites and delivering webcams? You seem pretty out and about for a ghost."

"Well," he sighed, "sorta." The status of his disappearing act was obviously not what Jerry wanted to talk about. "Would you please let me finish?"

"Sure." Jocelyn smirked while transferring the phone to her other ear.

"Thank you. So I go over to Gino's house to deliver the webcams and to recommend a respirator filter should he find himself under the test site. I had brought my respirator to show him. Anyhow, to my horror, Gina's there. I hadn't intended to see her. I hadn't showered or shaved, and I smelled and—"

"Okay. I get it. So what happened?"

"So she comes right up to me and gives me back the engagement ring that I had given her. She tells me that she doesn't want to be associated with any crooks—that her family has already been down that road. So now I'm just standing there like a stinky freak holding a respirator, a Walmart bag full of webcams, and the ring. Gino says something like, 'Gina, can you be more of a bitch?' And it's on. They start just wailing on each other. I mean, it was nuts! An old-school fistfight!"

"No way." Jocelyn went to sit up but quickly lay back down. She was starting to get into this story as she recalled her original phone call to Driver, aka Gino.

"Yes way! And she's a pretty good fighter, too. I wouldn't want to go up against her—"

"And what?" Jocelyn interrupted. "You thought Ethan, the ex-SEAL, was more your speed?" She almost regretted saying it after it came out of her mouth, but she'd seen the opportunity and, well ....

"Nice, Joss. Real nice. Thanks."

"I'm sorry. Go on."

"So they're just killin' each other, and Gino jumps back and threatens her with telling me something. She goes bat shit. Totally crazy. Picks up a lamp and starts swinging at him. Gino's laughing and taunting her. I'm thinking I should just leave the webcams on the coffee table and leave. That's when she says something about the FBI. I don't know, but of course it got my attention."

"Naturally," Jocelyn added.

"So while Gino is jumping around trying to avoid Gina's swinging lamp of doom, he finally gets so pissed off, he blurts it out."

"What did he say?"

"He said that she was never really pregnant with my kid in the first place."

"Oh, Jerry. That's gotta sting," Jocelyn said.

"Yeah, well, that's not the only thing that stung. Gina was so pissed Gino told me about the fake pregnancy that she spun around like a roid-ragin' Olympic hammer thrower with that lamp and threw it. Of course, she missed her brother and ended up whacking me in the head."

"Good Lord!" Jocelyn gasped, trying to imagine this whole scene.

"I was unconscious for ... I don't know. I'm not even sure. When I came to, Gina had already called an ambulance and was holding an ice pack on my head. Gino was sweeping up the remains of what used to be the lamp. They both looked really bummed out, and both of them seemed really sorry about what happened."

"Well, yeah, they were sorry! Did you get a concussion? Were you bleeding?"

"No, I wasn't bleeding—not that I noticed anyway. She got me on my left temple. I'm not sure if I got a concussion. But I didn't hang around to hear the official diagnosis. I wanted to get out of there before the ambulance showed up. I mean come on! I've gone like three years being a ghost. No way was I gonna let them send me to the hospital. No way!"

"Right. Way to keep the ghost alive, Jerry. Smart thinking."

"Well, before I left, they both told me that the FBI had been to see Gina about the ring that I had given her."

"Whoa! How'd that happen? Do you think they finally opened your file and put someone on the case?"

"I don't know. But that's why she gave it back. The FBI showing up freaked her out. She didn't want it anymore. Said it had lost its luster."

"That's crazy, Jerry."

"No, its not. That makes perfect sense. What's crazy is the helicopters that started following me around."

Jocelyn would have typically ended the call right there, had it not been for her own experience with the Early Bird Whirlybird. "Helicopters?"

"Yeah. I noticed one right after Ethan punched me in the nose and then one—"

She cut him off. "Wait. When did you come over to my house?"

"Huh? You know, when Ethan punched me."

"Yeah. Yeah, I know that. But you didn't come directly from Gina's house to my house, did you?"

"Well, yeah."

"Jesus, Jerry! You drove for almost three hours with a concussion only to end up at my house to get your nose broken?! What were you trying to do? Get in touch with your inner punching bag?"

"No. I was trying to see you."

Jocelyn suddenly felt too dizzy to deal with this. "You noticed a helicopter when you ... when you were at my house?"

"Yeah."

"At night?"

"Yeah."

"What did it look like?"

"I don't know. It was nighttime. But it seemed to be hanging out over your house."

"Like, directly over the house?" Jocelyn asked in alarm.

"Nah. It wasn't like that. It seemed to be flying around your neighborhood. I could hear it and see the lights. But I couldn't make out its profile or color. That camera you guys have up in that tree might have some audio of it."

Jocelyn cringed at the mention of the camera. She had hated it and was now thinking about how Ethan had said that there was no footage of that night.

"I got some good black and whites though when it was following me around over in my neck of the woods." Jerry paused as if considering something. "Maybe we could meet over at IHOP again? I could show you the pictures?"

Jocelyn rubbed her eyes, and she stopped in mid rub when she heard that. Maybe Ethan really was onto something with his theory of Jerry being sweet on her. "Ah. No. I don't think so. I'm really not feeling a hundred percent," Jocelyn said, grateful not to have to tell a real lie to get out of meeting him for pancakes in order to look at his blurry, black-and-white photos of helicopters.

"Oh, I'm sorry to hear that. Do you need anything? I can pick something up for you."

"You live more than two hours away, Jerry. Thank you, but that won't be necessary. I'm waiting on some medicine. It was supposed to be delivered two days ago, and it's still not here. Listen, let me get off the phone and call that mail-order pharmacy that the insurance company makes me use."

"Oh. Yeah. Right. No problem. I hope you feel better," Jerry mumbled.

"Thanks for the call, Jerry. You really did make my day. I hope your nose gets better soon." She actually felt kind of sorry for him as she dizzily hung up the phone.

CHAPTER TWENTY-EIGHT

"WHAT DO YOU MEAN I'VE canceled the order? Why would I do that? I've been on this medicine for more than a decade. And I've been receiving it from you guys every month for almost three years now. I don't understand."

"That's what it says in the notes area here in our database."

Jocelyn was not only dizzy, she was confused and angry. She used to just go to the neighborhood drugstore, but now she had to go through this call center pharmacy because of the insurance. Ethan had her and the kids listed on his policy. They'd had to sign some papers stating they were living together and have them notarized at the library, but that was all it had taken. The insurance was very good—at least that's what everyone said. She had been waiting days, without any medicine, for her monthly box of prefilled syringes to show up, and it never had. "Can you read exactly what it says in the notes to me, please?"

"It just says patient called and canceled order."

Jocelyn rubbed her forehead as she thought this through. "Okay. We've established that I'm the patient. Right?"

"Yes."

"I'm telling you that I, the patient, did not call to cancel the order. Please send me that Capaxone as soon as possible. I'm in the middle of a relapse right now, and I don't have any of the drug on hand." It was all she could do to keep from yelling this at the call center order fulfillment clerk. "By the way, when does it say I canceled the order?"

The clerk switched back to the appropriate computer screen and said, "Five days ago."

"Five days ago?" Jocelyn wondered what she had even been doing five days ago. Oh, that's right! The neurologist appointment. She hadn't called anybody that day. No one. "What number does it say I called from?"

The clerk read the number, and Jocelyn instantly recognized it. "That's my old cell phone number! I had my number changed recently when my phone got stolen." The woman on the other end of the line gave out an exasperated sigh. "No. You don't understand. Wait. Hold on, I'm getting my new cell phone out right now." The clerk waited patiently as Jocelyn rifled through her purse and found the phone. She wondered if, in her dizzy state, she had actually called them and somehow inadvertently canceled her own order. She scrolled through her recent calls list from the past week. Nothing. "My phone did not call your number last week. But I did call you eight days ago to request a delivery.

"That's interesting," the clerk said flatly.

Jocelyn got the distinct impression that this call center employee did not believe her. "How do the cancel order and phone number get entered into the notes area on the database? Did a person have to physically type that in?" Jocelyn wanted to know.

"Usually the phone number just pops up on the computer screen when the call gets patched through. But, ummm ... there's no entry here saying who the person was who took the call."

"Is that normal?"

"Well, ummm ..." Jocelyn could almost see this woman using her index finger to help navigate the database she was looking at. "I mean you don't *have* to put your name in, but usually everyone does."

"And there's no way to backtrack and find out who entered the note?"

"I don't think so. I guess you could get the list of everyone who was working five days ago and just ask everyone."

Thinking that sounded doable, Jocelyn asked for the list.

"Really? Okay. Do you want the call centers in Canada and Mexico and India, too? Calls can come through from there as well."

"I guess not," Jocelyn said, realizing that the attempt to play Nancy Drew in this little mystery was just too tedious to deal with. And to what end, really? The medicine was on its way.

Maybe it was just a computer error. Stop being so paranoid, she told herself as she hung up the phone. But she couldn't stop thinking about how someone had stolen her cell phone and not used it, and then this canceled order shows up. *Why?* She couldn't stop thinking about helicopters. *Why were they flying around her house and following Jerry?* She couldn't stop wondering why someone would break into her house and take her computer's memory cards. *Why not take the whole computer?* It was at this moment that she decided that she wanted off.

But off what? Sure, she was dizzy, but something was seriously not right. She would feel like a fool if she were to talk about it. She'd sound like some sort of whack-job conspiracy theorist. Even with her counselor, she wouldn't talk about stuff like this. But she knew it. She did not trust the neurologist, and she did not trust the mail-order pharmacy. Somehow, her health and her relationship with Ethan (or lack thereof) and her impending bankruptcy and the computer and the phone and the helicopters and— *Ding-dong*. The doorbell rang.

Jocelyn got out of bed and unsteadily made her way to the front door to open it. Her mom had taken the kids for the afternoon, and they were supposed to be back soon. It was probably them. The kids loved to press the doorbell.

"Hello!" Jocelyn dramatically called out while swinging the door wide open, only to reveal a middle-aged woman with meticulously-styled hair holding a clipboard and wearing an official-looking name tag.

"Well, hello to you, too!" the woman said enthusiastically in not quite a southern accent. Jocelyn had heard it before. Oh, yeah. Virginia. The woman had a Virginian accent. All the trips to and phone calls from the Conglomerate—that's how she knew it.

"Oh, I wasn't expecting you. But hello. What brings you here?" Jocelyn asked as she studied the clipboard and badge. "Are you collecting signatures for something?" She recalled the mad dash to collect signatures to get Ray Pierce on the ballot.

"Oh, no. Nothing like that." The woman smiled and shook her head while presenting her business card. "I'm offering families the opportunity to participate in a health survey. You may have seen it listed in the local paper." She produced a photocopy of an article in the localest of local newspapers—a small publication that Jocelyn never bothered to read. "We are offering fifty dollars per participating resident. May I come in?"

Now, perhaps if this woman had not caught Jocelyn at the height of her personal I-don't-trust-anyone rumination rally, Jocelyn would have graciously invited her in for a cup of tea, as she often did when the Jehovah's Witnesses would stop by. But today she wasn't up for it. In fact, Jocelyn didn't even address the issue of coming in and asked as she scanned the business card and photocopy, "What company is this for? Some sort of drug company?"

"No." The woman almost giggled. "It's a national study, and your neighborhood has been selected to participate," she said as she reached over and pointed to the small print of the photocopy. "I work for the government contractor that is organizing and collecting the data for this study."

Jocelyn looked more closely at the woman's business card. It had a local address. The woman took out a pen and started asking questions that Jocelyn, intentionally, wouldn't answer fully. The woman began jotting notes down on the long form on the clipboard. Jocelyn really was in no mood to be doing this. She was way too dizzy and weak to be standing, let alone answering questions. The woman offered to come into the living room so Jocelyn could sit while she asked the questions.

What the heck? thought Jocelyn as she studied the woman, who was almost vibrating with the same relentlessness as the *Drosophila melanogaster* salesmen she used to work with. She had called them that because they would hover like little fruit flies around her office, waiting for the government sales leads to be issued. *This woman is working on commission.* "You're not from around here, are you?" Jocelyn said, changing the subject. "But your business card says you work right down the street."

The woman smiled a smile that seemed like something a beauty pageant contestant might drum up during the final round of judging. "Oh, I've been here for a while."

Cagey bitch, thought Jocelyn. "You know, it sounds fascinating. But I'm really not interested." Jocelyn's smile was so sweet it dripped honey.

"Well, it's easy money. And who can't use some extra cash these days?" the woman replied back with NutraSweet. "All you have to do is answer some questions and visit this doctor." She pointed to the back of the business card. "Once he confirms that you have been there and that he has your blood sample, we'll send you the check—fifty dollars per person. How many children live in this house? They've all had their vaccinations, correct?"

Blood sample?! "Is this connected to the census?" Jocelyn asked with not as much honey this time. She wondered if Ethan had actually filled out the recent census form and mailed it in. There had been a lot of discussion within the remnants of the Raymond Pierce group about the questions on the latest census. People were concerned—no, make that upset to the point of paranoia—because the only thing a census is supposed to do, as per the US Constitution, is document how many people live at each house. This information is used to figure out how many representatives to Congress and members of the Electoral College each state gets. Jocelyn had noticed that some people were complaining about an overabundance of questions that were seemingly unrelated to the official business of the census. A few, not all, had gotten a longer form than others.

"No. This is just a public health study."

"Well, as I've said, I'm really not interested."

Not surprisingly, given she was dealing with a *drosophila melanogaster*, Jocelyn could not make the woman go away, but she gave it one last-ditch effort. "You know, I've heard through the grapevine"—Jocelyn lowered her voice while leaning in closer to the woman—"that the folks across the street might be looking for some extra cash. I think they are both out of work. Why don't you try them?"

"I can't," the health database contractor said as she searched though her paperwork. "It says right here." She paused, tipped the clipboard, and pointed to the notes area of her printout so that Jocelyn could see. "Residents of interest—yellow house, left side of street."

Jocelyn slammed the door in the woman's face.

Jocelyn then laboriously made her way to the couch but then decided to just lie down on the floor. It was closer. She recalled very clearly, as she lay there staring at the ceiling, one of the earlier RP Meetups she had hosted.

"They are trying to find out as much as they can about the Ray Pierce supporters," she had heard more than one person whisper at the Meetup. At the time, she had shaken the comment off. Jocelyn had come to accept that some of the group could be really conspiracy-oriented. She would have written the whole thing off entirely if she hadn't happened to notice the registered trademark symbol next to the words United States on the census.

Why would the census need a corporate logo? she wondered. And why would they need to trademark just the name United States in some sort of really nondescript serif font? And why didn't they use the full name, the United States of America? This had irked Jocelyn because, of course, she had been pretty much clubbed to death with all the branding and trademark legalities over at the Conglomerate.

So she had looked it up. The name United States in that nondescript font was, not surprisingly, registered with the US Census Bureau. What was surprising to find out during her cursory investigation was that, during World War II, the United States Census Bureau, which has consistently and proudly advertised that it would never share the information that it collects, assisted the federal government's internment efforts by providing confidential neighborhood information on Japanese Americans. The Census Bureau's role was denied for decades but was finally proven in 2007. "Prejudice, war hysteria, and a failure of political leadership" led to the US government eventually disbursing more than $1.6 billion in reparations to the Japanese Americans who had been basically thrown into concentration camps on US soil.

Apparently, that was what was making the Ray Pierce group edgy—that US citizens, Americans, could be hauled away by their own government and placed into places no better than prisons. Sometimes worse. That and the fact that the Census Bureau also had a history of helping the government track down and prosecute draft dodgers. Well, that sealed the deal. People did not like the long form census.

And Jocelyn did not like the fact that the equivalent of a paid-on-commission, traveling encyclopedia saleswoman was trying to extract private health information from her, not to mention a blood sample, for fifty bucks. *Like, when does that happen?*

CHAPTER TWENTY-NINE

THE KIDS WERE HAPPILY PLAYING in the backyard. In slow motion. Dandelion fluff lazily swirled in the air around her twins. Outfitted in OshKosh B'gosh denim overalls, they carried their buckets and shovels to the dirt pile next to the chicken coop. They were laughing. The scent of Casa Blanca lilies, the ones that Ethan's mother had given her as dry roots to plant in the yard, hung luxuriously heavy in the air. The sun beamed its nonviolent, after-3:00 p.m. rays, and it was magical. Simply magical. Feeling hugely content, Jocelyn made her way back inside to figure out what in the heck she had just been dosed with.

It had been about a week since Jocelyn had received her shipment of Capaxone, and she still hadn't given herself the injection. The day she discovered that the UPS shipment had quietly shown up on her front steps, she had been so relieved. Finally! Salvation had arrived! She had glanced up and down the street to see where the UPS truck was hiding. She must have missed it, although it was easily one of the loudest trucks that regularly passed through her neighborhood. She'd collected her package and brought it inside.

Once in the kitchen, she had hastily torn open the thick cardboard shipping box to uncover the Styrofoam sarcophagus inside. Using a sharp paring knife, she slit the packing tape around the KoolPac and removed the lid. Nestled inside were ice packs and the trademarked blue box that she had been waiting for. She opened the little cardboard treasure chest to reveal $115 per day worth of Israeli-made medicine nestled inside. Like some sort of futuristic shipment of life-saving ammunition, each prefilled syringe was packaged in its very own little plastic casing. Jocelyn grabbed one and tore it open. She popped the plastic cap off the needle and held the syringe between her middle and index fingers, thumb on the trigger. *Took long enough*, she thought. She was just about to jam the thing into her thigh when she noticed. Tiny little flecks.

Tiny little snowflakes were floating around in the medicine. This was unusual. Typically, the Capaxone looked like plain water. Squinting, she studied the fluid inside the syringe. And then put it aside. She grabbed another out of the box, unwrapped it, and, "What the heck? This one, too?" All of the prefilled syringes in the box, except one, contained nearly imperceptible flakes of white dust.

Jocelyn picked up the phone and, after several rounds of phone tree button-pushing, was finally able to speak with someone who told her to just take the clear one and throw out the rest. "It might have just gone bad with age or something. It could happen."

"This is bullshit," Jocelyn said as she hung up the phone and looked at the one lousy clear syringe. She didn't like that there was only one.

Why would there be only one good shot in that package of thirty? They all had the same expiration date printed on them. They were all from the same batch. And they're all supposed to be good for another year.

Maybe she'd been too influenced by her brief conversations with Jerry, but all she knew was that she didn't trust that singular, now-taking-on-ominous-dimensions syringe. She didn't like that she didn't have a choice in the matter. She didn't like that the person on the phone had to check the "notes area" in the database to tell her to just take it. She didn't like that she was trying to talk herself into taking it and then talking herself out of being paranoid.

Seems like the perfect way to get someone to poison herself—especially someone desperate for her medicine.

"Fuck this shit," Jocelyn said. It was right then that Jocelyn decided that she wasn't doing it anymore. She wasn't going to depend on Capaxone or that mail-order pharmacy. She wasn't going to depend upon that neurologist and his MRI images of her brain. Were they even of her brain? Or was that some sort of screen saver he had constantly looping on his computer? Lord knows, seeing as how he was clearly involved with the Tysabri sales team.

Jocelyn knew that the marketing material she would make up often had fake stuff in it, too. People didn't mind. In fact, they kind of expected it. Or at least that's what Jocelyn would tell herself as she produced the stuff. It was like visual candy. People loved it—smart bombs flying straight through open doorways, or the reporters in studios that were made to look like they were on rooftops of some nondescript Middle Eastern hotel. The visuals helped the Conglomerate's sales department while trying to convince whomever the ultimate decision-maker was on the purchase of a missile or the latest vaporware or some sort of democracy-training program to lay out the cash and sign on the dotted line. Great visuals always trumped written proposals. The rest was up to the sales team to hammer out the details of terms and pricing.

Could it be the same with the drug company? Well, the MRI images were probably hers, Jocelyn reasoned. But all she knew for sure was how she felt, and the neurologist never seemed to be listening to her at all. It appeared that he made his decisions based solely upon evidence he had gleaned from some sort of superexpensive, space-age technology. She picked up the phone and made an appointment with that naturopath/homeopath that her cousin had researched and recommended. There had to be a better way—or at least a different way—to deal with MS.

And that was what she was looking for when she went back inside on that glorious day with the dandelion seeds floating carelessly around her kids—the paperwork that the doctor had given her about homeopathic medicine.

Jocelyn had never experienced it before. With her mother being of the generation that got to escape the farm and go to nursing school, Jocelyn had been brought up with the idea that all the technology and all the medicine that the United States had to offer was not only the best way to handle illness, it was the *only way*. She had seen homeopathy and diet mentioned on the Internet as good alternatives for people with all sorts of illnesses. She knew that this approach was popular in Europe and figured she'd give it a try.

Enduring the nonstop skepticism of her mother during the drive in, Jocelyn had been rewarded with an hour-and-a-half long visit with the doctor. She hadn't expected to answer questions like, which side do you sleep on? Describe the color and consistency of your bowel movements. Do you prefer hot or cold water? How old were you when your parents got divorced? Jocelyn and this new breed of doctor spent a long time talking about the stuff that Jocelyn kept herself busy with—the kids, the Ray Pierce group. Although Jocelyn had no real idea as to why, the doctor seemed to have a favorable opinion of Ray Pierce, which made Jocelyn instantly relax.

"Have you had any dental work done recently?" the doctor asked.

Going on over an hour's worth of these seemingly random questions, Jocelyn started giggling. It all seemed so ridiculous. *Dental work?*

"Why are you laughing?" the doctor asked calmly.

"I'm not sure what all this has to do with multiple sclerosis."

The doctor sat back in her chair, folded her hands against her chest, and smiled. "I'm trying to figure out which type of approach would be best for you. We are definitely going to clean up your diet."

Jocelyn was surprised to hear that.

"America can be a tough place to live for some of us. The food is overly processed, and a good portion of what we eat is genetically modified. The body doesn't even recognize it or know what do with it. There are toxins all around us on a daily basis," the doctor said as she pointed out her window to a commercial jet flying overhead, leaving its white scratch on the sky.

"It's everywhere. In the air. In the water. The stuff we clean our houses with. Not to mention the relationships we have. Medicine in America ..." She paused, looking at the volumes of reference books she had neatly organized in the bookshelf only an arm's reach away. "It's literally fantastic. It does amazing things. I'm not anti–Western medicine by any means, but I know that everybody is different. The wholesale selling of one-size-fits-all medicine is big business, and more often than not, people don't need the full assault that a quick fix provides. Sometimes, it actually ends up damaging a body. If someone has to take these medicines, they might want to buttress with specific vitamins or supplements so that the rest of their body stays strong for the fight. Ultimately, it's the body that cures itself.

Jocelyn nodded.

"So when did the dizziness start?"

"I think it was when I was at Ray Pierce's political training in Minneapolis. But I wasn't dizzy at first. I was itchy—like I had bugs crawling on me. I thought it might have been that I was allergic to something. Then it changed to dizzy when I got home."

"What were you doing at a political training?"

"Oh, we were learning how politics isn't so much about winning elections, but more importantly, it's about moving a theoretical, philosophic box around the voters who, I was surprised to find out, are actually a very small percentage of the population. This group of concerned citizens usually sits right in the center of the box. It's up to political marketing campaigns to push the edges of the box around that group to the left or to the right. The polarization of just about every issue forces the locked-in voter to be perceived as more extreme than he or she most likely is, as that theoretical box slides past the voter, pushing him or her to one side or the other. It turns the whole political thing into an *us* versus *them* contest and motivates people to vote when they typically couldn't care less. I guess it's easier to move a concept around than to move actual people."

"Hummm dizzy ... left to right," the doctor mumbled as she scribbled something down in Jocelyn's file.

Jocelyn continued, "This pushing thing usually ends up boiling down to some splinter issue—stuff that most people don't usually think about on a daily basis. It's never about the real issues, like economics or monetary policy—stuff that actually impacts real people in their real lives. It's easier to get people to emotionally engage with the diehard, splinter-issue voters. They make decisions about the country and the world based on how they *feel* about something, that has absolutely nothing to do with their everyday lives—which ultimately comes down to how they want to feel about themselves. Honestly, it's just like a real corporate marketing campaign."

The doctor gave the emotionally detached nod that prompted Jocelyn to continue.

"The one thing that stood out to me in this training was that the guy who says he will end the war always wins. People like that. Even if he never gets around to getting the United States completely out, as long as he says it enough times, that guy will win." She paused and added, "And someone will probably give that guy a Peace prize, or something, just for saying it."

Jocelyn had more to say, but the doctor quietly took control of the conversation by nodding and asking, "And how did you react when you found out about the crash?"

"Huh? What crash? My father? Or there was that one at work that kind of freaked me out. But what does that have to—"

"Patriotism. There is a reason why the root word for patriotism comes from the Latin word meaning father. So what is it about the crash? Do you think that you could have prevented it? Saved everyone?"

Perhaps the doctor had changed gears too quickly, but Jocelyn stared at her, momentarily bewildered. Was she talking about a plane crash or some other, more far-reaching and devastating crash that she hoped to avoid and shelter her children from?

When Jocelyn finally left the doctor's office, she was holding a stack of photocopies about diet and "like curing like," as well as a little glass vial full of tiny white spheres. She was supposed to take two of those in the morning and another when she felt dizzy.

"Don't touch them. That's very important. That will ruin them. Just shake two into the lid of the vial—like this—and drop them under your tongue. Don't swallow them. Just let them dissolve."

So that's what Jocelyn had done a few minutes ago. And now she was looking through all that paperwork. Maybe it said something about those two, teeny, magic orbs that she had carefully placed under her tongue. Jocelyn was happily studying all the photocopies while wrapped inside a slice of sunshine that angled itself through the kitchen window.

Seriously, what did that homeopath give me? LSD or something? This is incredible.

Jocelyn smiled as she shook her head. Sure, she was concerned, but not really. This was nice. Then she saw it.

Homeopathy is an effective scientific system of healing, which assists the natural tendency of the body to heal itself. It recognizes that all symptoms of ill health are expressions of disharmony and unbalance within the whole person and that it is the patient that needs treatment, not the disease. Some patients experience a brief period of well-being and optimism immediately after taking a remedy ...

She read the entire photocopy again. How was it that she had never been exposed to any of this before? This style of medicine had been around for hundreds of years. When the obvious answer noiselessly fluttered into view and revealed itself to her, an unexpected single tear rolled down her cheek.

Big money. That's why. Millions of people owned stock in her suffering. And why not? It was the American way.

CHAPTER THIRTY

"DO YOU LIKE IT HERE?" Ethan asked Stojanka. He really wanted to ask her when she was leaving. He had been paying for this efficiency motel apartment in Newport for her for over two months now. He knew Europeans took long vacations, but come on. The landlord was pressuring him to sign a long-term lease. It wasn't like he was getting any special benefits out of this arrangement, either. In fact, at this point, it made him highly uncomfortable that she was nearby, and he was suspicious of the whole situation. *Why in God's name is she just hanging out? Doesn't she have anything better to do?* He knew, of course, that back in the day, he had said a lot of things to her about coming to America. She was just little then, and those were just words. He didn't realize that, after her sister got killed, those words would become an immovable peg for her to hang hopes on—that they had become the very reason for her being.

"Yes. Here it is beautiful," she replied as she gazed out over the Atlantic from the little porch of her apartment.

Ethan had set up collapsible lawn chairs the day she moved in. He had felt responsible for her in the way that an estranged father might. But now he was becoming somewhat resentful that this person would just show up and assume that he was going to take care of her. But what could he do? Simply give her a bunch of money and tell her to go away? That seemed cruel, considering how much of herself she had given to him as a child. Honestly, he was confused about how he felt about her. The fatherly thing corrupted the this-chick-is-hot thing, and when he added the fact that she was a better shot than he and was now obviously getting paid to kill people—well, he was downright jealous. She was a beautiful killer with no false pretenses to maintain. Meanwhile, he had kids and a house. Plus, he was still doing on-and-off consulting with the generals back at the Conglomerate. That was, of course, when he wasn't completely out of his mind.

The two of them sat in silence and watched as the gentle waves continued their eternal hello/good-bye with the beach. "You are married. No?" she asked from out of nowhere.

Ethan froze. He had not mentioned Jocelyn or the kids to her, at all, ever. He preferred that they not exist in the reality he was currently inhabiting. "No," he replied while still watching the waves. "I'm not married."

"But you have children. No?"

He turned to look at her as she produced a pack of Kent cigarettes out of her beach bag and nonchalantly lit up in a way that no American woman would ever be able to. She looked out over the water and took a puff, waiting for his response.

He sighed. "Yes. A girl and a boy."

"Precious. No?"

Ethan's vision was starting to close in on him, the danger-Will-Robinson signal that he had learned to live with. "Where are you going with this?" he demanded.

"Nowhere to go." She took another pull off the cigarette and let the smoke drizzle out of her mouth. "You are going to learn them to shoot?"

"I hadn't really thought of it. But yeah. Probably when they get a little older."

"Well, you a good teacher. You teach me everything I know."

He was very appreciative of her saying that and, in a bizarre fit of sentimentality, reached over to hold her hand. She just looked at him and moved her hand away. That's when he noticed it—the little tattoo on the interior of her left wrist, a jagged, broken heart.

His emotions were all over the place, and he thought he might cry seeing the little piece of embedded clip art. He had forgotten all about that. Or had chosen to forget about it. His vision was closing in on Cheerio status. *Heartbreaker.* That's what they called her. That was her professional name. She had been branded with the tattoo at eleven years old, right before Ethan had stumbled upon her and her sister. Her hands were very tiny then, and that had made him seem very big. He grappled with the thought of his own daughter or son having to endure what this woman had lived through. The humanitarian war.

"I'm sorry," he choked as he got up out of his lawn chair. She was still smoking her cigarette when he leaned over to kiss the top of her head and perhaps give her a hug. And that's when she kneed him in the balls.

"Fuck you, Colonel," she snarled as he doubled over.

CHAPTER THIRTY-ONE

TUCKED INTO THE TINIEST SLIVER of her side of the bed, Jocelyn slept. She had learned it was easier to stay out of his path and would even do so unconsciously. She cozied with the edge of the bed and was facing the blue Joan Miró print—the one Ethan had had hanging in his office when they had first met. Both of them were fast asleep when the phone rang at precisely 3:00 a.m. Jocelyn, being positioned closest to the phone, rolled over to answer it.

"Hum ... yeah ... hello?" she mumbled, not noticing the red digital numbers glaring at her from the nightstand.

"Is Colonel Lowe available?"

"Uh ...who?

"Colonel Lowe. Is this his wife?"

"What? What time is it?" She squinted at the clock. "Colonel? I think you have the wrong number."

"This is the number I was given. I need to speak with him. It's urgent."

Ethan sleepily rolled over and looked at Jocelyn.

"There is no one here who goes by the title Colonel. Good-b—"

Ethan snatched the phone from her. "Who is this?" he demanded. Jocelyn couldn't hear the caller but for some mumbled military-esque barking. She watched as Ethan's expression vacillated between confusion and anger.

"Don't *ever* call here again!" Ethan yanked the phone cord out of the wall and rolled over and resumed his former sleeping position as if nothing had happened.

"Who was that?" Jocelyn asked, intensely curious. "Do you know that guy? Why was he calling you Colonel? You're not a colonel. Are you? He sounded strange. And—"

"Go to sleep. It's nothing."

"But who was that?" She propped herself up on her elbow to face him.

"Just some drunk guy."

"How'd he get this number? Did you give it to him? Did you tell him that you were a colonel?"

"Please stop talking. Go to sleep. I need to sleep. I'm exhausted," he said, curled up, facing away from her, and decidedly done with this episode.

"Does this call have anything to do with the one we got a couple nights ago from that Krav Maga guy?"

Ethan didn't move, but Jocelyn saw that he opened his eyes.

"That's what it's called, right? That Israeli Special Forces hand-to-hand combat thing you told me about? It didn't sound like the same guy."

"Goddamn it, Jocelyn! Stop talking and just go to sleep!"

"Well, how the hell am I supposed to fall asleep when some mystery guy calls at"—she pointed to the alarm clock—"at three o'clock in the morning ... again!"

Ethan didn't say anything. He just grabbed his pillow and headed out to the couch.

"Ethan! Seriously, what's going on?!" she called down the hall.

Silence.

"Ethan! Talk to me!"

Silence.

"Uhhhggg! You are so infuriating!" she yelled as her head plopped back down onto the pillow. Jocelyn stared at the ceiling and tried to remember one of the breathing techniques that she had done back in her yoga class years ago. Not achieving the desired result of ... Wait. What was that syncopated breathing supposed to do for her again? Calm her down? Or stimulate her fifth chakra? Or ... "Oh, screw it," she mumbled and buried her head into her pillow.

At about 4:00 a.m., Jocelyn decided to take a different tact. *He's keeping a roof over our heads. We have health insurance. We are safe. Everything's fine.* She repeated that like a mantra, just like the one they had taught her at Executive Training for Women, the one about being awake and alive and feeling great. That ridiculous little ditty that the Conglomerate had taught the miserable female employees as they drank coffee like it was going out of style. Finally at about 5:00 a.m., she fell asleep. Of course, the kids woke up at 5:50. Ethan was still sleeping on the couch.

Jocelyn was dead tired, but she had decided, by 8:30 a.m., when Ethan had yet to wake up, that she was going out that night. Samantha Ballentine, or "Sam" as she would sign her business letters, had invited a few people from the essentially defunct Ray Pierce Meetup group over to her office for the evening.

Jocelyn had been reluctant to accept the invitation. *Who would watch the kids? Ethan?* She hadn't asked him about it when she was invited because she really didn't care to broach the topic with him. It wasn't that she thought he would say no. It was just easier to stay home. Jocelyn wasn't sure what the occasion was anyway. Nor did she know why the group was meeting at Sam's office, the place they had gathered to compile signature sheets during the election.

Regardless, after the scene last night, Jocelyn figured she owed it to herself to get out of the house—even if it was just to stop in and say hello. She wasn't devastatingly dizzy anymore, and she was going out.

CHAPTER THIRTY-TWO

SAM'S OFFICE, WHICH WAS FAMILIAR to all of the guests because of the goings-on of the previous election, was located in the basement of a completely nondescript, brick, two-story office building located not far from the state dump. Tiny strip malls flanked the building. Shear Madness; Tony's Pizza; Dance Artistry; Benton's Quality Used Car Dealership; and a small, locally owned grocery store were her neighbors.

No one would suspect that Sam's basement-level lair was the home of a much sought-after global investment advisory service—one that offered personal handholding to the, as of late, perpetually edgy likes of the Kingdom of Saudi Arabia and France's *régimes spéciaux de retraite* fund managers.

Everyone in attendance seemed thrilled to be there. A silver-haired massage therapist/tai chi instructor named Abigail brought veggie wraps for everyone. And one of the men, Peter, a tall, thin, blond man who was a subcontractor at a small software company that was currently positioning itself to be assimilated into the Conglomerate, shuffled in with a white pastry box full of generously proportioned sugar cookies. Everyone made a big deal, appreciating the unexpected delivery of food. Once a little table had been set up for the food and paper towels distributed, the dozen or so in attendance settled into the chairs that Sam had dragged out and set up in a circle in the fairly banal, beige reception area. It wasn't long before the group began riffing, as Ray Pierce supporters are apt to do, about what a mess the world was. The conversation, as it grew, despite its dismal content, decorated the walls and made the place much more colorful and inviting.

Sam, who was sitting comfortably in her chair, whipped out and unfolded the Letters to the Editor page of the *Providence Journal*. "Well, there isn't much we can do about it, guys, except to continue to educate the people around us. That's why I spend a lot of my time calling into radio shows and writing letters to the editor."

Jocelyn, unlike most of the crew there, knew some of Sam's backstory, and she liked her. She was nice enough. And Jocelyn would forever admire her for standing up to crazed Kris Jung at the library. Jocelyn suspected that Sam was smart by the way she was able to succinctly craft her thoughts about the economy into simple-to-swallow, sound-bite-sized chunks.

"Oh, I saw your letter, Sam!" Abigail enthusiastically commented while trying to rewrap her veggie wrap. "That was great how you basically shredded the *Journal*'s story about the Federal Reserve. Very classy, as per usual."

Abigail, the evening's sandwich bearer, was also startlingly direct in her communications and would often get her letters to the editor published in the newspapers, too. Because of her success with getting letters published, the Ray Pierce group called her Dear Abby. Although not as knowledgeable as Sam on the particulars, Abby maintained a reputation as a harbinger of simple common sense with her letters. One of the more memorable was the one she had written about the governor and how he should take a flying leap off the Newport Bridge.

Forrest and Palmeri were there, of course. These two Jocelyn had known since her first Ray Pierce meeting. While Jocelyn listened to the particulars of Forrest's latest job conundrum, Palmeri was snuffing out the remains of a ridiculously large cigar and tucking it away for later enjoyment. Palmeri was some sort of IT guy at yet another large defense contractor over by the now-defunct navy base that the state was trying to sell off to a huge biomed company.

A skinny man, with long, scraggily, white hair, who seemed to defy age quantification, was there. He could have been anywhere from forty to sixty-five in Jocelyn's best guesstimate. His name was Wesley, and for most of the evening, he sat cross-legged in a chair with a fashion magazine on his lap. Jocelyn had never met him, but others in the room seemed comfortable with him as he waited for everyone to be silent before he quietly spoke. The magazine that Wesley had been patiently holding had an article that he had circled, and it featured a picture of the former First Lady and the Queen of England. Jocelyn wondered why someone would take the time to bring this in as she watched the rest of the group munch their sugar cookies. She was looking for the others' reaction to this guy and his magazine.

When Wesley finally had everyone's attention, he excitedly pointed out that the two prominent women were wearing pins made by the same jewelry designer, which he must have assumed everyone would recognize. The designer was featured in a little square insert overlapping the photo of the Queen and the First Lady. Wesley looked around the room waiting for a response, and when none came, he produced, out of his courier bag, a coffee-table book of famous jewelry designers. He quickly opened to the page he had bookmarked and held the book open like a kindergarten teacher so that everyone could see.

"Oh! I've seen that designer's work!" Jocelyn said as she smiled, remembering that tacky butterfly pin her former employers had given her as a parting gift on her last day at the Conglomerate. "Or at least a knockoff of it."

Wesley eyed her suspiciously. "You are a fan of this man's work?" he asked with one raised eyebrow.

"Well, I wouldn't say that exactly," Jocelyn said as she brushed sugar off her lap. "I had one of those butterfly pins once—just like that one." She pointed to the one in the photograph.

"Did you now?" Wesley said as he crossed his legs and leaned back against the chair, still holding the book so that everyone could behold the butterfly pin.

"Yeah," Jocelyn sort of snorted. "It was the gift my coworkers gave me at my going-away party. Right before I had the kids. I thought it was kind of gaudy, actually." She omitted the part about someone snatching it from the dashboard of her unlocked car and motioned for the person sitting next to the little food table to send over another sugar cookie. Sure, she wasn't supposed to eat it while on that diet that the new doctor had her on, but what the heck. This was her first night out in a long, long time. One more wouldn't hurt.

The cookie box was passed, and she daintily plucked one out as Wesley, still seemingly quite put off by the revelation that Jocelyn had owned one of these pins, continued. "I would be sure that it was a knockoff," Wesley said in a voice so snooty that Jocelyn had a hard time not laughing as she bit into her cookie. "That brooch that you just pointed to is valued at just under a million dollars."

Jocelyn stopped chewing and leaned in closer to look at the picture. Yup. The one that Mimi had made sure to give her on her last day was definitely just like the one in the picture. Even the weird little antennae of the butterfly looked the same.

"This designer, Carlos Delohim, is a self-declared Satanist. Look closely at the filigree work," Wesley instructed as he ran his finger almost sensually over the page. "It's all tiny little pentacles. See them?"

Jocelyn did. "Oh, you're right! What delicate detailing."

"His work is popular with members of the Illuminati— or at least those who are trying to impress the Illuminati. They will wear Delohim like a badge signifying that they have made their alliance with Satan. They like to announce their plans right out in the open. It's like a sick little joke.

They'll slip their message into movies or in songs on the radio. I remember the first time I became aware of this, back when I worked for that music producer out in Hollywood—"

Forrest took the final bite of his veggie wrap and said, "Look, Wesley, this is all very interesting, but I'm not into that Satanist/ Illuminati/Freemason/Reptilian—"

His buddy Palmeri interrupted, "Reptilians are a totally different thing, Forrest. They're more aligned with UFOs, seraphim, and Nephilim. It's a completely different branch of the tree."

Jocelyn had no idea what the heck they were talking about, but it appeared that Abby had a clue as to what Nephilim were by the way she raised her eyebrows at the mention of the word.

"*Whatever,*" Forest countered. "I'm not into this conspiracy stuff. I'm into real-life stuff that I can vote out of office. So what if some art school graduate worships Satan? I'll stand by anyone's right to worship anything they please. I'm not a Satanist. It really doesn't affect me."

Dear Abby, a diehard and very vocal advocate for her Lord and Savior Jesus Christ, basically blew a gasket. "No! No! This country was founded by Christians! And—"

"Actually, other religions were represented at the signing of the Declaration of—"

Abby's head couldn't have looked more like that kid in the movie *The Exorcist* as it instantly spun around toward the source of that inconvenient truth. She shot a very un-Christian look at poor John P., another IT guy who worked at an accounting firm. (He was called that because nobody ever knew how to pronounce his really long last name).

"Unitarians," John P. said helpfully, "and they respect all different—" And then, suddenly sensing Dear Abby's pent-up wrath, he quietly acquiesced with, "Sorry. Forget I said anything."

Abby retuned her sights to Forrest. "This politically correct tolerance for the unholy is the reason why America is falling apart! And—"

Now the youngest of the party, twenty-one-year-old Joe Kurt, a talented graphic designer who Jocelyn saw as only hindered by his habitual and unbridled drug use, cut Abby off as the rest of the party, nibbling on their sugar cookies, watched on. Everyone seemed to be enjoying this hometown version of *The McLaughlin Group.*

"Artists have to go where the money is, Abby. Look at the Vatican and Catholicism," Joe Kurt said. "You can't blame this guy and his jewelry. Rich people like it. So what? What else are they going to do with their money, anyway?"

"I don't know. Mess with people for the fun of it?" Palmeri mumbled.

Joe looked up at Palmeri and giggled his stoner giggle. "Probably. Anywho, I wish I could get me some elite sponsorship like that."

Forrest broke in with, "If I had a ton of money, I'd probably be trying to engineer world events for my benefit. Sure. Who wouldn't? But you sure as hell wouldn't find me wasting any of my time with tacky butterfly pins to let people know I was the boss. A kick-ass Bugatti Veyron Grand Sport? Hell yeah! Absolutely. Nothing says 'I fucking rule' like a Bugatti." He nodded in agreement with his own comment and concluded with, "But I'd stay away from the lame-ass jewelry."

"Annnnd that's why you haven't gotten laid in like a year," Palmeri uttered at just the right volume as to let the rest of the room hear him. He licked the sugar off his fingers nonchalantly and said, "Chicks dig fancy jewelry."

Forrest rolled his eyes at Palmeri and shook his head. "Shut up. You don't have kids. You'll see. Kids jam everything up. You really shouldn't even bother offering me advice until you find a real girlfriend."

"Oh, I will," Palmeri said confidently, "when you find a legit job."

"You ass! You know I'm only working under the table as a favor for the guy who owns the machine shop."

Everyone smirked, and Joe Kurt giggled.

Abby's friend, Clint, the guy who had driven her to the party and who, not surprisingly, had maligned teeth, took a pack of cigarettes out of his shirt pocket and asked Sam where he might go to smoke. Palmeri joined him.

This, of course, led to comments about inflation. "Oh, I could never smoke now. I remember when a pack cost ..." And the role that the Federal Reserve played in causing inflation and fractional-reserve banking. And, of course, taxes.

Once Clint and Palmeri, accompanied by the heavy scent of stale smoke, reemerged and jumped back into the conversation, all talk turned to the particulars of driving over the state line to buy cartons of cigarettes in order to avoid state taxes. The bulk of the dozen or so nonsmokers in attendance were curious. Was it worth it? This morphed into an almost twenty-minute jam session about interstate commerce. And not surprisingly, for people familiar with RP supporters, the conversation included massive amounts of history about the Interstate Commerce Clause and gun restrictions.

Jocelyn suddenly realized that she would have found all this incredibly boring a couple of years ago. Even though she did not smoke, did not own a gun, and had not been this tired since the kids were in diapers, she was having a thoroughly enjoyable evening.

The party broke up well after midnight. As it was breaking up, Sam said while shaking Jocelyn's hand in farewell, "I'm so glad you came."

"Oh, me too. I almost didn't. Thanks for inviting me."

"I wish more people were able to attend a meeting like this," Sam said. "This is the sort of conversation that too many people are missing. People need to get off the couch, shut off the damn dream box, and educate themselves. Schools sure as hell aren't doing anyone any favors. And all these shows"—she sighed and waved absently over her shoulder—"they're just exercises in social engineering. They don't call it programming for nothing."

"I don't have a TV in my house," Jocelyn said. This seemed to please Sam. But Jocelyn was curious. "Why do you have a TV over there?" she asked, pointing to a large flat-screen television in the corner of Sam's office.

"Oh, that's so I can keep up with what my clients are going to be calling in and freaking out about next."

Jocelyn thought about what Sam had said as she drove home. She had never thought about it from the other side. After all, wasn't that Jocelyn's job at the Conglomerate? To push stories to affect stock price? And wasn't it Sam's job to be watching said stock market? Jocelyn knew that Samantha's late father had started the business before electronic trading became *de rigueur de jour* and that what Sam did was all based on studying trends and applying time-honored, solid economic principles. She and her father would document the twitches and subtle nuances of the stock market every day with colored pencil in a large, hard-bound, graph paper ledger. And Sam still did it that way.

That evening, at the get-together, Jocelyn had noticed the ledgers from decades past, when the firm was housed in an upscale office space on Wall Street in Manhattan, lining the bookshelves at Sam's office. Those handy, historical reference materials of stock market activity were not only proud reminders of Sam's father's American dream achieved, they also had the ability to conjure up the misty remains of the conspicuous consumption years—the years before those "in the know" began slowly becoming less and less visible. Anonymity had now become the new chic.

Sam and her global investment service were first adaptors to this trend. Her firm had no website; nor was the phone number listed in any directory or phone book. An interested potential client would only be able to reach her if they had gotten her number from one of her current clients. Sam made all new clients accept an agreement, under penalty of losing her as their advisor, not to distribute her contact information unless the interested party was holding more than the equivalent of $50 million.

Not everyone in attendance knew the story of Sam. Even the ones who knew part of it probably did not know all of it. And she preferred it that way. She rarely shared information about herself. Many of her clients did not even know that "Sam" was a woman.

Jocelyn drove her Hyundai through the deserted, late night, amber glow of streetlights and considered Sam's history, along with all of the other stuff that had been discussed at the party; she wondered if maybe there was something she could do that was proactive. Maybe she could start a book club or something—something where people could sit and talk like her RP friends had that night.

Jocelyn was so busy pondering this that she didn't notice the car following her home.

CHAPTER THIRTY-THREE

JOCELYN, FEELING QUITE SATISFIED THAT she had decided to go out that night, pulled into her driveway and noticed, in her rearview mirror, a silver Crown Victoria gliding past her house. She shut off her car and gathered up the remains of her cookie and the *Loss of Liberty* DVD, a documentary about the 1967 Israeli attack on the USS *Liberty*, that John P. had given to her. She headed into the house as quietly as she could. She had not expected to come home this late. The light was still on over the kitchen sink, and she tiptoed down the hall to check on the kids.

After straightening their blankets and kissing each of them on top of their sleeping little heads, she went to her room. She quietly entered the dark room and began taking off her clothes. She opened her drawer. It squeaked. Jocelyn cringed. She didn't want to wake Ethan. She felt around in the drawer for something to sleep in. She grabbed a nightie and slid it over her head. Then, as gently as she could, she lay down in bed. It was less than a minute before she realized that Ethan was not in the bed with her.

Jocelyn jumped out of bed and flipped on the light. "Ethan?" she said as she inspected the room. Then she went out to the living room to see if he was sleeping on the couch like he had last night. Nope. Now she was starting to get worried. "Ethan? Are you here?" she called out softly as she entered each room and turned the lights on.

Did Ethan leave the kids alone in the house? He'd never do that. Would he?

She walked back, confused, through the kitchen. The light switch was next to the basement door. That's when it kicked in. The dream—the dream where Ethan had shot and killed her, leaving her surrounded by nothingness. Her heart started beating in double time. Was Ethan down there? Should she check? Or should she just go back to bed? She knew she'd never be able to just fall asleep now.

Jocelyn braced herself as she pushed open the unlocked basement door. The dream and its nothingness were heavy upon her. "Ethan," she called out hesitantly. "Ethan, I'm here. Are you down there?"

She could hear something. She waited. Then Ethan rounded the corner. His face was very placid—almost a relaxed smile. *Just like that dream.* She swallowed and forced herself to smile back.

"I hope you enjoyed yourself this evening," he said as he slowly headed up the stairs, wiping his hands on an oily red rag.

Jocelyn was quick to move away from the stairway, the site of her untimely demise in the dream. She felt so vulnerable in her Victoria's Secret cotton baby-doll nightie that she absently grabbed an apron and started folding it—as if that would somehow provide an additional layer of protection.

"You look nice," he said as he finished wiping his hands and leaned against the counter. "You still have your makeup on. You look good."

"Oh, thanks," Jocelyn answered feebly while still folding the apron.

He watched her. Then he slowly approached her.

She slung the most potent joy kill topic she could think of at him. "How were the kids?"

He continued to smile. "Oh, they were fussy at first." He took the apron out of her hands and tossed it onto the table. She blinked and backed away. "But then they were fine. Just fine," he said as he put his arms around her to hug her.

She gave him a little hug back. But as she attempted to end the friendly hug, he slid his hands down her back. He squeezed and cupped her bottom, pulling her closer to him.

She arched her back, leaning away from him, attempting to avoid a kiss, but that only pushed his obviously aroused groin more firmly against hers.

"Playing hard to get tonight?" he asked.

"Uh, no. I just—"

"That's good," he said as he grabbed the back of her head and forced his tongue into her mouth. Startled, Jocelyn gasped for breath as his tongue hungrily prodded hers.

What is going on? Not only was Jocelyn freaked out by a dream she couldn't forget, she was exhausted and monumentally confused. Ethan had not shown a stitch of interest in her since, good Lord, she couldn't remember when. She tried to push him away, but he only clutched her more forcefully as he wedged her up against the refrigerator and started to peel off her little nightgown. When she tried to squirm away, he grabbed her firmly with both hands by her waist and then ran his hands up and over her breasts. They finally ended up on her neck, thumbs resting on the bottom of her chin as he continued thrusting his tongue into her mouth.

Jocelyn, without even thinking about it, reverted to life-saving mode. She moaned appropriately and ran her hands up the center of his chest up to his neck, hoping that she might be able to, she didn't know, force his hands away from her or something. Instantly, she knew that was not likely. Accepting defeat, she allowed herself to float away while Ethan peeled off the rest of the Victoria's Secret nightie. Her consciousness somehow watched on from the sidelines as he began pinching and licking her nipples. Her heart was aflutter. Maybe she wanted this? But not like this. Couldn't this wait until it made sense? Maybe if she hadn't had the dream, this would all be simply awesome.

Ethan had fallen to one knee and had started licking her stomach. He was working his way down when Jocelyn saw her chance for escape. She jumped away.

"What? What's wrong? Did I hurt you or something?" Ethan asked, looking up at her, confused.

Now that was a loaded question. And Jocelyn didn't quite know how to effectively address the full scope of it while standing butt naked in the kitchen at 2:00 a.m. "Um. No. I just ... I guess I'm just tired. I didn't really sleep last night."

"Oh. Right. Uh-huh. Sorry to inconvenience you. It sounded like you were into it. I thought that maybe you'd want to, you know, after I watched the kids and all—"

"I watch the kids every day, Ethan," Jocelyn said as she grabbed her nightie and held it close to her chest.

They stared at each other. Ethan broke the silence. "I'll sleep on the couch again tonight."

"I'm sorry," Jocelyn mumbled.

"Whatever."

The next morning when she got up with the kids, Ethan wasn't there. Unlike last night, he really was gone. A cryptic note let her know that he wouldn't be back for a while. It ended with, "If you need me, call me," and a series of letters and numbers that were clearly not a phone number scrawled across the bottom—3 X R 30 1 X L 40 1 X R 70.

"Great." She sighed as she hung Ethan's note on the refrigerator like some sort of melancholy memento from the night before.

After she had made the kids some breakfast, she turned on her computer. She wanted to look up that jewelry designer and pin that Wesley had mentioned last night. Sure enough, there it was—the picture of the fabulously expensive butterfly brooch that she had gotten as a gift. The caption under the picture read, "White and black diamonds with rubies, emeralds, blue and pink sapphires, garnet, and amethyst. Exquisite 24 karat gold filigree. It took designer Delohim almost four years to make this piece."

That butterfly they gave me sure does look a lot like this one, Jocelyn had to admit to herself. Even if the one she lost was a cheap knockoff, it had been a pretty convincing likeness. As she clicked around for more information about this crazy pin, her daughter ran up to her and tugged her arm, "Mommy! Mommy! There's a man outside! SpongeBob! Come look!"

"Where's your brother?" Jocelyn asked because usually the twins were like a roving unit and traveled together.

Her daughter pleaded while tugging at her mother's arm. "He's outside. Come on!"

"With the man?!" Jocelyn quickly hopped out of the chair and followed her daughter outside. Sitting at the picnic table as if they had been lifelong friends were her son and, across from him, a man in a dark blue suit with a tie that featured the popular cartoon character SpongeBob SquarePants.

Jocelyn quickly jogged up to her son and put her hand on his shoulder. She gave her kid a quick visual inspection and told him that he and his sister should go inside. *Now.* She'd give them the don't-talk-to-weird-guys-who-just-show-up-in-our-backyard talk later.

With the two of them tucked back in the house and watching her through the panes of the French door, she turned to face the stranger.

SpongeBob smiled and leaned forward over the picnic table to shake her hand. Jocelyn just looked at his extended hand.

"What are you doing in my yard with my children?" She paused as she looked around for his car, which wasn't anywhere to be found. And just as the man was going to answer she added, "You know what? I don't care. I don't know you, and you were not invited. Please leave the property." She noticed that the man was not moving. "I'm going to call the police." And she turned to walk back into the house. "What kind of freak ..." she grumbled.

"They should be here in about eight to twelve minutes," the man called back casually. "That gives us plenty of time to talk. Besides, I am sort of like the police." He reached into his jacket pocket and whipped out his credentials, just like they do on TV. "Won't you join me at the picnic table? We need to talk," he said holding his flaccid wallet like an old leftover pancake.

Jocelyn kept walking toward the back door and waved at the man over her shoulder as if to say, *buzz off, creep*, but instead said, "You might have tried the front door."

"You may be in possession of something that could get you in a lot of trouble! And I'd hate to see you get jammed up because of it!" SpongeBob called out.

This got Jocelyn's attention. She hesitated, but only briefly, as she entered her house and shooed the kids away from the door. She went straight to the phone and did the unthinkable, especially after last night. She called Ethan.

The phone rang and rang. He did not answer. She hung up and called again. And again he did not answer. She tried one more time. This time, he answered, obviously annoyed.

She didn't even let him speak. She just blurted out, "There's a guy in the backyard who says that he's *like* the police. I think he's a freak. He seemed interested in the kids. We're all inside right now. I'm gonna call the police, but—"

"Don't tell him anything, Joss. I don't care what he says. You don't have to say anything."

"About what? What could I possibly tell him? He says I have something that might get me into trouble and wants to talk with me about it. But I don't see his car. I don't even know how he got here."

"Okay, call the police. Do you still have that note I left you? You didn't throw it out, did you?"

"No, I didn't throw it out."

"That's the combination to the safe downstairs. It means go to 30 three times clockwise, then to 40 counterclockwise, and then 70 clockwise. Make sure you go past zero every time. Get the shotgun."

"But I don't know how—"

"That's okay. Just get the shotgun. It's the easiest. It's not loaded. I'll talk you through it. If this guy gets too close to the house before the police get there—"

Knock. Knock.

"Oh shit, Ethan. He's knocking on the front door right now."

"Okay, I'll call the police for you. Just see what he wants. But leave the door locked. If he's a real cop, have him leave a card or something. Better yet, tell him to type up whatever it is he's worried about in a letter and mail it. But don't let him into the house."

"Okay." She hung up so that Ethan could call the police, and she yelled, "Please go away!"

"Ms. McLaren," a different male voice called through the front door. "I am Special Agent McDonnell. I am with the Federal Bureau of Investigation. My partner and I would like to speak with you about your dealings with a company called DVIE. May we come in?"

"The guy with the SpongeBob tie? Well, tell him that he's creepy. Who goes sneaking around backyards and starts talking to the kids without the parents around? What is he? Some sort of child molester? That's not cool. Oh and how'd he get here, by the way? I didn't see a car. Like I'm supposed to believe the FBI walked here or something?"

"I apologize for Agent Dobson, Ms. McLaren. Our car is in your driveway right now."

Jocelyn looked out the window and saw the silver Crown Vic.

It was the same one she'd noticed in her rearview mirror the night before. "Please, just go away. If you have something you would like to ask me, please put it in a letter and mail it. This conversation is over." Jocelyn hunched motionless by the door, straining to hear whether or not they were leaving.

After she was convinced that Dobson and McDonnell had left, she stood up and looked out the window. Yup, the car was gone. She took a deep breath. She called to the kids. They could come out of their room now. The twins came barreling over to her, a bubbly mass of tiny arms and legs, stuffed animals, and colorful sneakers, wanting to go back outside.

This time, she accompanied her kids outside with a pitcher of lemonade and watched as they fluttered about the yard as only kids can do. Her son was purposefully building an airplane out of random things that he had procured from the shed. Her daughter was enjoying making herself dizzy as she spun around and around on the rope swing.

That's when they heard the sirens. The police had finally arrived. Jocelyn had forgotten that Ethan had called them. And that's exactly when she decided that she should probably make some time to learn about shotguns.

CHAPTER THIRTY-FOUR

ETHAN WAS STILL SOMEWHERE ELSE. To his credit, he had called to check on everyone at just about the same time the police had pulled up. The timing of his call was fortunate, because Jocelyn had been having difficulty communicating to the police as to what had prompted the call in the first place.

"You mean some FBI guys showed up and threatened you? That's why you and the kids were hiding in the house?"

"No," Jocelyn said as she poured her dizzy daughter a glass of lemonade. "This guy, Agent Dobson, the guy with the SpongeBob SquarePants tie, he looked like a child molester. He just showed up in my backyard—"

"And so why did this fella from a Pennsylvania long-range firing club call this in?"

"I have no— Oh, Ethan. He's in Pennsylvania? I didn't know that."

"How do you know Ethan?" The police officer looked at his clipboard. "Ethan Lowe, correct?"

"Oh, he's the kids' dad."

It went on like that for seemingly forever until Ethan's call came through and he spoke with one of the police officers. Jocelyn offered the other policeman a glass of lemonade, which was declined, as he waited for his partner to get off the phone. This man-to-man conversation seemed to settle the whole incident. The police tipped their hats as they departed, leaving Jocelyn to feel like a ditzy, overreacting, typical woman. In fact, she thought she heard one of them say exactly that as he got into the cruiser.

A few days later, the official correspondence that Jocelyn had requested showed up in her mailbox. It wasn't much more than a we-want-to-speak-with-you request and listed a phone number and address at which she could respond. Jocelyn picked up the phone and decided to call. Those guys were legit. But still, what kind of moron just walks into someone's backyard and starts making time with the kids while wearing a SpongeBob SquarePants tie? She'd write a letter expressing her disappointment to Dobson's superiors about that later. In the meantime, she was interested to hear what the FBI had to say considering all that Jerry Apario had told her. Clearly they must be onto something connected to those diamonds and gems he had been smuggling in. She wondered if Jerry was still a ghost.

She dialed the number and got patched through to Special Agent McDonnell, who, after thanking her for responding to the letter and apologizing again for Dobson, invited her to come to his place, the FBI office downtown. Jocelyn wanted to talk it out over the phone, but McDonnell said that he wanted to show her something, and it was probably going to make things much easier and quicker if she came to the office. Of course, he could always come back to her house ...

So Jocelyn made the appointment for the next day and met him at the FBI's branch office. It was located in a renovated office building down in the financial district of the city. It was a small office, smaller than she had imagined it would be. She noticed the cheap, battleship gray, indoor-outdoor, wall-to-wall carpeting and cube desks. How happy she was that she didn't work for the Conglomerate anymore.

McDonnell ushered her into a tight conference room. A poorly erased whiteboard welcomed her like some sort of graffiti-inspired modern art. A small, oblong, white Formica conference table sat in the center of the windowless room. With fluorescent lights adding to the ambience of the setting, the agent pulled a chair out for Jocelyn and offered it to her as he placed a thick, brown file on the table. When she was settled, he sat down.

"Thank you for coming today," he said as he smoothed his very non-noteworthy gray tie and folded his hands in front of him on the table. "I am very, very sorry about the way we first met."

Jocelyn nodded. She had already sent the letter complaining about Dobson, and she wondered if McDonnell had caught wind of that. Probably not yet.

"We wanted to ask you some questions about things you may have witnessed a few years ago."

Jocelyn nodded again. McDonnell opened the brown file and flipped to a page that apparently included information about her.

"Are you familiar with DVIE?" he asked.

Jocelyn sort of wiggled her head no.

"It was a company that shared the building with your division when you worked for the Conglomerate."

Jocelyn furrowed her brow and thought about it, "Oh! You mean Randy Veritas's company? Davis Veritas Electronics, Inc.? They were doing something with circuit boards and had to make sure that there wasn't any static electricity. I'm not sure, but I know they had to wear shower caps and booties. Nice guys."

Now it was McDonnell's turn to look like he was trying to recall something. He wrote down everything that Jocelyn had said.

"Umm. No. I'm talking about DVIE, Darling Vintners Import Export. Have you ever had to deal with them?"

Jocelyn thought about it. "No. But"—she hesitated as the memory fell into place—"now that you mention it, I do remember a gigantic shipment that was sent to Davis Veritas. The shipping company wouldn't take no for an answer and just dropped tons of stuff off. I think it was because of a typo. You know, the initials DVIE and DVEI. I guess that would be an easy mistake."

"You don't say," McDonnell muttered while scribbling feverishly in his file. He circled something and drew an arrow up to something higher on the page. "Can you remember anything else about Darling Vintners?"

Jocelyn looked arbitrarily around the room. "I don't think so."

"Okay." He nodded. "Now I'm going to change gears. Did you ever have to deal with Miriam Stein?"

"Who?"

"Miriam Stein. She was a board member at the Conglomerate."

Jocelyn flipped through her mental rolodex. The name sure sounded familiar ...

"She was the only female board member. She died right around the time you left the Conglomerate," McDonnell continued. "You may have seen her death notice. It was mentioned in the financial publications."

Jocelyn instantly thought of the bonus someone must have gotten for placing a story about a board member's funeral in the financial section of the *New York Times*. But to be honest, she had been so focused on being secretly pregnant and getting out of that place, she wasn't surprised she didn't remember an obituary. "I'm not sure. I'm really not that great with names. I never forget a face though," she said brightly.

"Does this ring a bell?" McDonnell asked as he slid the first from a set of photographs over to her. It was of the board member that Jocelyn had met in front of Robert's office right before Stan the congressman had sauntered in to tell them about winning the Malaysia contract years ago.

"Oh, yes! I've met this woman. She swung by the office one day and left with our congressman. I only met her once."

"She was an interesting woman. As well as being on your board of directors, she had been involved, on and off, since the 1970s with various attempts to develop a diamond index. The diamond index, if it ever got approved, would allow for the trading of diamonds as a commodity on the New York Stock Exchange. There have been a lot of problems with this project, but right before her death, it seemed like things might actually take off." McDonnell paused, looking for a reaction. When none came he said, "She seems to have had something in common with you."

"Really?" Jocelyn looked up from the photo, not able to imagine what she could possibly have in common with this woman other than ... *Okay, here we go. He's gonna hit me up about Jerry being a mule.*

He slid four more photographs over to her. These were not like the last. Jocelyn blinked as she tried to process what she was even looking at. When it finally clicked, she took a quick, short breath and swallowed.

They were crime scene photos—the body of a woman. The victim was partially naked and badly cut up. Obviously someone had just gone nuts methodically making tiny cuts all over this woman, which had produced lots of blood. One of the victim's eyes had been plucked out, and it was on the floor not far from her nearly dismembered head. The other eye was still in place, but you couldn't see it. A jewel-encrusted butterfly pin had been very purposefully pricked into the center of the victim's pupil.

Almost as if relaying the particulars of the crime scene bolstered McDonnell's concept of his own masculinity, he got up from the table, straightened his belted trousers, and strode around the tight, little conference room. He stopped only to lean over Jocelyn, who was sitting in horrified silence, to point out specifics in the photos.

"We theorize that the perp wanted Stein to be found like this. The attention the murderer paid to her eyes makes us believe that she had seen something that she shouldn't have. Obviously, the pin was the final act. See how it is placed very carefully. It's not haphazard at all. It's perfectly aligned with her face. Whoever did this cared enough to make the perfect photo op. The room was absolutely clean of fingerprints, but yet this mess remained. We have a very dramatic killer on our hands." McDonnell paused as if punctuating the drama. "We can conclude from the wounds and other elements at the scene that the entire event probably took about six hours. It was a slow death. We think that Ms. Stein was probably tortured for some sort of information." McDonnell leaned over Jocelyn's shoulder again to point to the picture. "See? See how both her legs are broken? And how she's tied to the chair?"

Suddenly remembering that it was this woman who was responsible for her promotion at the Conglomerate, Jocelyn's eyesight got blurry. She felt her heart in her throat and swallowed hard. "Uhhh ... I ... uhhh. I'm not sure what to say. Am I supposed to say something here? This is absolutely horrible!" Jocelyn blinked and pulled herself together. "Ummm ... you had said that she and I had something in common ..."

"Yeah. Malaysia."

Jocelyn's heart skipped a beat. *Is this where I say I want to speak with a lawyer?* Instead Jocelyn said, "Malaysia? I don't understand."

"Apparently, Miriam Stein had contacts in Kuala Lumpur who were interested in the diamond index project she had been working on. These people were well placed within the government. They were, like most of the Malaysian government, anti-Zionists and, apparently from the communications we are in possession of, they had made some sort of deal." He stopped to watch her reaction to that statement. "Jocelyn, do you know anything about these contacts she had in Malaysia?"

"No," Jocelyn said in confusion while mustering all of her resources in an attempt to appear composed and not vomit. "I honestly don't know anything about this."

"Are you sure?"

What kind of question is that?! Of course I'm sure!
"Yes, I'm sure. Look, I didn't even know this woman, let
alone her contacts in Malaysia."

Special Agent McDonnell just stared at her as if
considering something. He bit his lower lip, took a deep
breath, and nodded. "E-mail can be deceptive."

Oh shit. This *is where I'm supposed to say I want a
lawyer!* But Jocelyn didn't. She was violently rummaging
through her memory banks trying to confirm that she was still
in possession of that beige floppy disk. The last time she had
seen it, it had been in her hardly-ever-opened jewelry box,
empty but for two gold coins and some love notes. Thanking
God that she'd had the foresight to make copies of those e-
mails to Robert about the Royal Malaysian Navy proposal,
Jocelyn decided to just sit. She concluded that uttering the
words, "I want a lawyer," was tantamount to confessing to a
crime. And she didn't have the time or, more importantly, the
money to deal with that. Besides, she was the one who had
questions for the FBI. She wasn't going to feel intimidated.
She knew that she didn't have any connection to some
freakish murder.

"I bring this up, Jocelyn, because we have records of
your Conglomerate e-mail account communicating with the
highest levels of the Malaysian government."

Jocelyn couldn't help but smirk in disbelief. She was
just about to open her mouth and say something stupid like,
"Well, I did work on a proposal once," but McDonnell didn't
afford her that opportunity.

"These e-mails," he said as he flipped through the
papers in his thick, brown file, "were sent after you left. Your
account was still active."

Now instead of smirking in disbelief she was smirking
because she could totally see the disastrous IT department,
composed of Dr. Betty Lambert and Jerry Apario, never
getting a memo from the equally disastrous human resources
director to shut down her account.

Thankfully, Jocelyn hadn't opened her mouth about her e-mails to Robert or about the signatures needed for the Malaysian proposal. Clearly, that was not what they were looking for. Right? So why bring it up to confuse matters and incriminate herself? And McDonnell obviously knew that it wasn't her communicating with Malaysia. So why was she there? It couldn't be just so that McDonnell could show her some over-the-top snuff photos and freak her out. Could it? There had to be something more. So Jocelyn, being Jocelyn, just asked.

"Special Agent McDonnell, this is all morbidly fascinating, but I don't understand why you needed to show me all of this. I don't get what's going on here. Am I a suspect?"

"No. You are technically a person of interest."

"Oh," Jocelyn said as if she knew the difference.

"This case has basically gone from lukewarm to cold, and it appears that the higher-ups would like nothing more than for this whole sordid scene to just go away. Dobson, who unfortunately couldn't be here today, has not given up on this. He's the reason we ended up at your house. He feels as if he's found a new angle."

"Have you been watching me for a long time?" Jocelyn wanted to know. She really wanted to ask about the helicopters, but she didn't want to sound like a crazy person.

"Long enough to know that we wanted to speak with you."

Jocelyn lifted her chin and nodded ever so slightly in recognition of the ground rules. McDonnell wasn't going to be answering any of *her* questions.

The conversation was soon over. Special Agent McDonnell gathered up the contents of the brown folder and walked Jocelyn to the door of the office suite. He produced a business card and handed it to her as she made her exit.

As Jocelyn drove home, she realized that she was, not surprisingly, in some sort of functioning state of shock. She thought that she had held it together pretty well during that interview. But now that she was in the car, *What the hell?! Why was that woman stabbed in the eye with one of those ridiculously gaudy pins?! And who was that guy in the parking lot on my last day of work who told me that those pins could make or break a person?!* That was the real mystery for Jocelyn. She could care less about diamonds, Malaysia, and anti-Zionists.

She wondered if Jerry had been found by the FBI and was thankful that she hadn't mentioned him. Now she wondered if she was a person of interest because of him. She wanted to contact him. Of course, now that she knew she was being watched, she didn't know how to go about that. She'd figure it out. But what was the most important thing for her to be focused on right now? Jocelyn tried to prioritize as she drove the mommy mobile back to her kids, and *staying safe* quickly became number one on her list.

What would be the best way to do that? Well, of course Ethan had that gun safe downstairs; she should probably familiarize herself with some of that. But seriously, she couldn't just stay locked in the house with the kids holding a shotgun all day. That was insane.

"That murder happened years ago," she told herself in an attempt to rationalize away her fears. "I'm gonna be fine. I mean, I'm nobody. I'm just some stay-at-home mom. I have MS for God's sake. If someone wanted to kill me, it would be pretty darn easy, and they would have done it by now." That helped ... sort of.

As she approached her house, she waved to her next-door neighbor, who was watering the lawn. She never spoke with the woman, but they always waved hi. She pulled into her driveway. Still holding the steering wheel as she sat in the parked car, she looked at the little yellow house. It was not giving her any comfort. Not at all. *We have a roof over our heads. We have health insurance. We are safe* was not cutting the mustard right now. If she could, she would pick up the kids and just run away and hide. They could all be ghosts together. Wouldn't that be fun?!

After less than a millisecond of imagining herself and two toddlers living off the grid, evading all outside contact, a resounding *no* was all she was left with.

Maybe she should call Ethan? *Ummm, no.* Not now. She'd tell him in person when he came home. Tell her mom? *Oh, jeez, no!* Or how about her counselor? She pictured herself describing the crime scene photos to her, and ... Oh, forget about it. As if the counselor didn't already think Jocelyn was nuts. As she unlocked the front door, she glanced and smiled again at the woman watering the lawn. She decided that she needed to get to know her neighbors.

CHAPTER THIRTY-FIVE

THE LANGUAGE. ARABIC. ALL THE online ads started appearing in Arabic. At first, Jocelyn assumed it was her computer. So she spent way too much time fussing with the settings and turning the thing on and off. She could still check e-mail, and the search function still worked. But the ads were coming up humorously, or not, obviously geared toward a devout Muslim. Finally, she concluded that it was some sort of glitch with Google or Gmail. Palmeri had called during the on-off segment of her computer fix, and she'd mentioned it to him.

"They must have me on the wrong marketing preferences list or something," she said casually as she clicked around with her mouse.

"Oh, man, it's not the marketing preferences, Joss," Palmeri said. "You're on *the list*."

"What list?"

"That crazy MIAC report list. It's all about domestic terrorists, and they single out Ray Pierce supporters. They must have gotten their wires crossed or something, and they have you down in the Muslim extremist database or something."

"Shut up! You're kidding me," Jocelyn blurted incredulously. "What's MIAC?"

"No, I'm not kidding. Look it up. But don't worry, Joss. They'll figure it out soon. I'm sure they're on it," Palmeri said with typical Gen X sarcasm. "Pretty soon you'll probably be seeing ads for Tricorn hats and Gadsden flags."

And so, after she hung up with Palmeri, Jocelyn did just that. She looked it up. Sure enough there it was, the Missouri Information Analysis Center. It was confusing, but random mentions were scattered all over the Internet announcing that the MIAC report was the product of some sort of new Department of Homeland Security thing called a fusion center. Ray Pierce supporters, Constitution and Libertarian Party members, and a whole host of others were included on "the list" as possible terrorist threats.

In complete disbelief, Jocelyn went outside and begrudgingly took her Raymond Pierce for President bumper sticker off her car. Sure, the election was over and all ... As if worrying about the FBI stalking her and/or being stabbed in the eye with a butterfly pin wasn't enough, she simply didn't need the hassle of being associated with domestic terrorists. But it baffled her as to why Ray Pierce supporters, of all things, would be considered a threat.

Clumping up the remains of the sticky blue bumper sticker, she headed over to the garbage can to throw it away and glanced over her shoulder at the car. It looked naked. She sighed, tossed the sticky wad into the trash, and decided to check the mail. When she opened the mailbox, she noticed something new stuck inside. It was a round sticker used to color code the files at work. This one was red. *What's this doing here?* She stood and looked at it for a long time, for about as long as her gut could handle it because it felt like someone was wadding up her insides just like that bumper sticker she had just tossed. She carefully plucked the red circle off. *I'm going to show this to Ethan.* She handled it carefully. *This might be important.*

Ethan still hadn't reappeared, but he had sent an e-mail that he'd be home sometime that weekend. And she had a lot of important things to tell him. He still didn't know about the butterfly pin, the FBI, and all that. And now this. She really hoped that he would be in a decent mood when he finally showed up.

When she got back inside, Jocelyn was getting pretty fed up with being fearful. She checked on the kids—*still napping, good*—and sat down at her computer again. As an animated GIF advertisement, for what she could only imagine was some sort of Koran Home Study Program, flickered in the banner ad of her local newspaper's website, she hatched a plan. She was going to do the very opposite of Jerry and his ghost approach. Screw the hiding and avoiding everyone. How was that safe?

Jocelyn picked up the phone and called the library. "Yes. I'd like to book a meeting room." She was going to hold a public meeting. It would be just like the Ray Pierce Meetup but without all the campaigning nonsense—and more like that get-together at Sam's office. Jocelyn was going to finally meet her neighbors, and they would know that she wasn't a terrorist. She was honestly just a normal, concerned mom. She only kept her computer on long enough to make the flyers for the library meeting next week. Then she shut the thing off.

> Book Club Meeting
> Next Wednesday, 5:30 p.m.
> At the Library – Large Conference Room
> !!!Free!!! Coffee and Snacks!!!! Free!!!

Discussion of the book *Blowback* by Chalmers Johnson

Jocelyn held the flyer she had made while her son pushed in the final thumbtack. "Looks good, guys," she said as she gathered up the kids and walked them over to the children's section of the library. Once the kids were contently wandering around the bookshelves and playing on the Reading Rowboat, Jocelyn sat down at one of the public computers. She took the library card from her purse and glanced at her daughter's signature scrawled across the back. Her first name. All in capital letters. As she typed in the library account number allowing her access to the Internet, Jocclyn recalled how proud her daughter had been getting that card.

Jocelyn knew full well, of course, that if someone really wanted to keep an eye on her, they would be able to tell that she had used her kid's library card and had sent the message. But at least it wouldn't be sent from her home computer, which had suddenly been plagued with Arabic.

She had no idea if Jerry would get the message or not, but she had banked on her hunch that he was the webmaster over at ChemTrailTails.com. And if he wasn't? No big deal. She was pretty sure ChemTrailTails got weirder e-mails than hers.

By the time Jocelyn had sent her simple message from the children's section of the library, which read, "I hop church day ten and a half," Federal Bureau of Investigations Special Agent Dobson had figured out how to make $9.99 + shipping Gadsden flag advertisements appear in the sidebar of Jocelyn's Gmail.

CHAPTER THIRTY-SIX

STOJANKA WAS OUTFITTED IN SKINTIGHT black jeans, combat boots, and a cropped leather jacket. Her dark hair was pulled back into a long ponytail. "You must be a very special lady," the Harley Davidson salesman remarked. "He's getting you a very nice bike."

Stojanka didn't smile and just kept her eyes locked on Ethan as he signed the sales slip for the two new motorcycles. A Sportster Iron 883 for her and a VRSCDX Night Rod Special for him. Both black. "Would you like me to show you how to start the bikes?" the salesman, who now knew not to talk to Stojanka, asked Ethan.

Ethan glanced at Stojanka and replied, "Naw. No thanks, man. We're cool."

The salesman handed him the keys to both motorcycles. Ethan shook his hand, and he and Heartbreaker mounted the bikes.

"You get me small bike. Yours is better."

He sighed. "I'm bigger than you. I need this bike," he said as he turned the key in the ignition. A satisfied smile spread across his face when the patented Harley sound erupted. "That one's too small for me!" he shouted over the rumble.

Stojanka smirked, started hers, and they both pulled out onto the road. As they zipped through the tree-lined back streets, Ethan had to give Heartbreaker credit for smashing him in the nads. Of course, now he wanted to call her Ballbreaker, but she had been right. He really did have to snap out of it.

With a gratifying gear shift, he recalled how, after the testicular trauma, Stojanka had calmly gone off on him and explained that there was work to do and that he would be needed—that he needed to "grow a pair." Ethan, of course, was feeling a bit sick and really wasn't listening to her at the time. The vision Cheerio had completely collapsed upon itself, and he couldn't see anything but grizzly black-and-white static. Once he pulled himself together, she explained that she didn't really care—that he shouldn't really care. And it made sense. She would be relocating to Florida soon. And she wouldn't see him anymore. That's when Ethan got the idea to just buy the bikes. Screw it. They were Harleys. The purchase was like an investment.

They sped off to the east and followed the shoreline south. It wasn't a particularly sunny day, but it wasn't cloudy either. The sky was an uninspiring bluish gray with random white streaks running through it. They had been riding for more than an hour when Ethan pulled into a bank's parking lot in Connecticut. Stojanka followed and stopped next to him.

"What is plan?" she asked over her engine as he hopped off the bike.

"I just have to run inside." He motioned across the street. "There's some shops and a restaurant over there. We'll get some lunch when I'm done."

She nodded and headed across the street.

Ethan went into the bank and waited to speak to the manager, who allowed him entry into the vault to collect the contents of his safe-deposit box.

It was quiet in there—spooky silent—as he slid the box from the wall as if he was pulling a corpse out of its refrigerated holding bin at the coroner's. He opened the thin, stainless-steel box and instantly grabbed for some US dollars. He left his bounty, the gold coins and Euros, in there and shut and locked the lid. He pushed the box back into the wall, thanked the manager, and headed out to the parking lot.

He scanned the street, looking for Stojanka's bike. He didn't see it, and his heart sank. Then he got pissed. *That wacky bitch just stole my bike.* He resentfully headed over to the restaurant across the street and made himself comfortable there. He ordered a coffee, and when the busboy passed by, he motioned for him to come over. The busboy knew him from his previous visits and nodded. When the coffee arrived, so did his coke. He nodded and handed the waitress a balled up hundred-dollar bill. Just as he was taking a gulp of coffee ruminating about how Stojanka had screwed him over, in she wandered holding a boutique's shopping bag.

Much relieved that his new Harley wasn't getting sold on the black market, he smiled and said, "You went shopping?"

"You give me gift of motorcycle. Now I give you gift." She pushed the overly feminine bag over to him.

"Well, I didn't actually give it to you." He cringed. "I'm planning on selling it when you leave for Florida."

She squinted at him and grabbed the bag back. She opened it up and made a big deal about peering at the contents.

"So ... um ... you're not gonna give me your gift now?" he asked as the waitress came over and poured some coffee for Stojanka.

"Oh, I love that shop," a different young waitress said, motioning toward the bag Stojanka was holding. "They have such nice things there."

Stojanka smiled, and the coffee bearer made her way to the next table.

Now Ethan was curious. "Aw, come on. You're not gonna give me the gift unless I give you the bike?"

Stojanka took a sip of coffee and raised her eyebrows. He took another swallow of his coffee and made a face like he couldn't care less. She started poking through the bag, and Ethan looked at the menu. After an uncomfortable silence, he asked, "You sure you don't want to give me that?"

She sighed, "I do not know. Maybe."

Ethan didn't have patience for this and just grabbed the bag. He opened it up and spied a shoe box bearing an illustration of a woman's high heel and, tossed in next to it, a red, lacy negligee.

"So you want the bike for this?"

She looked at him expectantly as he stood up and started walking toward the door. "Deal!" he shouted back over his shoulder.

Heartbreaker grabbed the bag and ran after him.

CHAPTER THIRTY-SEVEN

JOCELYN INTENTIONALLY WORE A SHOCKINGLY red dress so that he would see her. She waited at the same table where she and Jerry had sat before. It was just about 10:30 a.m. when she saw Jerry walk through the door in his Wayfarers. He quickly trotted over to her table, grinning.

"I hop church day ten and half! That was great! I knew it was you!" he whispered excitedly as he plopped down in the chair.

Jocelyn grinned back. "I thought you'd figure it out if you were on the other side of that website." She was astonishingly pleased with her encryption prowess. Of course, the fact that she had created and logged into ChemTrailTails.com with the user name ithinkiusedtoworkwithu had probably helped too.

"So what's up?" Keeping his sunglasses on, Jerry twisted around and hung what reminded Jocelyn of a 1980s Member's Only jacket on the back of his chair.

"Has the FBI been in touch with you?" Jocelyn asked.

Jerry shook his head. "No."

Jocelyn leaned in close and whispered, "Well, they know me now—or have known me. They called me in for a person-of-interest interview the other day."

A waitress suddenly appeared, offering coffee.

Somewhat startled, Jerry accepted. "Bring it on," he said, pushing the mug that was already on the table toward her.

Jocelyn asked for decaf.

"Whoa. Decaf? Jocelyn, I think my world just tipped off its axis mundi."

The waitress pouring the coffee grunted in mild amusement at Jerry's remark.

"Yeah," Jocelyn said, holding her mug as eight ounces of tepid decaf was poured in. "I've changed how I eat, and now I simply cannot tolerate caffeine. It's weird." She didn't want to mention that she was having problems sleeping lately.

The waitress distributed the menus, letting them know she'd be back for their order.

When the coast was clear, Jerry leaned over the table. "Well, what did they say?"

"Dude," she glanced around and whispered, "it's fucked up. One of the Conglomerate's board members got killed right around the time I left. They showed me the pictures." She paused and shook her head. "It was gross. I think it might have to do with those gems and diamonds you were smuggling in."

"Don't mess with me, Jocelyn. You're serious?"

"As serious as a heart attack. That woman was the reason I got promoted. And it has something to do with Malaysia. The guy said that my e-mail account was communicating with the muckety-mucks of the Malaysian government after I left. I guess that's why I am now officially a person of interest."

"Did you mention me and the packages?" Jerry was eager to find out.

"No."

"Why?"

Jocelyn sighed and said, "I don't know. I guess I was freaked out seeing that board member woman all mutilated. And I didn't want to bring up something that was not directly related. I don't know. I suppose if he had asked a question about you, I would have told him what I knew. I don't know," she said for the third time. "I guess I didn't really trust the guy. I didn't like the way he and his partner contacted me." She proceeded to tell him the whole SpongeBob thing while

Jerry nodded vigorously, as if it confirmed for him that stuff like that happened all the time.

The waitress showed up again. Neither one of them was very hungry. "Just keep the coffee coming. We might be here for a while," Jerry said.

The woman walked away with what Jocelyn perceived as a disappointed smirk.

"Jerry, by the way, are you still a ghost? I mean, how do they *not* know about you?" Jocelyn asked.

"I guess I'm a good ghost."

Although Jocelyn was highly skeptical of this, she took his explanation at face value and didn't bother to comment. They stayed at that table and sipped mediocre coffee for the next two hours. Jocelyn relayed the graphic details of the crime scene photos and filled him in about the Darling Vintners discussion.

"Dude! That's the company!" Jerry almost jumped out of his chair, pointing at her. "That's the company I was supposed to deliver the packages to!" He sat back in his chair and rubbed his neck. "Remember? I knew it had to do with wine. It was one of Adam's companies. Or was it his girlfriend's?"

"Probably why his girlfriend had that enormous emerald ring," Jocelyn recalled. "Did they ever get married?"

"Nah ... I don't think so. When the Conglomerate finally announced that the Indonesia contract had fallen apart, I think that was when I heard that the wedding was postponed or canceled or something."

"Figures." Jocelyn couldn't help but wonder how it went down with "Dad," Adam's girlfriend's father, who had been paid handsomely as a consultant to help manage the ill-fated Indonesia contract. She could only imagine. She took another sip of coffee and took a good look around the restaurant. There wasn't much to notice other than a few people munching on hash browns and French toast. A group of elderly ladies were happily and loudly bragging about their great-grandchildren. But there was this one middle-aged guy wearing jeans, a gray sweatshirt, and a black baseball cap, who had been sitting at the same table since she came in. He was obviously drinking coffee, but oddly, as he sipped from his IHOP issued mug, he kept fiddling with a Starbuck's paper cup. She noticed him because he was so nondescript, unlike Jocelyn in her nearly neon red dress, and Jerry, who had not removed his sunglasses the entire time.

Looking at Jerry in what she guessed were his eyes behind the sunglasses, she twitched her head toward the unassuming patron. "That guy has been here longer than us. All by himself," she said softly.

Jerry looked over and pointed. "Him?"

"Shhh!" Jocelyn sort of hunched down in her seat. "Yeah. Him."

"Maybe he likes pancakes or something."

Jocelyn frowned. "I haven't noticed him putting anything into his mouth other than coffee. And look, he has another coffee sitting there next to him, too."

"Well, we haven't had anything but coffee, either."

Jocelyn was astounded that she was acting more like Jerry than Jerry. So she backed off and changed the subject. "So, have you had any more helicopter sightings?"

"Nope. You?"

"Nope. I guess they found what they were looking for and went home." They both nodded. Jocelyn continued, "Hey, speaking of which, I should head home soon. If I need to get in touch with you, should I just send a message through the ChemTrailTails website?"

"Yeah. Definitely. That's probably the best bet."

They waved to the waitress and asked for the bill. Jocelyn felt sorry for the waitress as the check for the two bottomless cups of coffee was slapped on the table. "Oh ... we should probably leave her a nice tip. We've been here a long time," Jocelyn said as she noticed the business card that she still had floating randomly around in her purse. John P. from the Ray Pierce Meetup had made these cards up. It was a little reminder to vote for Ray Pierce because of his stance that tips should not be taxed. Of course, Pierce wanted to shut down the IRS all together, but this tip-taxing language seemed an effective way to get the word out quickly to Main Street's Joe the Bartender. Still fussing around, Jocelyn put the card on the table as she looked for some cash.

"Oh, don't worry, Joss. I've got it." Jerry plunked down a fifty-dollar bill as he stood up to put his coat on.

Jocelyn looked up at him, hands still buried in her purse. "Well, thanks, Jerry. Aren't you going to wait for change?" she asked while scooting out of the booth.

"Nah. She probably depends on her tips to live. And you're right. We've been in here for a long time."

"Wow, Jerry, that's supercool of you." As she followed him to the exit, Jocelyn momentarily wondered how he was afforded the luxury of fifty-dollar coffee while living as a ghost. Jerry held the door for her, and she glanced back at the man with the two coffees. She stopped in her tracks and her stomach tightened up. A familiar-looking woman was now seated with the man.

"You all right?" Jerry asked, still holding the door.

"I feel like I've seen that woman before," she whispered while attempting to discreetly point at the newcomer. Jerry glanced over her shoulder as she reached into her purse and pulled out her prescription sunglasses. She popped them on just as Jerry tipped his sunglasses down for a better view and concluded that he had never seen the lady before. With her glasses on, Jocelyn felt sure she had run into this person at some point but she couldn't place where or when. In fact, now that she had a clearer view of everything, she felt like maybe she had seen the guy before, too. She watched him as he picked up the paper coffee cup and spit into it. "Ew, he chews tobacco," she whispered.

"Come on, Joss. Let's just go," Jerry urged. Somewhat begrudgingly, she nodded and headed out. They shook hands in the parking lot and said their good-byes, promising to keep each other "in the loop."

It wasn't until she was almost home that she remembered where she had seen that woman. It seemed like a lifetime ago, but she was sure of it. *That was the chick I mistook for Shelly-the-temp at the doctor's office. What she's doing here in Rhode Island with that tobacco-chewing guy?*

Jocelyn was pretty pleased with herself that she had figured it out. *But the guy. The tobacco chewing. Chewing tobacco ...* She was flipping that around in her head and was so distracted that she almost rear-ended the white Camry in front of her. As she smashed on the brakes and swerved to avoid impact, the almost unimaginable dawned on her. Not sure if it was due to the fact that she had averted a car crash or if it was because she was so startled by the recollection, she realized that she was trembling. She had always been good with remembering faces, but this surprised her. *What the heck is that guy doing here?*

Jocelyn pulled over and shut off the Santa Fe. She saw, in a slow motion flash, a man scurrying out of her boss Robert's office with a coffee cup. He had spit into it. This man had been followed by Robert and Miriam Stein. The hurried man had been a board member at the Conglomerate. She knew that because she had met him again in Virginia when she had gotten that promotion. His name was ... She wasn't so great with names. She couldn't remember that, but she was pretty sure that's who the guy was and it scared her. *This doesn't even make sense. Maybe I'm losin' it.*

As the traffic whooshed past, Jocelyn sat for a long time in silence questioning her own mental health. Just when she decided that she should call her counselor or something, another memory smacked her squarely on the brow. "Oh, my God," she muttered and rubbed her forehead. She was thinking about the guy in the parking lot on her last day of work. The guy who had given her the warning about that obnoxious butterfly pin and had disappeared. He was chewing tobacco, too. "No. No, way," she said out loud. She blinked, trying to remember the out of focus figure. It was all too much. It was a stretch, and she knew she was probably letting her imagination run away with her. *That meeting with the FBI really messed with my head.*

Forcing herself to calm down, she started the car, cautiously pulled back into traffic, and headed home.

CHAPTER THIRTY-EIGHT

"WHY ARE YOU LOOKING AT me like that?"

"Like what?"

"Like this." Ethan made an exaggerated stare and turned to walk away.

Jocelyn grabbed him by the shoulder and forced him to face her. "Well, I'm trying to figure out what you're thinking. I was, and still am, really freaked out, Ethan!" She waved her notebook around so that he would have to look at the red sticker she had removed from the mailbox. "I mean, wouldn't you be if the FBI called you in to look at pictures of some dead lady with a butterfly pin sticking out of her eye? And then you find this on your mailbox?"

Exasperated, Ethan shot back, "It's a fucking sticker, Joss. Calm the fuck down."

She was attempting to control her emotions while trying to communicate with him. She was confused as to why he was not exhibiting a mutual concern about this whole situation.

"Ethan." She took a deep breath through her nose. "Let's forget about the sticker. Just forget I brought it up, okay?" She threw the notebook onto the kitchen table. "The critical thing here is the pin." She rubbed her forehead and continued. "I swear to God, it was the same type of pin that I got at my going-away party at work. Don't you think that's just a little, oh, I don't know, weird?!"

"Oh, for shit's sake. Joss, give it a rest already." He pushed, half-kicked his carry-on luggage with his foot. "I just got through the door, and you hit me up with this crap. Like who wants to come home to this?"

"I'm sorry. You're right. I should have at least let you get unpacked." She leaned over, picked up his luggage, and leaned it against the wall. "But I'm scared and—"

"Stop being so dramatic, for Christ's sake. Like some piece of random jewelry couldn't look like some other piece of random jewelry?" He took off his pea coat and draped it on the kitchen chair. "Honestly, take it down a notch. You were probably so shocked at seeing the pictures that you *imagined* it was like the thing they gave you."

"No. It was the same. You never saw it." She was fighting back tears. "You weren't even at my party when they gave it to me." Her lip trembled. "I thought it was god-awful. It was wicked tacky and—"

He cut her off. "Joss, Joss, honey, look, just calm down." He pulled her in and hugged her. "I'm sorry I wasn't at the party. You know that." His voice was now as smooth as silk, and Jocelyn was crying because *that* wasn't why she was upset either. *Why does he always misunderstand me?* She wrestled with her urge to push him away and debate him—to make him fully understand that it was all about that crazy pin and its connection to the Conglomerate. She just wanted him to talk it out with her, to solve the mystery with her. But she didn't push him away. Being hugged felt nice. Comforting.

He whispered, "No one is going to hurt you. I won't let them. You're the mother of my children. You're safe."

CHAPTER THIRTY-NINE

THE BOOK CLUB STARTED OFF small—seven people, to be exact. Jocelyn knew all of them except for one woman, who seemed to be some sort of angry throwback to her 1970s counterculture self. But that was cool. The book club was open to anyone. And Jocelyn enjoyed hearing the angry hippie woman's take on the parts of *Blowback* that described how Japan had made a deal with the United States for a base in exchange for some economic stuff and military protection and how all around the base, new industries had grown up, built specifically to service the incoming Americans. Namely bars, prostitution, and drugs.

If the statistics mentioned in the book about the drunk driving around the base weren't horrifying enough, the part about sexual assaults and the little girl out to buy stationery getting gang-raped by US soldiers was just heartbreaking. No, make that nauseating. Even more disturbing was the commanding officer's bewildered response. "Why didn't you guys just go get one of those tiny whores? That's what they're there for."

With that episode being just the tip of the iceberg of related stories about the unintended consequences of US foreign policy, the author illustrated what the CIA calls "blowback"—namely, that actions of the United States, or people representing the United States, can cause a lot of animosity, fueling resistance and retribution conspiracies. This was pretty much old news to the folks in the room.

"That went well," remarked Sam Ballentine after saying good-bye to the angry hippie. Jocelyn just noticed the irony of Sam wearing a sweatshirt that read "The Good Guys," surrounded by the insignia of each of the US military branches. Jocelyn and Abby were cleaning up the remains of the brownies and chocolate chip cookies that she and the kids had made especially for this meeting. Sam joined in on the cleanup effort.

"I had hoped more people would show up," Jocelyn said in disappointment.

"Well, you've got to advertise it better," Abby matter-of-factly stated while handing her the well-wrapped remaining cookies.

"I think it was great. Just do it again," Sam suggested optimistically. "What if you invited the state chair of the Republican Party?"

"Yeah!" Abby said. "I wish the whole GOP were here tonight. The reason they treated Ray Pierce so poorly is because they have no concept of stuff like this. Everyone is so afraid of getting bombed by some far-flung, third world nation, it's pathetic."

"They are courting the military interests while the Dems go for the other big money voting bloc, the teachers and the unions," Sam said.

"When did the Republican Party become so hawkish? I remember I voted for them when they were the antiwar party."

Sam smiled almost wistfully at Abby's remark, and Jocelyn was confused because she didn't realize that the GOP had ever been antiwar.

So after that meeting, Jocelyn ended up taking her friends' suggestions to heart. She invited the GOP chair, Mike Zachari. And every month, she would hold a book club meeting. It was like a special night out among grown-ups. She picked books that she had read or new ones that seemed interesting to her. She quickly found out that, although the group had grown to over thirty people, much to her chagrin, not many of them actually read—even folks who seemed pretty intelligent. So she decided to show films and recommend related books. That grew the group to about fifty people.

Soon, authors wanted to speak to her book club, and politicians were lining up to say a few words before the meetings. And Jocelyn liked it. A lot. The group grew again to over 100 people. Skype interviews were introduced, and—*bam!*—the group grew yet again to over 120 people. People trudged in each month to just talk about real-life concerns that they had with other real-life people. Jocelyn had only one rule for her club. *Respect the fact that someone came all the way here to say something, even if what he or she says is stupid.*

People liked that and felt free to speak freely. Every so often, someone would roll in with a completely jarring tale about mind control or FEMA camps that somehow tangentially related to the book club's original theme. Eyes would open wide, but everyone listened, even those who were shaking their heads in disbelief. People were getting introduced to new ideas. They were educating each other—or, at the very least, widening their fields of view.

Thinking about what the topic might be for the next book club as she did her daily chores around the house really helped her take her mind off the stuff that had started causing her mild anxiety attacks—namely, the fact that Ethan was spending less and less time at home. She liked having him around, not so much because she was missing his companionship (heck, they hardly ever spoke) but because his presence psychologically meant that she and the kids were safe.

That security meant a lot—especially since that FBI visit. It meant so much, in fact, that she could put up with his silence and his sitting in the dark staring out into the distance and even the uncalled-for bursts of anger. The bizarre changes in his attitude or wardrobe, the sporadic arrival of the FedEx deliveries that jammed up their hallway with mail-order boxes, the two brand-new Harley Davidsons sitting in their driveway—she could deal with all of that.

That was until she found the size 8, black stiletto and experienced Ethan's reaction to it.

"That's your shoe! Don't even look at me like that!"

"I'm a size 10, Ethan. I was just wondering how the heck a shoe got in our yard?" she had questioned as she skeptically picked it up with her index finger and thumb as if it were a dead rat and dumped it into the recycle bin. That was a few weeks ago.

Now, she knew confronting him was pointless. Jocelyn had learned long ago that Ethan lived in some sort of alternate reality. No matter what approach she would take trying to broach, oh, just pick any old topic (a news story, what they should have for diner, the kids' doctor's appointment), it would somehow result in Ethan thinking that she was accusing him of something. Then amazingly, it would be twisted around, and the nonissue would turn out to be her fault. It was very draining.

But because her counselor had explained what Ethan was doing in technical, medical terms, somehow, instead of saying, *Oh wow, that's messed up. I'm outta here,* she had always been able to look at his behavior with a sympathetic eye. Even though that metaphorical eye was now effectively very black and blue.

Somehow along the way, she had decided that she would help him with what she now had come to understand as a medical problem. And that gave her license to feel badly for him and to start looking though his wallet, you know, for his own good. She had been doing that for months now, and she hated it; but she couldn't not do it. Little scraps of paper with mysterious phone numbers and random receipts from faraway places were what she would typically find and carefully put back exactly as she had found them. Looking through his belongings when he wasn't around was like a bizarre compulsion. She would always justify her actions by telling herself that she would help him get help and all that. But collecting the shards of a shattered person and trying to reorganize the pieces so that they made sense only left her with a distorted reflection of herself.

Jocelyn heaved a heavy sigh and headed through the French door, out to the raised garden beds that Ethan had built for her. Of course, construction of the garden had not occurred without significant disagreement. But these squabbles were pretty much par for the course now when she and the man she once loved deeply would have occasion to speak. She tried to be thankful for all the beauty that they had created together in spite of their bickering. Their children were primary examples as they hustled around with Tonka trucks building a rudimentary fort out of some random stuff from the shed. She took the time to appreciate the moment. She knew that things were always changing. Kids grow up, and flowers bloom and eventually wither away. Give it some time, and everything would be different. She knew that. Seasons changed.

Jocelyn admired the scraggle of overgrown, late-season tomatoes. Random fruit still hung on the vine, and more had fallen, littering the raised bed. The squash and pumpkins were beginning their season, and the flowers along the path to the grape arbor could use some deadheading, so she set to work picking and weeding. When she was officially in the nirvana-like state otherwise known as the Gardening Zone, something started beeping somewhere. She brushed off her dirty hands as best she could and checked her pockets. Nothing. *What* is *that?*

The beeping stopped, and she started gardening again. And as soon as she was knees down in the dirt, the beeping would start up. She ignored the beeping until it became omnipresent and demanded to be discovered. She called the kids over to help find whatever it was that was beeping, and they happily started searching with her.

Beep, beep, beep, beep.

"I found it!" her son cried out.

"No! I found it!" her daughter yelled while trying to snatch Jocelyn's cell phone away from her twin brother.

Jocelyn wandered past the Rose of Sharon bushes that she and Ethan had planted, over to the kids who were at the picnic table fighting about who had found the phone. She sneakily grabbed her little girl and hugged her. "Thank you for finding the beeping noise, guys." She winked at her son who held out the phone to her.

"Awww. I wanted to find it," her daughter whined.

"You both did as far as I'm concerned. I forgot that I had left it there," she said as she tickled her daughter and then accepted the phone from her son. "But why is it beeping? Is it out of batteries or something?" She flipped the phone over in her hand and studied it. It wasn't out of batteries, and it had never made that sound before.

Suddenly the phone started vibrating and beeping in her hand, and it startled her. That's when she received her very first text message. She didn't even know that her phone could do that.

"Oh, Daddy just sent us a message. How cool is that?"

The kids looked on as she tried to figure out which button to press to read the message. When she finally did, it was as if pressing that button had crushed her chest. The message read:

Heartbreaker, I found the other shoe.

The kids watched as she started trembling. His response to her discovery of the size 8, black stiletto that she had found a while ago, along with this cryptic text message pushed Jocelyn over the edge, and she started crying.

"Mommy, are you crying?" Lillian asked.

"Mommy, don't cry," William said as both the kids, with looks of bewilderment scratching their faces, attached themselves to her legs and started hugging her. It was at that moment she heard Ethan's Harley Davidson Sportster rumbling toward their house. She wiped her tears and tried to appear as put together as possible and gently extracted the kids from her side.

In a few moments, he was walking toward her and the kids wearing a placid smile, not unlike the one he had been wearing in the dream she had been dragging around with her. He came up close to all of them and asked with now-furrowed brow, "What happened? What's wrong?"

It wasn't that she didn't know what to say. It was that she had so much to say. She couldn't speak and just looked him in the eye and shook her head no. He looked at her, confused.

"What, Joss? What could be so bad?" And he went to hug her.

She pushed him away and handed him the phone. Still seemingly confused, he took the phone and read the message. Jocelyn could tell he was acting, for about ten seconds, as if he had no idea what was going on, but then she watched while, as if changing mental gears, he got mad. Before he could even finish his first full exclamation about how crazy she was, Jocelyn stopped him. She put her hand on his chest and just shook her head no and then glanced over at both the kids.

"They need you to not be freaking out. I need some time. Please take them somewhere for a while." She wasn't even sure how she was able to get that all out. But as she watched her children walk away with their dad and get loaded into the cab of his truck, she began to cry for real.

Not without serious tears, she decided that, bankrupt or not, she was going to have to follow through on Operation Easy Extraction. Once again, a country music song was being crafted somewhere within the depths of her temporal lobe, and she couldn't shake the D-A-G three-chord progression. She didn't even like country. Roots rock maybe, but not country. Auditory hallucinations of country music had gotten tiresome for her the year before.

Anyhow, after she settled on roots rock as her mental soundtrack, she went to her computer and clicked on craigslist, looking for a new place to live. She found three places and then made her way to her room—specifically, to that little jewelry box she kept on her dresser. It was a small and not very feminine thing that her mother had given to her as a gift, but it was large enough to hold a floppy disk. And waiting for her under the beige floppy disk, like patient grandparents, were those two gold coins that had mysteriously appeared in her desk at work.

She picked up the coins and turned them over with her fingers. This was the first time she had bothered to really study them in almost seven years. She knew that they were valuable. Maybe they could help finance the first month's rent. While looking at the coins, she wandered over to the phone to call the first rental she had found and just ask. But then she hung up, knowing that it was probably useless to even try. *What landlord in his right mind was going to take a Krugerrand gold coin as payment?*

She had to figure out how to trade these coins in for money she could actually use. Maybe Sam Ballentine would know how to offload these things. First, she figured, she might as well know how much she was looking at. So, still holding the coins and with a new sense of purpose, she trotted back to her computer and did a web search for "price of gold." She ended up at a website called KITCO.com, and that had all sorts of informational live charts about the spot price of silver and metals and ... *holy Toledo!*

One ounce of gold was $1,738. Jocelyn looked specifically at that 1984 Süd-Afrika Krugerrand coin sitting on her desk. *This is nuts! I remember checking the price of gold when I first got this thing! It's gone up in value like—*

And that's when the computer and all the lights in the house suddenly went black.

END OF BOOK 2

Sneak peek at
Security Through Absurdity
BOOK THREE: THE BIG SHOW

North Kingstown, Rhode Island, USA
Autumn

THE ANGLES OF THE TINY yellow house were closing in on Jocelyn as the shadows grew longer and more defined. Sure, she had just busted Ethan for some sort of affair, and he had taken off with the kids about fifteen minutes ago. That was depressing enough, but now a power outage?

"Great," she grumbled as she stared at the lifeless computer screen staring back at her. Jocelyn rubbed her temples and then hoisted herself out of the chair. She pushed open the Home Depot French doors that Ethan had installed and cut through the Martha Stewart color palette of the living room with its hardly-ever used fireplace and random sampling of the kids' toys.

As she walked into the kitchen, she pulled her long strawberry blond hair back into a loose ponytail and zeroed in on the refrigerator. She had to check. Yup, it wasn't working either. She slowly closed the stainless steel door and tried to remember what the deal was with the circuit breakers. She knew they were in the basement, so she reached behind the fridge, got the key, and unlocked the basement door. They kept the door locked because there were guns down there.

Jocelyn had insisted when they moved into the place, right before the twins were born, that the kids never have access to Ethan's guns. Ever. This request (well, it was more like a demand) had taken Ethan by surprise. Ethan Lowe was a former Navy SEAL, and guns were a big part of his lifestyle growing up. Of course, they had both worked for the Conglomerate, a huge private defense contracting operation. He had worked for the mercenary division, and she, Ms. Jocelyn McLaren, had been in the marketing department while he had been rolling around in Iraq. Mr. and Ms. America, really.

But that was five years ago, back when Ethan still loved her, and they were both all excited to have left their jobs and started a new life. They had made plans, and it was going to be a great little family. But things changed. Now Ethan was barely ever around, she was bankrupt, they had two little mouths to feed, and she felt like she spent most of her time doing laundry.

Jocelyn fiddled with the basement key. She didn't like going down those basement stairs. Not only were they something of a physical challenge because she was managing multiple sclerosis, but the basement steps were downright creepy. She had a really bad dream about these stairs once, and since then she rarely went down into the basement. She braced herself and ended up lumbering down the dank stairway while en route to randomly flip circuit breaker switches. Finally, she decided to just call the power company and report an outage. She concluded that someone must have crashed into a telephone pole or something.

While searching for her cell phone, a terrible thought struck her: maybe the person who crashed into the pole and left her in the dark was Ethan. Maybe he had been so upset and distracted by their earlier confrontation... *I really hope he and the kids are okay.*

She headed out to the front yard with her cell phone because, of course, the reception inside the house wasn't that great. She got through to the power company, and after dealing with the phone tree and waiting on hold for way too long, she was informed that no lines were down. According to them, everything was functioning perfectly.

But things weren't perfect. She thought about it,

cringed and decided to call Ethan. It was his house after all. He had done the re-wiring during the renovations. Maybe she was doing something wrong. Maybe it was an easy fix.

As soon as he answered, Jocelyn knew something wasn't right. He was way too calm. Uncharacteristically calm. He didn't even sound like himself and she wasn't prepared for what he told her.

"You mean *you* shut off the electricity *and* the phone?"

"Yup," Ethan answered casually.

"But... I'm here. I'm still here," she blurted into the cell phone.

"I know. That's why I shut it all off."

"Huh? But why?"

"Because I'm taking the kids to New Hampshire. To go camping... I think. Hey, kids! You wanna go on your first real camping trip? I'll show you how the gun works!" Her heart sunk to her stomach at the thought of him with a gun and the kids. She heard an overwhelming shout of approval from the peanut gallery and Ethan continued, "I'll be back with them soon. Don't worry. They'll have a good time." Jocelyn was at a loss for words as he kept talking. "But I'm not leaving *you* there with the Internet and electric that *I* pay for. I'm not paying for you to sit in front of a computer, Jocelyn. And I don't need to be paying for the phone. You've got a cell phone."

The sun was starting to set. Bright slashes of the dwindling daylight sliced through the trees. Jocelyn couldn't believe this. She wandered over to the driveway to get better reception. She stood right where his truck had been when she last saw him loading the kids into it, and that's when she noticed the dangling cables on the corner of the house. *He cut the wires to his own house?! When did he...?*

Jocelyn spoke cautiously, "Ethan. The wires to the house... The wires aren't connected anymore."

"Joss, you're breaking up. The juice boxes are in the red cooler, Lilly," she heard him shout to her daughter.

A swelling wave of anxiety rushed through Jocelyn's body, and she almost dropped her phone, the same cell phone Ethan's misguided text message to someone called Heartbreaker had showed up on earlier that day and prompted her to tell him to leave. She could hear her twins, Lillian and William, babbling in the background. Still holding the phone to her ear, she ran back into the house to get her car keys and asked, "Where are you now?" Maybe she could cut him off somewhere and wrangle the kids back.

"What?"

"Where are you now?!" she shouted into the phone.

"In the Super Stop and Shop parking lot. We just loaded up."

"So, you're leaving this minute? It's pretty late to be leaving on a road trip with five-year-olds, don't you think?"

"Nah. They'll be fine. I've packed a cooler with everything they could ever want. We'll sleep in the truck and be home in about a week." He said like it was no big deal.

"Oh, okay, so you're all suddenly going camping, and I'm staying here alone in the dark?" She was completely confused by what was going on. Sure, their relationship had gotten strange for her a while ago, but he had never done anything as whacked out as this before. Jocelyn tried to stay calm. She didn't want to ignite any sort of internal fuse in him because he had the kids and was armed, and he certainly wasn't thinking like a normal person.

"*You* told me to take the kids somewhere—that *you* needed time. Well, that's what I'm doing. I'm helping *you* out here, Joss," he said over the sound of his truck starting up. "I can't pay for all this. I mean, I came back in the house to get the Glock, and you didn't even hear me. You were so involved in whatever it was you were doing on the computer."

"You did?" Jocelyn thought back to what she was doing before the lights went out and realized that she had, in fact, been completely engrossed in finding out the current price of gold. "Well, it's not like you let me know you were back."

"Well," he said, mocking her tone, "it's not like you would have cared. You only seem to care about that Ray Pierce campaign and his cult and..."

She cut him off as she swung open the car door and hopped inside. "It's not Ray Pierce! It's a book club, and I don't think..."

"Whatever. I'm not paying for it. You can go to your mother's and let her finance your apathy." He hung up. Jocelyn threw the phone onto the passenger seat and tore out toward Super Stop and Shop.

NOTE FROM THE AUTHOR

MANY OF THE TOPICS IN THIS BOOK, as well as this trilogy you have just read, are based on real life events. I got the inspiration for the character of Jocelyn McLaren when I was elected to attend the 2012 Republican National Convention. Being disillusioned by the entire political process, I unaffiliated from the party as soon as I got home.

I'd like to thank Catherine Austin Fitts for her insight into the topic of Shadow Banking and Dark Money as well as all of the people in my life who have inspired this story. Unknowingly, their influence has shaped characters who I love and are now a part of me. I genuinely hope that you have enjoyed inviting these characters into your life as well.

To see my real time tweets from the 2012 RNC, where I did dress as Jocelyn and pass out business cards just like the ones in this book, please visit Twitter **@JocelynMcLaren**. You are, of course, invited to visit **www.rachaellmcintosh.com** to stay up to date with my writing and appearances.

See you there!

Made in the USA
Middletown, DE
08 January 2022